# SHADOWS

# OF THE

# SERPENT

\* \* \* \* \* \*

BOOK SEVEN

\* \* \* \* \* \*

D.W. Neuman

# ALSO BY D.W. NEUMAN

## FICTION

<u>Shadow Series</u>
*Shadows of the Mind – Book One*
*Shadows of the Soul – Book Two*
*Shadows of the Service – Book Three*
*Shadows of the Past – Book Four*
*Shadows of the Heart – Book Five*
*Shadows of the Sand – Book Six*
*Shadows of the Serpent – Book Seven*

ISBN (978-0-9907247-2-8)

Connie;
my wife, my love.
You perpetually surprise me
again and again, and
I love you for that more
then you'll ever realize.
Where did you come from?
(Oh, I love you more and now
it's in print so I win :p).


Carol.
Is this the end of their
world as you know it?
My novels are a direct result
of your "over-the-top" involvement
which never seems to slow down.
Thank you and have a great trip!
(11/20-12/1/14)

We do not remember days,
we remember moments.

-Cesare Pavese

# 1
## May, 2001

"Clear the bay. I repeat, clear the bay. Prisoner transfer in progress."

Site 43 wasn't on any map. Originally it had been an old missile silo that had been converted, secretly, into a prison. It was designed for housing high value assets that didn't officially exist to the rest of the world anymore. Within its depths interrogators would take their time prying information out of their subjects without any subjective laws to hinder their progress. The process was efficient and sometimes terminal to the assets housed within Site 43.

The Arizona sun was at its peak when Site 43's large steel reinforced doors cracked open. The external hot air rapidly entered the black book facility and warmed up the chained prisoner and his three guards who stood behind the large entryway. The large, slow moving doors completed their cycle and sixty-two year old Robert Aleman, previously a General with the codename Raven, emerged from within its blackened depths.

The sun struck his face and immediately soothed his tired and haggard body. He hadn't seen or felt the sun in years.

"Move it asshole," one of the guards commanded and pushed Robert from behind.

The man known as Raven stumbled, hindered by his leg restraints, pitched over and landed on the ground.

"Pick his ancient ass up. We're going to be off schedule if we don't hurry it up."

The two other heavily armed guards forcibly pulled Aleman to his feet and steered him towards a van fifty feet away.

"Where are you taking me this time?"

1

"Shut the fuck up. Another word out of you and I promise you you'll be eating through a tube for the next week."

Robert Aleman didn't have the energy or the will to fight back. For the past twelve years he'd been incarcerated at one location after another. At each new facility he was constantly questioned about the other Organization's members he'd been running drugs with into the United States. Over and over they told him they already had all the evidence they needed to take the Organization down. All they wanted, they kept saying, was to fill in the blanks and tell them where the money was. If he told them they'd make his life more comfortable.

*Yeah right. I didn't believe anything they promised me at any point. I kept my mouth shut and they put me in one hole after another trying to break me.*

Inside the rear of the van Robert Aleman was placed in a floor to ceiling cage. His hands and feet were secured to eye-rings and then the cage door was locked from the outside. One guard sat across from him while the other two got in to the front.

The guard in the passenger seat used the mounted radio as the van turned over.

"Viper nest. Viper nest. This is Viper One."

"Viper One. Go ahead."

"Viper One is on the move. ETA fifty-five minutes."

"Roger that Viper One. GPS is live. We have you on our scope. Viper nest out."

Robert smiled and his guard caught it.

"What the hell are you smiling about shithead?"

"Nothing really. Just an old memory about the individual I used to call my father." *Serpent.*

"Well, you've got fifty-five minutes of alone time before you're someone else's problem. Smile all you want but keep your fucking mouth shut."

2

Robert nodded and closed his eyes. He knew for certain that the next hour was his to enjoy without the threat of sleep deprivation, needles, hunger, beatings or anything else he'd experienced in the past twelve years. He'd grown accustomed to enjoying the little things because, in his reality, that's all he had left.

The van excited the outer security fence and headed down the dirt road towards the highway ten miles away.

*I wonder where I'll end up this go around? Why haven't they killed me yet? Why this change of scenery after four years? Could it be that they haven't gotten their hands on our drug money after all this time?*

Robert allowed himself to smile yet again.

*Maybe. Maybe not. It's not like that matters now anyway. I've been forsaken for twelve years. Forsaken and forgotten. Even my Anna. I can't believe Anna would forget me like this.*

His mouth tightened in to a snarl.

*No one has come for me. Nobody at all. But I wouldn't have been tortured and caged in horrible places if it wasn't for those two do-gooders, Sam and Bill. I should have killed them when the group ordered me to. But I thought I could turn them; bring them in to the Organization after all. I couldn't have been more mistaken and it cost me my freedom and my life.*

His mouth grew even tighter. His face seemed to transform in to something else altogether as the rage built up inside him.

*I would very much like to rip their family's hearts from their chests, show it to them and then take their lives. I would make them suffer for what they've done to me.*

The van exited the dirt road and shifted to pavement. On this stretch of road, this far off the beaten path, vehicles were few and far between. Robert was jarred, in his cage, during the transition and he opened his eyes. He couldn't see outside but he knew his

3

time was ticking down before he was going to be handed off to his next 'caregivers'. He was not looking forward to that so he promptly closed his eyes again.

But before he could take another breath the van's front end violently pitched upwards, turned laterally and landed hard, and skidded down the asphalt on its side.

Robert was knocked around his small cage, hit his head on impact and blacked out.

The van slid to a stop and all three guards were dazed. The guard that had been sitting in the passenger seat was dead while the other two were bleeding from multiple wounds and were unconscious.

"Go get him."

"Yes sir," his subordinate replied as he put away the remote detonator to the bomb that had been planted in the road.

Two vehicles, off the side of the main road, quickly removed their camouflage netting and drove the short distance to the downed transport van. A total of eight armed men exited both vehicles and their plan was quickly put in to motion. An elderly ninth man took his time as he stepped out and observed.

Two men watched the road, one in each direction.

Four other men immediately inspected the transport for any threats. Two verified the guards up front were incapacitated while the other two attached a small charge to the rear lock and then backed away.

"CLEAR!"

The explosive detonated and the rear door swung down and open, its lock destroyed.

Two remaining men removed a body bag from the back of one of the vehicles and carried it towards the rear of the transport.

Robert Aleman lay prone inside his cage, unconscious.

They quickly breached that lock and using bolt-cutters snipped through the chains that held him in place. They pulled his body from the transport, laid him down on the road, un-cuffed his wrists and legs and then stripped him.

The body bag was unzipped and the naked corpse inside was dressed in Robert's clothing.

"FORTY SECONDS!" the elderly man yelled out with a surprisingly deep voice.

Robert's unconscious body was dragged to its feet, wrapped in a sheet and two men took him to the rear car and placed him inside.

The corpse was shackled and placed back in the cage.

"TEN SECONDS!"

An incendiary device was tossed inside the back of the transport and it counted down from twenty as the remaining men collapsed back to the two vehicles and raced away from the scene.

Behind them the transport van exploded with flames which began to eat away at all four of its occupants, two of which were still alive. The two unconscious guards woke up and began to scream as their flesh charred at a rapid pace in front of their eyes. They passed out from the immense pain and were burned alive.

\* \* \*

"Viper One. Viper One. Come in Viper One."

"Anything?"

The man operating the radio looked up at his superior. "I still can't reach them sir. Their last known GPS position puts them here," he said as he pointed to a location on his console's virtual map. "Their vehicle data shows them at rest; not moving at all."

*Shit.* "Understood. Ready a team and get them out there."

"Roger that sir."

Two helicopters and a ground unit lifted off and headed towards the GPS coordinates. Twenty minutes later the air units arrived and began to circle the area. The smoldering remains of the transport van were seen in the middle of the road. A few civilians had stopped and were on their phones, presumably calling 911.

"Viper nest. Viper nest. This is Viper Seven."

"Go ahead Viper Seven."

"Viper nest. The transport van is destroyed. It's on its side and looks like it burned from within."

"Roger that Viper Seven. Land and contain the area. I want a sitrep in five minutes."

"Yes sir."

* * *

"Viper nest. Viper nest. This is Viper Seven."

"Report Viper Seven."

"Situation is as follows. Four bodies are inside."

"And the prisoner?"

"Yes sir. He's one of the four. He's still in the cage and his shackles are secure."

"Understood."

"It's a clusterfuck out here sir. We're going to need more men and a team to handle the forensics right away."

"They're already in route to you. Hold and preserve that scene."

"Yes sir."

* * *

Robert groaned as he began to regain consciousness and soon realized he was on his back. He tried to sit up but a torrent of pain rippled through his brain.

"Ouch," he mumbled.

"Sir. He's coming to."

The elderly man got up from his comfortable chair, onboard the private jet, and made his way to the back of the plane where Robert lay on the couch.

"Robert? Robert, can you hear me?"

*Who's talking to me? Am I hearing things?*

"General Robert Aleman, can you hear me?"

*General? I don't remember the last time I was called that.*

Robert slowly sat up and opened his eyes. He blinked a few times as he looked at the face of someone he thought he'd never see again. *I don't fucking believe it.*

"Hello son."

Robert's face clearly displayed the shock he felt. "Dad?"

The man in the organization known as Serpent stood over his son, Raven. "How are you feeling?"

"Like shit. What the hell happened?"

"We used a road bomb. We then replaced you with a corpse and torched the van."

Robert shook his head. "They'll figure it out."

"Oh, I'm sure they will, but by then it won't matter. We'll have disappeared. Besides, who are they going to tell? Officially you don't exist anymore."

Robert rubbed his head. "I could use a drink. Scotch. The bottle."

"Bring me a glass as well," Serpent added.

One of the men brought two glasses, poured two helpings and left the bottle as he returned to his seat. Father and son each lifted a glass.

"To freedom," Serpent said.

"To freedom."

They both drained their glasses and Robert made a face as he swallowed. He hadn't tasted any alcohol for over a decade. Serpent refilled them.

"So, I'm grateful for the rescue but why now after twelve years?"

Serpent emptied his glass for a second time and sat down next to his son. "The short of it is I couldn't find you. You just disappeared."

"And the long of it?" he asked as he drank his scotch.

"Well, that's where it gets tricky."

"How so? I've been rotting away for over a decade. Shit, I'm sixty-two now dad. How tricky could it have gotten?"

"I may be old son but you don't get to bark at me. You have no fucking idea the level of hell you brought down on the Organization."

Robert's eyes narrowed as his father continued.

"It was a fantastic idea for you to keep such a large amount of incriminating evidence in one place. The information in your goddamn briefcase shut everything down."

"It was already happening," Robert countered. "The congressional investigation…"

"I had it handled until Pandora's Box was opened. Decades of work, planning and execution all spiraled down the drain. All of the Organization members were left with little choice but to point their fingers at you. Backroom deals were made to soften the blows and the fallout to our country."

"So what happened to you?"

8

"I was forced in to retirement, along with our partners. Certain accounts, containing vast sums of money, were handed over in lieu of jail time. I called in every favor I had to get out of the iron shackles you put us all in."

"That still doesn't explain why you sprung me."

"As much as I hated you for what looked like an obvious betrayal, the fact remains that you're still my son."

"But twelve years?"

Serpent shook his head. "I wasn't lying when I said they made you disappear. I've been out of the loop for a long time and I financed this with accounts they never knew about. I've spent years looking for you and I finally caught a break."

Robert looked his father in the eyes. "You never stopped looking?"

"No son, I didn't."

"So I haven't been forsaken?"

"Forsaken? Hell no. I may be twenty years your senior but life has been boring without you and the Organization."

"What are you saying?"

"Anna still asks about you. She was thrilled to hear I had finally found you."

"Anna's alive?"

"Very much so. And there's more."

"Such as?"

"Well, I've been using your old friends over at SANDBOX."

Robert bristled. "I don't understand. Those are the two that put me away."

Serpent nodded. "Indeed. But I took your idea and ran with it. SANDBOX has grown global. They're still relatively small but I've got some of our own personnel on their payroll."

Robert perked up. "No shit."

9

"I thought that would get your attention. In the last few years I've been using them to traffic merchandise back to the U.S., just like old times."

"You should have plenty of money tucked away. Why the fuck are you using them rather than destroying them?"

"Calm down and find some patience son."

Robert stood up. "Patience? Are you kidding me?"

"Relax."

Robert placed his hand on the bottle of scotch. "You fucking relax. Do you have any idea what I've been through in the past decade? What they did to me in there? Do you have any clue whatsoever the absolute hell I've been through?"

"Oh boohoo. Grow up and be a man. You deserved whatever you got for fucking us over as much as you did."

Robert's face twisted as he stared at the man he once looked up to and tightened his grip on the bottle.

"You know what dad, you're right. I'd be interested in learning more about what's happening at SANDBOX."

"Good. Glad to hear it. I prepared an informational packet for you when you're ready to review it."

"How about right now?"

"Now? You're injured and need to rest. You're hardly ready."

"Actually dad, using SANDBOX was my idea in the first place. I've been ready. I think I'll take over for you at this juncture."

Robert quickly lifted the scotch bottle and smashed it against the side of the table. What was left in his hand was a jagged and makeshift device that he deftly sunk in to his father's throat. Arterial blood sprayed all over Robert as he pushed the bottle deep. His father's eyes bulged and the look of betrayal appeared on his face.

10

Three of his father's men produced side arms and pointed them at Robert who was engrossed in another task; watching his father bleed out in front of him, eyes locked with one another.

"It's my turn now father. Hurry off to Hell as I take over what's left of our family business."

Serpent gurgled. His blood quit pumping out of the hole in his neck as his heart finally stopped beating.

"Stay where you are," one of the men ordered.

Robert turned to face them. The entire front of his body was awash in his father's blood.

"My name is General Robert Aleman, but you will refer to me as Raven. You work for me now."

A full ten seconds passed before all three men slowly lowered and then holstered their weapons.

"What are your orders, sir?"

\* \* \*

## July, 2001

Two months later and Raven was well on his path of revenge. Members of his old organization, all forced in to retirement a decade before, began to turn up dead. Wolf, Bear, Eagle, Panther and Wolverine had all been assassinated.

Some had died in car accidents while others had heart attacks, poisoned by his old friend and confidant, Anna Garland, who was only too happy to be back by his side and in the game.

# 2
## Monday September 10, 2001

A warm, soft breeze danced over eight year old Gavin Clark as he sat in the sand and gazed out over the vast ocean. The single palm tree in the center of his small island provided some shade. He often came to this place to think; to get away from his family and everyone else. He stared intently out into the distance.

*I wonder what's out there?*

Gavin's right arm was nudged and he looked down at Stir, his imaginary but very real monster that he was able to conjure from the depths of his mind; one of his genetic anomalies he realized he possessed when he was only four.

"What is it boy? Did you want some attention?"

Stir's small form, red eyes and wispy black body ended in a short tail that thumped somewhat loudly on the sand. He nudged Gavin's arm again until his master relented and began to pet him.

"We've been through a lot together, haven't we Stir? If it wasn't for you I don't know where I'd be right now. Maybe even here."

Stir looked in to Gavin's eyes as if he understood every word he said, a slight smile on his jowls from the body rub he was currently receiving.

"I get it now though. I understand why we've been targeted all these years. I'm special, my sister's special and now my parents are special."

He stopped petting Stir and gazed off. Stir cocked his head to one side and then nudged Gavin's arm again. When that didn't work he began to gently whine.

Gavin looked down at his best friend. "Really Stir? Whining?"

13

His tail went in to overdrive and whacked the sand even louder. Gavin smiled and resumed petting Stir's smokey body much to his delight and then looked back out at the horizon.

"It's weird how it's always sunny here. Don't you find that curious?"

Stir wasn't listening as one of his back legs began to spasm as Gavin hit his sweet spot. Gavin suddenly yawned and brought the hand he had on Stir up to his mouth to cover it as Stir gave him a displeasing glare.

"It's late," Gavin said offhandedly as he stood up. "Let's go home."

Gavin took one last longing look in the distance and then turned towards the other side of his island, the shore a mere twenty feet away. With Stir by his side Gavin walked up to the only other item of interest on his island, besides the palm tree, and regarded the bleached skeleton that lay haphazardly on the sand with disdain.

"You're not that scary now, are you?"

All that remained of Victor Bannon, the former Director of Central Intelligence, was his skeletal form. Gavin recalled that it had been nearly four years prior since he and his family had been held hostage by Victor. Victor had tried to shoot his mother but his father Thomas, at that very moment, discovered and used his power to save them all. It was shortly thereafter, knowing full well that Victor was never going to stop coming after them, that his father asked Gavin to open a portal. Victor was pushed through and was never heard from again.

Gavin, when he came to his special place, often took the opportunity to look at Victor's skeleton that lay in the sand. At first he'd been frightened of it, not knowing what to do. But over time he got used to Victor's presence and he hadn't been scared of it for a long time. His father had forbidden him to use his portal soon afterwards, not wanting his son to see what happened to Victor, and Gavin had nodded his head in agreement but had never listened. This was his place and his alone.

Gavin looked away from the skeleton, formed the portal and both he and Stir went through it. Instantly they were back in his bedroom. He looked over at his clock. It read 12:06 a.m. They had been on the island for over an hour but here, on this plane of existence, only a second had passed by. Gavin didn't know how or why it worked that way and he never gave it too much thought. It just was what it was.

On his bed Stickers arched his back and stretched. The cat had become immune to the portal appearing, Gavin walking through and then reappearing again a second later. Stir jumped up on the bed and the two of them began to playfully tussle like they usually did. In no time Stickers raced off the bed, out of the room and down the hallway with Stir on his heels smiling the entire way.

In the next room over Emily, his ten year old sister, screamed. Gavin rolled his eyes and climbed into bed. His sister screaming from her nightmares wasn't anything new. She'd been having them for some time now and she had confided in him that past events haunted her from time to time. Gavin knew exactly what she meant. That was probably why he decided to visit his island more often than anyone really realized.

In his sister's room he heard his mother calming Emily down. It took a few minutes before he heard movement and then his mother's form appeared in his doorway. This wasn't his first rodeo.

"Gav, are you…"

"I'm fine. Goodnight," he said matter-of-factly.

Laura, now forty-six, paused in the doorway briefly, indecisive on whether to pursue her son's indifference in the middle of the night. Deciding against it she began to close the door just as

Stickers and Stir careened off one of her legs and bounded up on his bed. Within moments they cuddled up against Gavin and closed their eyes.

"Okay. Goodnight Gav. Sweet dreams."

"Maybe you should tell that to Em," he mumbled under his breath.

"Did you say something sweetheart?"

"No. Goodnight."

*He's lying but it doesn't matter.* "Goodnight."

Laura left his bedroom door open a few inches and headed back to the master bedroom.

"Nightmares again?" forty-four year old Thomas asked her. Laura nodded.

"Did she say what they were about this time?"

"No. She doesn't talk about them."

"Well, there was that one time."

"True," Laura replied, "but she knows I can tell when she's not telling the truth. I know it infuriates the kids."

Thomas opened his arms and welcomed his wife into his arms as she got back in bed. She cuddled up next to him.

"Well sweetie, you can't really blame them. Kids lie all the time. The issue is that they have a mother who knows when they're doing it."

"I know. I guess it just hurts. It feels like they're shutting me out of their lives."

"Just give it time, they'll come around."

Laura looked up at Thomas and caught his eyes. "Even you don't fully believe that."

Thomas chuckled. "Okay, okay. You got me. That was a half lie. How about I say I hope they come around in time? Is that better?"

Laura smiled. "Better," she said and lay back down on his chest.

Thomas waited a few seconds and then asked her a question. "Do you wish you'd never used the syringe I offered you?"

Nearly four years ago Thomas' DNA had been cracked wide open by Dr. Yamato Takuma Matsushita, deep within Facility 13. His father's mentor, Richard Moore, and he had been held prisoner. During that time Thomas and Emily had been interrogated and experimented on, ending with an experimental serum that was based off Thomas' DNA. Before Dr. Matsushita could perfect the process, or the serum, Thomas was able to escape the facility with the help of Rebecca Cross. During that escape the secret research and development facility caught fire and Richard had bravely sacrificed his life to save Thomas'. His mother and father, who appeared out of nowhere, also came to his aid to help their son and granddaughter escape. Doctor Matsushita, with a badly burned right hand and arm, escaped but not before he had stuck Thomas with what he thought was a sleep agent during their tussle.

Thomas discovered another syringe on the floor and pocketed it thinking he could use it to put someone else to sleep later if necessary. It wasn't until later that Thomas realized the extra syringe he'd pocketed, during the escape, was in fact one of the few test serums Dr. Matsushita had been working on. The syringe he'd been injected with was also from the same batch. Thomas' power of telekinesis emerged, at a heightened state of stress, and deflected the bullet meant to kill Laura. In the days that followed Laura begin to feel left out. It was then that Thomas gave her the final syringe and offered her the choice.

"Do you wish you'd never used the syringe?"

"Yes and no," she eventually responded. "It's like a curse."

"Why do you say that?"

17

"Some days I don't mind my power, the ability to know when someone is lying. And then there are other days when I just wish I could turn it off."

Thomas understood. "I get it. You're probably amazed at how often people lie to each other."

She nodded in the dark. "All the time. It's bizarre."

"Well, at least you know I'm not lying when I tell you I love you."

Laura softened up and a small smile appeared. "Well…"

"What? What do you mean well?"

"I guess the question is how much do you love me?"

Thomas finally caught on and moved his hands to tickle her. "Why you little vixen!"

Laura laughed and tried to get away but he held her down.

"You think that was pretty funny, don't you?" he said.

Laura nodded. "Hilarious."

"Tsk tsk," he responded as they begun to get comfortable in bed again. "Using your powers for evil. You should be ashamed."

Laura took that opportunity to rip off the comforter.

"What are you doing?"

"I'm not the only one who's used my powers for evil. Do your trick to me again and I'll show you how much I love you…"

\* \* \*

Thomas and his family sat around the kitchen table eating breakfast. The kids looked tired, and so did the adults, but for different reasons.

"Would one of you please pass the salt?" Thomas asked. Before anyone could react he spoke up again. "Never mind, I got it."

Thomas twiddled his fingers and the salt container levitated off the table and zipped over to his outstretched hand.

"My power is fun, even in the bedroom," he said with a twinkle in his eye.

Laura kicked him in the shin under the table. "Shh."

"I don't get it," Gavin stated.

"They're talking about sex," Em flat out told her brother.

"What's sex?"

Thomas and Laura froze for a second as their ten and eight year old started up on each other.

Emily rolled her eyes. "You're dumb."

"Nuh, uh. You're dumb."

"You're so dumb that you don't even know how dumb you are."

"Alright," Laura interjected, "that's enough of that." She turned her attention to her daughter. "Are you excited that school starts today?"

"Yes," Emily replied.

"What about you sport?" Thomas asked his son.

Gavin shrugged.

Laura couldn't help herself. "Em. Why don't I believe you?"

Emily dropped her toast back on the plate and stared at her mother. "I hate that you can do that."

"I'm sorry. You're right. But why aren't you excited? Is it your nightmares?"

"It's nothing. I don't want to talk about it."

"Okay, okay," Thomas said trying to smooth things over before the first day of school. "Hey Em. Maybe later, after you get home, we can try to see if you can summon your grandfather again. What'ya say?"

Emily stood up. "You two are unbelievable. It's all about what you want from me and what my powers can do for you. I'm

19

sick of it. And I'm tired of trying to get grandpa to show himself. It hasn't worked for years and you know it. I don't want to do things for you anymore. Just leave me alone."

Emily stomped back to her room and slammed the door.

Gavin spoke up. "She's been through a lot, and so have I. It's taking its toll."

Thomas and Laura sat there and eventually nodded.

"You're right Gav," Thomas replied. "You've had to experience the ugliness of the world, and from that you both have grown up too quickly. I'm afraid your mother and I don't always remember that."

Gavin shrugged. "But Em and I do. It just is what it is," he said as he took another bite of toast.

Laura stood up and started to collect plates. "Thanks for the reminder Gav."

"You're welcome. And I know what sex is."

"You do?"

"Sure. I just like messing with Em."

Thomas and Laura shared a quick glance.

Thomas looked at his watch. "Why don't you go get ready for school? Rebecca's going to be here shortly to take both of you."

"K." Gavin headed off down the hall and back to his room.

Laura paused as they looked at each other. "They are not getting any younger."

"No shit. We're going to be in for a wild ride."

Laura started to clean up breakfast and Thomas headed to his office. He sat down in his chair and began to recollect the past four years of his family and friends, Sam and Bill.

Unanimously they had all agreed to abandon Hawaii and move back to the San Francisco Bay Area. SANDBOX was headquartered in Marin and they had all grown up in the area so it was familiar territory for their wives and all of their children to come back to.  Naturally, before and during their time in Hawaii, they had all felt like targets.  However, moving back to Marin felt like the right move, and once again they were able to procure three houses that were next door to each other, for the right price.

For the first full year after they returned, in 1998, Sam made sure all three families were under twenty-four hour protection. And even though their paranoia was at an all-time high, there were zero incidents.  No one came for Thomas, Emily or Gavin.  No one shot at or ambushed the women on a deserted stretch of road. Even Sam and Bill, back at work expanding SANDBOX, hadn't taken any bullets to their bodies.

All six children had grown older.  Sam's kids, Amanda and Craig, were now thirteen and nine.  Bill's children, Sarah and Edward were the same age.  Julie and Kim had just turned forty-one a few weeks prior but constantly gave their husbands a hard time that their birthdays, when they'd turn forty-four, were right around the corner.

Life was peaceful, routine and boring.  But that didn't stop any of them from remaining vigilant.  They all carried semi-automatic handguns, either concealed in a purse or under a shirt nestled in a belt holster.  And they all made regular trips to SANDBOX's indoor range to stay on top of their shooting skills.  Thomas took it a step further and, without telling Laura, embedded all of his children's clothing with small GPS tracking devices.  He wasn't taking any chances with his children's lives and knew if he ever had to utilize the technology one day then Laura would understand.

Thomas swiveled in his chair.  He knew he and his children would always be targets but he also knew that he'd continue to do whatever it took to keep them safe.  The past four years had zipped by, but the memories of what they'd all been through still haunted each of them in one way or another.

Laura walked into his office.

"What're you up to today?"

"More running with Sam and Bill to start things off."

"You've been doing that for a while now and I 'm enjoying the results," she said with a grin.

"I bet you do," as he returned her smile. "After that I'll come home and figure something out. What about you?"

"It's the first day of school. I'll check in with Julie and Kim since I didn't see them over the weekend."

"That's a first," Thomas joked.

"Yeah yeah."

"You still provide them an ear to talk to?"

"It's not like they can go talk to someone else about what they've been through, right?"

"True enough."

"Anyway, I'll see where their heads are at with the kids finally out of the house and out of earshot."

"And you could use a break too I imagine."

"Definitely."

A knock on the front door interrupted their conversation. Thomas got up and looked through the side window of his office, hand on the handle of his Glock. He relaxed.

"It's Rebecca."

Laura walked out of his office, around the corner and opened the front door.

"Good morning Rebecca," she said as she let her in and they hugged each other.

Rebecca Cross had a strong affinity with the Clark family. She worked for SANDBOX and was in a charge of a group of other operators that had provided protection for all three families in Hawaii. Over time she had come to realize that Emily and Gavin had extraordinary powers. During the family's ambush in Hawaii, orchestrated by Nikolay Dmitriev, she was critically injured. At the hospital, in an induced coma, Gavin had hastily healed her before the family fled with no other choice but to leave her behind. It was during that Hawaiian attack when she received the scar that began under her right eye and travelled part way down her cheek. She knew Gavin saved her life and had witnessed more amazing things since then from all four of the Clark family members. When it came right down to it she had become a member of the family.

"Hi Laura. I hope I'm not too early."

"Right on time, as always. Can I get you a coffee to go?"

"Not this morning, thank you."

"Becca!" Gavin yelled as he ran around the corner from the hallway.

She smiled, knelt on one knee and gave him a huge welcome. "How are you? Ready for school?"

"Yes!"

"Wow," Laura said. "All I got was a shrug from you this morning young man."

"It's all about the delivery mom," he retorted and both Laura and Rebecca couldn't help but chuckle.

"I see. I'll remember that." Laura turned her head and spoke up. "Emily, Rebecca's here. Time to go."

Emily emerged from her room, trudged past her father as he emerged from his office, and stood by the front door.

"Hi," she said.

"Good morning Em. Ready for school?"

"Whatever."

Rebecca raised her eyebrows and looked at both Thomas and Laura. "I'll let you know how it goes. They're in good hands."

Thomas put his arm around Laura. "We know they are. Thank you."

"You're welcome."

"Where's my hugs?" their mother asked the two of them.

"Awh mom," Gavin whined but hugged his mother.

Emily ignored the request and headed straight for the vehicle.

Rebecca shrugged and then turned to Emily and Gavin. "Alright, get in the backseat of the Suburban. Move it you little freaks." Gavin giggled and even Emily cracked a smile.

"Have a good day you two," Laura called after them.

# 3
# Monday September 10, 2001

Forty-three year old Sam Paige jolted awake, opened his eyes and sat up in bed.

"Are you alright?" his wife Julie asked him.

He looked over at her, still resting on her pillow, and stared deep in to her dark, black eyes. Her eyes used to be brown when he married her but turned black after Gavin brought her back to life from the other place. He turned away.

"I'm fine."

"You want to talk about it?"

"Talk about what?"

Julie sat up and began to gently rub Sam's back. "You were having one of your nightmares. They don't happen that often anymore, but from time to time I can see they still bother you."

Sam was irritated that he wasn't able to control what his mind chewed on when he was asleep.

"What's there to talk about? There are moments when I relive you dying. I'm halfway around the world, patched through by radio and all I can hear is Laura telling me that you've been shot."

"But I was brought back."

"I know that now, but when it happened I didn't know that. I lived with the truth that you were dead for a long time and it tears me up."

Julie wrapped her arms around her husband. "I'm right here."

He embraced her as well. "I know. Hell, you'd think I'd be over it by now after four years."

"Maybe you should talk to Laura about this."

"Maybe," he hesitantly replied.

25

She pulled back and looked at him. "She's helped Kim and me through everything we've experienced more than you realize. She's a good person and, if you remember, she did have her own practice. Chat her up sometime."

The alarm next to the bed went off suddenly. Sam reached over, turned it off and got up.

"I'll check in on the kids and get them motivated being the first day of school and all."

"Thank you," Julie said. "Those two can be a pain in the ass to get out of bed. I'll start making breakfast."

\* \* \*

"Amanda! Craig!" Julie loudly said from the kitchen as she finished washing dishes. "We're leaving in one minute so finish up whatever you're doing. I don't want you being late for school."

Sam smiled from a kitchen chair and Julie caught it.

"What's that smile for?"

"You."

"Me?"

"You make me smile. That's all."

Julie walked over to him, bent over and gave him a quick kiss before she grabbed her purse and keys. "I'll take it."

"You bet you will," he replied with a smirk.

She smiled back at him. "So I'm going to take the kids to school and then have Kim and Laura over."

"Girl's morning, eh?"

"Well, it is our first day of freedom. And as much as I love our kids I feel better that it's the teacher's problem to deal with them all day now."

Amanda and Craig appeared in the kitchen. Julie handed each of them their lunch.

26

"Do you both have everything you need?"

Craig, only nine, hadn't fully developed the upcoming teenage aura like his sister had. "I'm ready."

"Yes mom," thirteen year old Amanda replied with an air of annoyance.

Julie ignored her daughter's attitude and turned back to Sam. "And you? Should we plan on a fourth wine glass?"

Sam shook his head. "More running with the boys."

Julie grinned. "Good. Just make sure you stinky men don't walk in on our clubhouse meeting. Everything we talk about is completely secret, you understand."

Sam put his hands up in mock compliance. "Roger that wifey," and then turned to his kids. "Who's got a hug for their old man?"

Craig gave him a huge hug. Amanda reluctantly held back until Sam pushed out his lower lip and cocked his head to one side. She finally relented.

"That look is so dumb," she said as she gave her father a quick hug.

"I know, but I got my little girl to hug me didn't I?"

"I'm not a little girl."

"Regardless of your age, young lady, you'll always be my little girl. Now, I want both of you to have a good day."

They all walked to the front door together.

"Be careful out there," he cautioned.

"Always," she replied as she patted her purse and felt the outline of her gun.

Sam closed the door behind his family and headed back to the master bedroom to get ready for his run.

# 4
## Monday September 10, 2001

"Honey?" whispered forty-three year old Bill Nicholson as he lay in bed. "You awake yet?"

Kim rolled over and her hand inadvertently brushed over her husband's crotch.

Her eyes opened and a sly grin appeared on her face. "I am now. You appear to have a little problem down there that needs taking care of."

"Did you just say it was little?"

Kim chuckled. "Awh. Should I whisper so your penis can't hear me?"

Bill smiled back at his wife. Their constant banter and shit-talking was one of the real joys of his life.

"Well, maybe you should go down there and talk to him yourself. You know, say you're sorry in person. He's pretty sensitive."

"Oh I bet he is," she replied as she wrapped her hand around him and squeezed tightly.

"Hey now!"

At that exact moment their bedroom door flew open and nine year old Edward ran over and jumped on the bed, barely missing Bill's crotch. Bill turned sideways and Kim withdrew her hands from underneath the sheets.

"Well, guess that takes care of that."

Kim smiled and then pulled her son close to her. "Are you ready for school my little man?"

"Uh huh," he replied as his head bobbed up and down.

29

"Good to hear champ," Bill said and then began to tickle Edward who started to laugh as he struggled to free himself from his mother's arms.

"What's going on in here?" thirteen year old Sarah stated from the doorway.

"Oh, just a little morning tickle fest," Bill replied as he started in on his son's tummy again.

"Dad! Quit it!" Edward managed to say between gasps.

"What? You want me to stop?"

His son nodded.

"Okay," Bill said. He grabbed hold of his son's right arm below the elbow and gently began to tap his son's head with his own helpless hand. "What are you doing? Quit hitting yourself. Quit hitting yourself."

Edward giggled even more as Sarah walked over. Bill turned his attention to his daughter.

"Oh, I see how it is. You must want in on some of this."

Sarah placed her hands on her hips. "We want a dog."

Bill's face faltered and he let his son's arm go.

"What?"

"I said we want a dog."

"Yeah dad," Edward added. "We want a dog. Please?"

"No," he immediately replied. "No pets."

"That's not fair," Sarah retorted.

"Why not?" his son added.

"The answer is no."

"But…"

Kim spoke up. "This isn't the time to discuss this. I want you both to go get ready for school. Breakfast will be in twenty minutes. Move it."

Edward climbed off the bed and headed out of the room while Sarah took her time, contemplating her next move.

"Now young lady," her mother urged.

Sarah finally relented and stomped back to her bedroom.

Kim looked over at Bill. "So no dog, huh? What aren't you telling me?"

He stared back at her.

"Well?"

"It was a long time ago but I don't want to talk about it."

"You can't keep telling them no without a reason. They're just kids."

Bill looked at Kim and relented. "I've never talked about this with anyone else. This doesn't go any further."

She nodded slightly and decided to stay silent.

"Back in the days, when Sam and I were going through training to become members of Special Ops, one of the requirements was that we each look after a pet rabbit. We were told to name it, feed it and clean up after it amongst all the other training we were put through. It seemed like a stupid necessity but you do whatever the instructors tell you to do. Anyway, Sam and I picked out our rabbits and named them. Sam decided to call his Mitsy."

"Mitsy?"

"Yeah."

"And yours?" she gently probed.

Bill didn't reply right away, but eventually he told her. "Bun-bun."

Kim smiled. "That's cute."

"I thought so too, at the time."

Kim pushed him a little. "What happened?"

Bill blurted the harsh truth out. "The motherfuckers made us gut, cook and eat our pets."

Kim covered her mouth in shock. "Oh. That's horrible."

Bill got up from the bed and headed to their private master bathroom where he turned on the shower. A few seconds later Kim walked in.

"Listen. I have no idea what you've been through, mostly because you won't talk about it."

"Can't," he countered.

"It doesn't matter. The issue is that you've got some baggage and you're entitled to it. But what you're not entitled to is preventing our children from experiencing things because of that baggage."

"But…"

Kim held up her hand to stop him. "I'm not overriding you, right now. But, sometime in the future I may have to. Our kids have been through more than they remember, and so have we. There are days when all I can think about is the attack in Hawaii, my sister dying, running for our lives on the open sea and being held hostage. Those images continue to haunt me. Luckily for us our children don't remember them because we had Emily wipe their memories. Can you imagine how fucked up our kids would be if they had all that shit running around in their heads?"

Bill nodded. "I might have an idea about that."

Kim softened her voice. "I know you do. You're a complicated man, but you're also a good man. Our life together is not what I was expecting, nor could have ever predicted. But because I get to spend it with you it's all been worth it. I love you."

"I love you too."

"I know you do." She slapped his naked ass. "Now get in that shower while I go check on our children's status, first day of school and all."

Bill stepped in and closed the shower door behind him. "What are your plans for the day?"

"I'm taking the kid's to school and then meeting Laura over at my sister's."

"For a freedom wine tasting session?"

"You bet your ass. What about you honey?"

"Heading out to run with the boys and then off to the office."

"Okies. I'll see you in the kitchen and hopefully we can get these two off to school without too many hassles."

"Good luck with that," Bill replied with a smirk. "You know that you're talking about our kids, right?"

"Oh, I know," she said with a grin as she walked out of the bathroom to begin the day.

# 5

# Monday September 10, 2001

Even though Thomas had been running with Sam and Bill for weeks now he still couldn't keep up with his friends as they crested the large hill ahead of him.

"Come on slowpoke," Bill said.

"Shut up," Thomas replied between breaths. "At forty-three you two make it look easy."

Sam smiled at his friend's discomfort. "We've had some practice."

"No shit Sherlock," Thomas shot back as he caught back up to them on the plateau.

"But in all honesty," Sam added, "we're proud of you for getting in shape."

"Especially at your age," Bill quipped.

"You assholes. Just because I'm forty-four doesn't mean your birthdays aren't right around the goddamn corner."

"But they're not here yet," Sam added with a chuckle.

"Yeah," Bill said, "let's go old man."

The trio kept pace along the top of the plateau. They finally came to a stop on a very familiar knoll that overlooked the bunker where it all started four years prior. The bunker where Joshua, the CIA rogue, had taken Thomas' children after he discovered they had powers. It was in that bunker where Gavin saved his life and Thomas had met Stir for the very first time.

After moving back to Marin Sam setup round the clock security on all three families and it wasn't until a year later that they finally reduced the twenty-four hour security. Nearly three years after that and still no one had come for them. Sam, Bill and Thomas often ran up this way, since they returned to Marin, as a reminder to always remain vigilant. All three of them carried side arms and remained cautious everywhere they went.

"So how's Rebecca?" Sam asked.

"Are you kidding me?" Thomas replied. "She's family, even though she's staying in the small guest house in the back. She needs her privacy and she likes to stay close. The kid's adore her and they don't have to hide who they are from her. She's really been one hell of a big sister since Hawaii. I know she'll look after our kids and do whatever it takes to protect them. Thanks again for letting Rebecca look after my family."

Sam and Bill nodded. They understood exactly where Thomas was coming from.

"Well, it was that or we figured you'd hire her away from us and pay her more money."

Thomas smiled. "Well, there is that. Speaking of SANDBOX personnel…"

Bill piped up. "I hear a segue incoming."

Thomas ignored his friend. "So what's the current state of the business?"

Sam spoke up. "You mean aside from the fact that we're taking contracts from all over the world now?"

"Yes, I know you're global now you bragger. Give me some details."

"Well, we've got contracts everywhere and I'm sad to say we're stretched extremely thin right now."

"He's not kidding," Bill added. "We're stretched to the max so much that Sam and I might have to start doing jobs again, and you know what our wives would have to say about that."

Thomas did. Sam and Bill had spent most of their time growing their business over the past four years which left them with little time to actually participate in active contract work. Their wives had gotten used to them being around and remaining safe. It was a bone of contention between them but one the men understood. Still, Sam and Bill continued to train with their operators as time allowed. They were who they were and their wives knew it.

Sam picked up the conversation. "The five hundred million your father gave us Thomas went one hell of a long way. Bill and I each netted twenty million and deposited the rest in the company coffers. That gave us the viability and bankroll to extend overseas."

"Is that when you bought the private jet?"

Sam nodded. "Our Cessna Citation Encore."

"You haven't traveled until you've gone four hundred and ninety-five miles an hour in a private plane," Bill added.

"Sounds fun," said Thomas.

"Anyway, we bought the jet and use it to quickly get boots on the ground wherever they're needed."

"And where are these contracts happening?"

"You'd be amazed. Quite a number of protection details in the Middle East have sprung up; oil executives and what not who are fearful of being kidnapped. Those sorts of contracts."

"Sounds lucrative."

"And expensive. We've had to bring on more internal personnel to handle everything. From linguists to lawyers. Name it and we've got it."

"But Roberta's still running our show for us," said Bill. "I don't think Sam or I would know what to do without her at this point. How long has she worked for us?"

Sam thought about it for a second. "Way back in eighty-six. What is that, fifteen years now? That would make Thomas forty-four, now wouldn't it?"

"Seriously? Back to that? Fuck you guys."

Sam and Bill started chuckling.

37

"We're just playing brother," Bill said as he lightly hit Thomas in the shoulder. "Besides, if I hit you any harder there's a chance I might break something."

Thomas grabbed Bill and managed to get the crook of his arm around his neck as the two of them playfully began to wrestle.

"Get'em," Sam urged.

It wasn't long before Thomas had been subdued. Bill let his friend go and helped him up, both smiling from ear to ear as they dusted themselves off.

Thomas spoke up. "Speaking of bringing new people on, how's Hobbes working out for you?"

Charles Hillburg, who went by the handle Hobbes, had previously worked for Victor Bannon, the former DCI. Hobbes, and his co-worker Calvin, had been the computer techs that Victor privately utilized to take down Nikolay Dmitriev. Ultimately Calvin and Hobbes were drawn in to Victor's plan of holding Emily and Thomas, not only as hostages, but to experiment on. Hobbes, as it turns out, was a reluctant participant and ultimately helped them take Victor down.

"Hobbes is working out well. Emily did a great job on his selective memory wipe. He doesn't remember a damn thing about what he did for Victor. Once we turned him loose at SANDBOX he proceeded to completely revamp our computer network, firewalls, communications and servers."

"Basically he's is nerd heaven," said Bill.

"That he is," agreed Sam. "Anyway, let's head out. We need to get to work."

The trio began to jog back the way they came.

"Oh," Bill exclaimed. "Let's not forget about completely redesigning the top floor of SANDBOX."

"I remember that," Thomas said.

38

In early 1998 Sam and Bill took the top floor of their office and gutted it. In its place they created living quarters, much like a penthouse suite. It was an open space concept that contained a central living area, kitchen, entertainment room and multiple living quarters, all with private bathrooms. The idea behind it, as always, was security. In case of an emergency all three families could head to SANDBOX and bunker down. In the three years since it had been built they'd only used it a few times. The first time was when they wanted to take it for a test run. Subsequent visits were mostly because the kids had whined about wanting to spend the night where their father's worked.

"But enough about us," said Bill as they continued to jog back home. "Sam and I haven't heard any recent updates about you and your writing career."

Thomas sighed because he knew it'd been years since he'd put pen to paper. In his head he had already made the decision to give up writing children's books, much to the chagrin of Nick Raynes, his agent. Thomas figured that maybe one day he'd pick it up again, but until that day he still had to live with the memories of what he, his family and his friend's families had all been through. Through everything Thomas' mind, although still very creative, had managed to become a tad bit darker.

Thomas opened his mouth. "With what we've all been through I've been mulling over writing a biography."

"That could never be published," Sam said offhandedly.

"Yeah, something like that."

"Well, it's not like you need a paycheck anytime soon," Bill joked.

"I don't know. I'm just tired of looking over my shoulder. It weighs on my mind and messes with my head. I'd have one hell of a time coming up with a children's book that wouldn't scare kids to death rather than lull them off to sleep."

"Any thoughts about what you're going to do about that?" Sam asked.

"I have no idea. Laura and I talk from time to time about it, but staying at home is slowly driving me crazy. I feel like I'm back in Running Springs again trying to block out the world around me."

"And now you know how we felt trying to get you off that damn mountain in the first place," Sam said with a smile.

"Fuck you two very much."

"Maybe it's something else." Bill said.

"What do you mean?"

"Even through all the hell we've been through, maybe you've just gotten a taste for it."

"A taste for what?" Thomas asked.

"Part of what you're saying sounds like you're quite the adrenaline junkie and you haven't gotten your fix."

"That's crazy," Thomas countered.

"No," said Sam, "not really. Take a second and breakdown what you've been through since nineteen ninety. Your mind was fucked with. You shot and killed Albert Clemmings. Your daughter and son now have special abilities based on the mind controlling chemicals they pumped you full of. Your children's abilities saved your life," Sam said as he thumbed his hand over his shoulder, "right back there in that bunker. We moved to Hawaii where your father, your long deceased father, spun us a tail about Nikolay Dmitriev. That led us to the microfilm and a whole new bevy of adventures that we're all very familiar with.

"Whether you want to acknowledge it or not Thomas, you're an action junkie now. Bill and I went off to the Army to spite our parents. In doing so we found our calling, and thanks to your generosity we built our business. You, on the other hand, knew from the beginning that you wanted to create. But, in the end, I think you're conflicted as hell. Who knows, maybe you just don't want to admit it to yourself."

Thomas stopped jogging and just stood there. Sam and Bill took a few more steps before they turned around and looked at their best friend.

"What's up?" Bill asked.

"You know, I was always jealous of you two heading off to the service together. I didn't hate you, but what I did hate was that you still had each other to lean on for all those years. I felt alone and I quickly grew accustomed to that condition. To answer your observation Sam, yes, I always knew I wanted to write, to create. And I was successful at that for a while. But when I needed you two the most you came to my rescue and together we took Albert down. It was at that point, along with meeting Laura, when I broke out of my isolated shell. All of us were together again, for better or for worse, and over the years since then the shit has significantly hit the fan."

Thomas paused.

"I'm not the same person that I once was, that's for sure. My family is what matters the most to me and, given the opportunity, we would all be locked up and probed for the rest of our lives. My point is that my path in life has changed, drastically but I'm thrilled to death that the two of you are still part of it."

"We are too brother."

"I think you're right Sam. I think I'm an adrenaline junkie. It's not that I wanted to be one, it's just what I've become from what life has thrown at me."

Sam walked up to Thomas and gave him a hug. "Welcome to the club."

Bill started to walk over. Thomas twitched his hand and an unseen force forcibly yanked Bill's shorts halfway down his legs.

Bill fell over before he could stop himself and tipped over onto the pavement. Thomas and Sam chuckled as Bill picked himself up.

"And then there's this Jedi power that I enjoy using from time to time," Thomas managed to say with an immense smile.

"Run," Bill said. "Because when I catch you it's all over."

Thomas took off like a shot with Bill after him. Sam continued to laugh as he raced to catch up.

# 6

## Monday September 10, 2001

Rebecca pulled the Suburban into the school's large drop-off area and put it in park. She turned around in her seat and looked at Gavin and Emily.

"I'll be back at three to pick you up and I'll meet you right here, okay?"

The two agreed.

Rebecca smiled. "Good. Now get out of here before I end up taking you both to Disneyland instead of school."

"Really?" Gavin tested.

"No," his sister retorted. "She's just messing with your head, just like all grown-ups do."

"I know."

Emily took that opportunity to exit the Suburban and head off into the school.

"What's up with Em? I haven't seen her like this before."

"She's not handling the family secrets as well as I am," he replied.

"Is that right?"

Gavin nodded. "I'm glad I don't have her powers. Too much pressure."

He scooted across the seat and into the vacant spot his sister had occupied.

Rebecca spoke up. "Speaking of powers…"

"I get it; no powers. I know the drill."

She smiled. "Have a good day. Knock'em dead."

"I will. I love you Becca."

"Love you too kiddo."

Gavin closed the door behind him and raced off. Rebecca watched him go and then put the Suburban in drive and headed out to the office.

Gavin looked around, finally located his sister in the throng of students and made his way over to her.

"What do you want Gav?" she demanded.

"That wasn't very nice. Becca was just making a joke."

"I don't care."

"Why not?"

She pulled her younger brother off to the side and lowered her voice. "If you haven't figured it out I don't want my powers anymore."

He understood. "It's your nightmares. They're getting worse, aren't they?"

Emily just stood there, open mouthed, staring at her brother. Her response was barely audible. "Yes."

"That's okay. I want to take you someplace tonight."

"What do you mean? What are you talking about?"

"To my special place. But it has to be our secret. Mom and Dad can't find out."

Surprise swept across her face. "But you're not allowed to go back there."

He shrugged. "So?"

Emily smiled. "Wow. Look at you being defiant. Okay, you're on."

Gavin smiled back at his sister and then headed off to his classroom.

A small sense of peace washed over Emily as she watched her brother weave through the sea of backpacks. She turned around and came face to face with a large sixth grade girl and two of her friends.

"I can't believe you left the house dressed in 'that'," the girl teased as all three of them giggled at an unphased Emily.

"You're not worth my time," Emily replied as she tried to push through the three girls.

The leader grabbed a fistful of Emily's hair and yanked her backwards. "You're not going anywhere."

Emily winced, placed her right hand over the girl's hand that held her hair and came face to face with the older bully.

"We're not done with you," the girl snarled in Emily's face. "You think you're soooo special being driven around by a bodyguard don't you."

"Let me tell you a story…"

"We're not interested in…"

"Shut up," Emily willed.

She still had the girl's exposed hand in her own and the bully immediately stopped talking, much to the surprise of the other two.

"You picked the wrong day and person to mess with. Before you interrupted me I was going to tell you a short story. But now none of you deserve to hear it. Instead, all I have to say is how unfortunate it is that so many spiders decided to nest in your hair. It'll take at least a minute for them to leave."

The girl released Emily's hair and began to shriek uncontrollably, swatting at her face, arms and body as her mind convinced her that spiders were coming out of her hair and crawling all over her body. Emily backed away as the two other girls were stunned by the sudden change in their leader's demeanor. They didn't know what to do but the girl's bloodcurdling cries began to bring numerous teachers over to her as a multitude of students looked on.

Emily knew she shouldn't have used her powers of suggestion but she didn't really care. She let a smile creep across her face as she headed off to her first day of class.

*Maybe I do want to keep my powers after all.*

# 7
## Monday September 10, 2001

After Thomas met up with Sam and Bill to go running Laura poured another cup of coffee and just enjoyed the silence. Stickers eventually made his way out of Gavin's room and into the kitchen where he politely meowed for his morning meal. She fixed it and then petted him while he ate. He purred from the attention.

"You have it pretty easy compared to the rest of us Mister Stickers. I don't know if our lives have gotten more complicated on their own volition, or if that's just what happens when everyone in this family has crazy abilities."

Stickers looked up at Laura briefly as if to answer her question, but then returned to his bowl instead.

"It's okay Stickers, you and I have both seen more than we could ever explain."

Laura stood up, dumped out her remaining coffee as she saw a familiar vehicle pass the front of her house and park next door. She locked the front door behind her and then headed across the lawn to Julie and Sam's house. When all the families decided to move back to Marin they initially thought about trying to obtain their old houses. However, after some discussion they determined that starting fresh was better for them as well as their children. They were able to convince the current owners of their houses that moving would be more profitable than staying, but only after they shelled out a few million dollars each to make it happen.

Laura met Julie in the driveway and they walked to the front door.

"How was dropping off your kids this morning?"

"Busy. As you know they go to two different schools. I just wish they were closer together. I should have Craig take the bus but I worry too much."

Julie unlocked the front door just as Kim pulled up and parked in her driveway. The two waited for her to join them before all three headed inside and sat down in the kitchen.

"I was just telling Laura that the two schools seem too far apart."

Kim nodded. "I suppose we could trade children in the morning. I drop our youngsters off at elementary while you take the teenagers to middle school."

Julie chuckled. "Sounds like you got the best end of that deal. What a handful our teens can be; unpredictable and opinionated."

"Just like Emily," Laura added.

Julie perked up. "Oh yeah? What's going on with Em?"

"That's the million dollar question right now. She seems angry and she won't talk to me. Every time I try to engage her she withdraws."

"That sucks," said Kim. "I wonder what's eating at her."

"It's frustrating to say the least. Just this morning I asked her if she was excited about school. She said yes but I knew she wasn't telling the truth."

Julie and Kim shared a glance and Laura caught it.

"What? What is it?" Laura asked.

"Well," Kim started, "that ability of yours has taken a bit for us to get used to as well."

"What my sister is politely trying to tell you is that even though we don't have secrets between us, or anything to lie about, your ability does present some fundamental issues."

"Such as?" pressed Laura.

"Such as when you ask either of us whether a certain item of clothing looks good on you," Julie answered.

"Little things like that," Kim said.

"I understand."

"You do?" Kim asked.

Laura slowly nodded her head. "Think about it from my perspective. I decided to take Thomas up on using the syringe because I felt like the odd man out, or woman in this case. Afterwards I feel like I have the flu, but other than that nothing happens and I didn't feel any different. It's not until a week later when I'm at the mall, kids and all, when my ability to sniff out the truth materialized on its own."

Julie and Kim knew exactly what Laura referred to. At the mall Laura had come across a small boy, separated and standing alone in the food court. She had walked over, squatted down and began to engage the youngster when a middle aged man came over and said he was the boy's uncle. Alarm bells went off inside her head and her entire body seemed to scream at her all at once....'*he's lying*'. Laura asked the boy if this was true and, with wide eyes, shook his head no. Moments later his distraught mother appeared and told Laura she was the boy's mother. This time Laura's head remained silent. The man disappeared into the crowd but it was from that point when Laura couldn't help but acknowledge a new voice in her head; the voice that told her if someone was lying or not.

"I'm still not completely used to the feeling my ability instills in me. If I'm in a crowd I hear people talking. You can't imagine how many of those conversations, even bits of them, are wrapped up in lies. When that happens it's hard to concentrate and block it all out."

Julie and Kim looked at each other and then back at Laura. "Sorry, we weren't aware it was quite that debilitating for you."

"It's okay," Laura replied. "I should have realized I was putting you on the spot. I just look at you two as my best friends

49

and that's all that matters to me." Laura smiled. "You're always free to tell me my outfit looks like shit."

The two sisters smiled back.

"And with that I think it's time to open our first bottle of wine," Julie said as she opened a cabinet.

"I second that," said Kim.

Julie opened the white wine, poured three glasses and they all held them up.

"To friends, family and our kids back at school," toasted Kim.

They all drank and were quiet for a bit before Laura spoke up.

"I don't mean for this to sound weird or anything."

"But…," said Julie.

"But…, are we really destined to continue to fill the role of stay-at-home mom?"

"Being a stay-at-home mom takes its toll on us," Kim replied. "Why? Are you bored Laura?"

"I don't know. I think I am. Sam and Bill have SANDBOX to keep them busy."

"And you used to have your psychiatrist practice. It was something to call your own and be proud of."

Laura nodded. "That's it, exactly. My life changed so drastically eleven years ago after Thomas came to me for help. Afterwards it was easy for me to give my practice up when we moved from southern California to Marin."

"But now you feel something's missing."

"I do. Don't get me wrong, I love my kids. It's just that I feel like I want more out of life."

"You've always been the go-getter of the three of us," Julie praised. "Kim and I are content knowing that we'll never have to work. The worst we've had to worry about is whether our husbands will come home."

50

"And that'll always be a battle we'll have to fight," Kim added.

"You, on the other, aren't satisfied with the homemaker title, and there's no reason you should be. Are you thinking of starting up a practice again or something?"

Laura shook her head after she took a sip of wine. "I'm just bemoaning my situation right now. I should be happy with what I have but I'm not totally satisfied, that's all."

"What about Thomas?" Kim asked.

"What do you mean?"

"You told us months ago he hasn't been writing. Has that changed at all?"

"Thomas used to write but he still hasn't picked that back up for a long time."

"If you don't mind me asking, what does he do all day?"

"I think he just worries. He's pretty paranoid that someone else is going to come and take the kids. You know he's been running with Sam and Bill for some time now, right?"

"We heard. Sam says he's been getting a lot stronger and training more often at the indoor range."

"It's true," said Laura. "I think he just wants to be ready for anything that life throws at us down the road. And I don't blame him. The road we've all been on has been excruciatingly difficult. It's taken a few years for all of us to put that past behind us."

"Well," said Kim, "you really have been a godsend taking so much time to help us work through the shit that happened to us in Hawaii."

Laura reached over and grabbed Kim's hand. "We all suffered but we all made it. That's what matters."

Julie refilled all their glasses. "And on that note I think we should change topics."

"Next topic!" Laura exclaimed.

51

All three of them chuckled knowing full well how easy it would be to rehash what they'd all gone through. But they also knew this wasn't the time or the place. They'd been down that road too many times and they wanted to concentrate on the future rather than the past. Besides, it was their first day of freedom and hell if they weren't going to do their best to enjoy it.

# 8
## Monday September 10, 2001

Rebecca pulled the Suburban into the SANDBOX parking lot, killed the engine and headed inside.

"Good morning Rebecca," greeted Roberta.

"Good morning to you as well Roberta. What's on tap for today?"

The two women had been working together ever since the families had moved back to Marin. Initially Rebecca insisted she be part of the Clark's security detail, but a year later that protection had been terminated. Not wanting to stray far from Emily and Gavin, Rebecca started to work part-time with Roberta as SANDBOX continued to grow larger.

"Sam and Bill have a conference call with a potential new client at eleven. Six of our operators should be landing in Saudi Arabia in the next hour for a temporary security contract. They should be back in a week, week and a half. Other than that it's business as usual. How're Emily and Gavin?"

"I think feeling anxious and trepidatious at the same time," Rebecca replied.

"Well, they're kids. They'll adapt to being back at school quickly enough."

Rebecca nodded. "I'm sure they will. But ten year old Emily already has preteen inclinations."

Roberta chuckled. "Attitude at ten. Oh boy. Look out world."

Rebecca smiled. "Absolutely. She's going to be a force to reckon with in no time, that's for sure."

Hobbes entered the lobby and as soon as he saw Rebecca a smile instantly appeared on his face.

"Hey Rebecca, good morning," he said as he walked up to the reception area.

"Hey Hobbes. How're things in the tech world this morning?"

"No complaints. No one's computer has died and the servers are running perfectly."

"Don't mind me," Roberta said. "I must be invisible."

Hobbes was thrown off but quickly recovered. "I'm sorry Roberta, good morning to you too."

Rebecca smiled at his discomfort. Hobbes tried so hard to act like a normal human being, but the only real connection he had was to his computers. Rebecca figured out long ago that Hobbes can work with people, but relating to them was a different story altogether. He'd tried to ask her out on a few occasions, but she had politely turned him down. That hadn't prevented him from being overly nice to her and Rebecca thought it was cute how he doted over her.

"Sam and Bill have a video conference call at eleven."

Hobbes nodded. "No problem. Are they calling us or are we initiating the call?"

"They're calling in. I've already sent the clients your protocol via email."

Hobbes smiled. "Oh good. Thanks. I'll just pop in to the conference room and make sure the system is working. See you later Rebecca."

"Bye Hobbes."

Roberta watched Hobbes head off before she spoke up. "He really has taken a liking to you, hasn't he?"

"It is what it is. I look at it as an adorable fascination. One of these days he'll pull himself away from his computers and find someone."

"I hope so. Anyway, back to business," said Roberta.

"Right."

"I'm catching up on the weekend email overflow and payroll."

"Gotcha. I'll take a look at the recent resumes that have come in and see if there are any potential candidates I can weed out."

Roberta and Rebecca worked diligently in silence. Thirty minutes later Sam and Bill strolled through the door after they showered from their run at home.

"Good morning ladies," said Bill as they walked over to reception. "How are my two favorite women this morning?"

"I can't wait to tell your wife you said that," Rebecca joked.

Sam smiled. "She's quick."

"Too quick," Bill agreed. "Maybe it's time to downsize around here?"

Rebecca didn't miss a beat. "We'll all be sorry to see you go Bill."

"But..."

Sam chuckled, put a hand on Bill's shoulder and led him away as the two headed for the elevators. "Let's cut your losses before your brain starts to hurt." He looked over his shoulder. "Always a pleasure Rebecca."

Roberta and Rebecca smiled and went back to work.

# 9

# Monday September 10, 2001

Thomas stepped out of the shower, for the second time that day, and dried off in front of the mirror. He liked the look of his new body, honed from his exercise routine he'd started a few years back, in an effort to tire his restless mind. Even though he'd been building up his body he hadn't begun running with his friends until a few months prior, joining them one day, very much to their surprise.

Laura hadn't come back from Julie's yet so he dressed casually and headed to his office. After he sat down he accessed a specific webpage, plugged in his credentials and watched as an overhead map appeared on the screen. Thomas watched as two unmoving GPS blips materialized in close proximity.

*Hello children. Nice to see that you're safely at school.*

Thomas closed the browser and looked around his office for something to do. His eyes eventually came to rest on one of his bookshelves that contained copies of his work.

*Thanks a lot eyes. Why'd you have to focus on that?*

Thomas turned around and reluctantly picked up the phone. He dialed an old but familiar number.

"Hello?" said the voice on the other end.

"Still keeping busy without me?"

"Thomas! You old dog," Nick Raynes, his agent, replied. "It's good to hear from you. It's been forever. What the hell have you been doing with yourself? Tell me you decided to start writing again?"

"You only wish Nick."

Nick sighed. "We had a good run, you and I, back in the days. You do understand the publisher hasn't come back to me once you reneged on the contract."

"I know Nick. I paid the fine. All in all it was fun while it lasted."

"So, if you don't mind me probing, what made you stop?"

"We've been through this. You know I have other priorities in my life that took precedence."

"I understand. Family is important. It's just too bad you gave it up completely."

Thomas sidestepped the comment. "How're Susan and little Lisa?"

"Not so little anymore. She's twelve going on thirty."

"Sounds like a handful."

"You don't know the half of it. Well, maybe you do. What age is Emily now? Ten?"

"Ten going on what feels like twenty. She's going to give me my first gray hair before I know it."

"Welcome to the club then my friend. Ahh kids. You can't live with them but you can't stop loving them. So, what's going on? I can't imagine you decided to call your old friend and agent, after all this time, just to shoot the shit. The last time we really talked was after you had moved back from Hawaii. That was..., damn, quite a long time ago."

"I know, I know. Too long I'm afraid. I'm a sucky friend. My family and I were caught up in a few things and there was no way I could concentrate on writing new children's books. It just wasn't in the cards and fell to the wayside. I'm sorry about that. I know I let you and your agency down."

"Forget about it. Is everything alright? I mean, I tried calling you a few times but always got the machine. I just gave up trying when I assumed you didn't want to talk to me anymore."

"It wasn't anything like that Nick. I didn't mean to make you feel that way. I guess if anything I'm calling to apologize for being such an asshole about how I handled our friendship and our business relationship."

"Apology accepted."

"Thank you."

"So what's up? Is everything alright?"

Thomas didn't know how to respond. He could never go in to any detail with his friend about working with his dead father to track down an old Soviet spy, the Hawaiian attack and subsequent incarceration, in an undisclosed medical facility, as he was experimented on.

"Everything's fine actually. I've been watching my children grow up and come in to their own and I've become more involved in my friend's PMC lately."

"PMC? A Private Military Company? What do they have you doing there?"

Thomas backtracked. "Oh, I'm not involved in anything they're doing. They just let me shoot at their indoor range and things like that."

"Oh. Oh good." Nick sounded relieved. "For a second there I was envisioning you in full tactical gear kicking in doors or something."

*If you only knew.* "Ha. Wouldn't that be a hoot. Other than that I've really just been hanging around the house, trying to figure out my next move."

"And you're sure it's not writing?"

"No, I'm actually not sure. But writing hasn't felt like what I've needed to do for the past few years."

"It's okay. I understand. Maybe someday you'll get the bug again."

"You never know," Thomas replied.

"We should get together one of these days if you're ever down in the LA area. It's been far too long."

"If I'm down there I'll give you a call. You do the same if you find yourself up in the Bay Area."

"Will do Thomas, will do. Anyway, I need to run. Thanks for calling. It meant a lot."

"You're welcome Nick. Take care."

Thomas replaced the phone back on the cradle and leaned back in his chair.

*Well, that didn't go as badly as I thought it would. His disappointment in me was obvious but there's not much I can do about that.*

On a whim Thomas opened his top right desk drawer and verified one of his many Glock Seventeen's was inside, ready to be used. He'd stashed a number of handguns around the house and knew that wherever he was he could have his hands on a weapon in less than three seconds. His overwhelming desire to protect Laura and the kids had slowly turned in to an obsession. He had remained paranoid that someone else would come, take them and the experiments would start all over again. Laura knew he'd do whatever it took to protect their family but worried that his energies weren't always focused in a positive direction.

Thomas looked back over at his bookshelf one last time before he headed out of his office and into the family room. He sat down and turned on the television. Stickers appeared out of nowhere, jumped up and curled up on his lap.

*Maybe watching a movie will help me relax.*

\* \* \*

Rebecca appeared in the doorway shortly after Laura had let Emily and Gavin inside.

"Thanks Rebecca. Please, come in."

As the two kids scampered down the hall and into their rooms Thomas came out of his office and greeted her as well.

"Thanks Rebecca."

"Don't mention it. You know how much those two mean to me."

Laura and Thomas smiled. "Dinner's at six," said Laura.

"I'm going to go relax in the guest house for a bit but I'll be back."

"See you then."

Rebecca headed through the house and out the back door to her small cottage as Thomas and Laura watched her go.

"She's been amazing," Laura commented.

"I always feel safer when she's around."

\* \* \*

Dinner included a recap of how their first day of school ended up. Gavin enjoyed it and had already made a new friend. Emily proceeded to spin a tale of how exciting class ended up being, all the while purposefully leaving out her run-in with the bully.

\* \* \*

That night Emily crept into Gavin's room shortly after they had been tucked into bed.

"Gav?"

"Shh. Hurry up and close the door."

She did as she was told and then joined him in the middle of his room.

"What's it like?" she asked.

"It doesn't hurt if that's what you mean."

"Okay. What do I do?"

"Take my hand," he said as he held his out.

Emily did.

"Here we go."

Gavin made a small motion with his hand and a bright, shimmering portal opened in front of them. The two stepped forward and the portal disappeared behind them. Instantly Emily felt sunlight on her face. In front of her was a large palm tree and beyond that fifteen feet the water lapped gently against the sandy shore. She smiled and looked around.

"We're on an island?"

Before Gavin could reply his sister shrieked but Gavin only smiled.

"It's fine. It's just a skeleton."

She couldn't take her eyes off of it and took a few steps closer. "Is that…?"

Gavin nodded. "That's Victor, or what's left of him."

"And that doesn't bother you?"

"Why should it? Think about it. He can't hurt us anymore, right?" He sat down on the sand close to the water.

Emily mulled over her brother's words and then looked away, checking out the rest of the small island he called his special place.

Gavin patted the sand next to him.

"How often do you come here?" she replied as she made her way over and sat down.

"As often as I want. Sometimes I just need to get away."

"And mom and dad never know you're gone?"

"Apparently time is handled very differently here. By the time we go home only a second has passed."

"Seriously?"

Gavin nodded.

"Cool." She looked out over the ocean. "It's really beautiful here Gav."

He smiled. "Tell me something I don't know."

She smiled back at her brother, closed her eyes and then let the sun bathe over her.

\* \* \*

Thomas looked in on his children before he and Laura headed off to bed. Emily was snug in her bed. He kissed her lightly on the forehead and closed the door on his way out. He slowly opened Gavin's door and made his way over as he heard his son softly snoring. Thomas planted a light kiss and as he was heading to the door his barefoot stepped on something soft.

*What is that?*

He bent over, touched it with his hand and felt sand.

*Sand? Great. Now I have to remind him to take his shoes off outside before coming into the house. There's nothing like recess time that will trap sand in children's clothing.*

# 10
## Tuesday September 11, 2001

In New York City, at 8:46 a.m., American Airlines Flight 11 flew into the World Trade Center's North Tower.

Media coverage began immediately and First Responders arrived at the scene and began to make their way up the 110 story stairwells towards the ensuing fires.

At 9:03 a.m. United Flight 175 crashed into the South Tower and fires engulfed those upper floors as well.

At 9:37 a.m. American Airlines Flight 77 flew low and into the outer ring of the Pentagon, penetrating 310 feet before coming to rest. Fire broke out immediately and a good portion, of that section of the Pentagon, collapsed.

At 9:40 a.m. the FAA ordered all aircraft, within the continental United States, to land immediately. All international flights were either cancelled or redirected to Mexico or Canada. In addition all international flights were banned from landing on United States soil for three days.

At 9:59 a.m. the South Tower collapsed, much to the horror or everyone present as well as to those watching on television.

At 10:03 a.m. United Flight 93 crashed in a field near Shanksville, Pennsylvania.

At 10:28 a.m. the North Tower also collapsed.

\* \* \*

The telephone rang and Sam sleepily looked over at the clock. It read 6:03 a.m. He picked up the phone.

"What?"

"Turn on the TV right the fuck now," Bill said urgently.

Sam came awake at the sound of his friend's tone. "What channel?"

"It doesn't matter."

"What's going on?" Julie managed to ask as Sam hurriedly searched for the remote.

"Are you watching yet?"

"Hold on," Sam replied.

He clicked the remote, the television came to life and the image on screen displayed one of the World Trade Center's towers burning. Smoke filled the air.

"What the fuck?" Sam said.

"They're saying a plane crashed into the tower," Bill informed him.

"On purpose?"

"I don't kno…"

Just then a large passenger jet appeared on screen and purposefully flew right into the second tower. Huge explosions ripped through the building and a large fireball filled the sky.

"Holy shit!" Sam exclaimed.

"Oh my God," Julie said at the same time as her hands flew up and covered her mouth.

"Jesus Christ!" Bill shouted on the other end of the line. "We're under attack!"

Sam couldn't tear his eyes away from the screen as his stomach began to tie itself in knots. A full minute passed as he and Julie took it all in.

"Bill, are you still there?"

"Yeah."

"We're in lockdown mode. School's going to be cancelled so we should gather everyone together in one place for the day."

"I agree," Bill said. "It's too early and the kids aren't even awake yet. Let's talk in an hour."

"Roger that. I'll call Thomas."

And with that Bill hung up and Sam dialed his friend's number.

"Hellllo?"

"Thomas, it's Sam."

"What's wrong?" was Thomas' instant reply.

"There's been an attack on the United States."

"What?"

"Turn on your television. I'll wait."

Less than a minute later Thomas and Laura were fully cognizant of the issue.

"Fuck," Thomas breathed out.

"No shit. I've already talked with Bill. We think it's best if we gather everyone together in one place today. There's no doubt that school's going to be cancelled."

"Makes sense. It's early though and…"

"I get it, the kids aren't awake."

"Yeah."

"How about eight o'clock you all come over? We'll get breakfast going and take it from there."

"We'll see you then."

* * *

"This is absolutely horrifying," Kim said as all the adults continued to watch the news.

Their children were collectively frightened just like their parents, who tried not to show it. Tears were not in short supply and some of the children clung to their mothers. And overall no one had really touched their breakfast. Rebecca had joined them and watched over the kids.

The constant barrage of repetitive footage, starting with the planes hitting the towers and up to each tower collapsing, created rage in all of them. But over time that transformed to numbness as the same images looped over and over and over. The attack was unbelievable, sickening and horrifying all at the same time. All of them cringed as the footage showed bodies plummeting from the towers of those people that attempted to escape the fire and smoke.

"Turn it off," Laura said.

Julie hit the power button on the remote and the TV blinked off.

"Horrible. Just horrible."

Sam and Bill looked at each other. They were amped up and seemed ready for a fight.

"Bill and I are going to head to the office for a bit."

"Don't leave," Julie and Kim said in unison, definitely rattled.

"As terrible as this tragedy is," Sam said, "you'll all be okay right here. Thomas and Rebecca are going to look after everyone and make sure nothing bad happens."

Laura nodded. "Go. I've got this."

Sam returned her nod, gave Julie a kiss and headed out the door. Bill took ten more seconds to reassure Kim and then followed suit.

As soon as the two got in their Suburban and closed the doors Bill couldn't help but make a comment.

"I am fucking pissed off right now."

"No shit."

"I just know that whoever orchestrated this is fucked beyond belief."

"You can say that again brother."

* * *

At eight the parents gathered all six children at Julie's house and tried to get them to eat, but they were still shaken up. Rebecca took them off to the side, except for Edward and Craig who clung to their mother's side, and tried to keep the other four occupied. That didn't work out as intended and while the news was running Gavin and Emily managed to sneak away upstairs, but not without Rebecca spotting them out of the corner of her eye.

"What are we doing?" Emily asked.

"Let's get out of here. Do you want to go to the island again?"

His sister genuinely smiled back at him and then nodded her head. Seconds later they were through the portal and standing on the soft sand.

"You have an amazing power Gav."

"Your powers are pretty awesome too," he replied.

She shrugged and walked over to the water's edge, careful to keep her distance from Victor's skeleton.

"What's wrong Em? Is it your nightmares?"

"I don't know. Maybe."

"What are they about?" he asked as they both sat down.

Emily grabbed a fistful of warm sand and then slowly let it sift out of her hand and mix back in with the rest of the beach.

"They're about everything I guess."

"People shooting at us?"

She nodded.

"The explosions?"

She nodded again.

"When you were experimented on?"

A single tear appeared and trickled down her face. Gavin put his arm around his older sister.

"I used to have similar nightmares."

"No, you had a monster in the closet which is totally different."

"Well yeah, there's that. But you're not the only one that those things happened to."

"You're right. Sorry."

"It's okay. But I started coming here and it's really helped me."

"I can see why. It's peaceful here." Emily lowered her head. "an...can I tell you something?"

"Okay."

"I...I don't know if I want my powers anymore."

"Why not? They're great."

"Speak for yourself. You've got a protector you can summon. You can heal people and you can come to, well, whatever this place is."

And what about you? You can summon dead people and make people do whatever you want just by touching them. That's pretty cool."

"Well..., maybe, when you put it like that. Still, if it wasn't for our powers then none of the bad things that have happened would have happened."

"Probably not. But you know what sis, we didn't have a choice. I like my powers and so should you. We're special and even though we have to keep it a secret that's okay."

"I got bullied yesterday," Emily blurted out.

"Wait. What? What are you talking about?"

"Three sixth graders cornered me. The ring leader grabbed me by my hair."

Gavin was concerned. "Are you okay? We should tell someone."

Emily smiled and Gavin caught on right away.

"Okay, wait. What did you do?"

"I made her think she had spiders crawling all over her."

"No you didn't!"

"It's okay. I only made them last a minute. You should have seen it. It was hilarious."

"Well, on one side I don't think they'll mess with you again. On the other hand you shouldn't have done that. We can't expose what we can do. I don't want you taken away again, okay? Promise me."

Emily's smile faded. "Okay Gav. I promise."

"Good," he replied in relief. "Now, let's just sit back and make a sand castle or something."

Emily's smile instantly returned. "I haven't done that in years."

\* \* \*

Rebecca walked up the stairs and she saw a brief flash of bright light come from the next room. She stepped into the doorway and Emily and Gavin's faces turned to shock.

"What are you two doing?"

"Uhh...nothing Becca," Gavin replied.

"Really? Nothing Gav?"

"Nothing at all, honest," Emily added.

Rebecca looked her straight in the eyes. "You don't get to lie. I may not have the power that your mother does but I damn well know when someone's bullshitting me."

The two children were taken aback at Rebecca's tone, not to mention her use of bad language.

"Now, I have a suspicion that you two were someplace you've been told not to go, am I right?"

"Umm," Gav stammered.

Rebecca leaned down and changed her demeanor. "I don't care if you went to your special place or not."

Emily and Gavin shared a glance.

"The only thing I've ever wanted is for the two of you to be safe. To do that I need you both to be honest with me from here on out. Deal?"

"You're not going to tell on us?" Emily asked.

Rebecca shook her head. "Nope. That should save you the effort of making me forget that I ever saw you both in here, wouldn't it Em?"

"I wouldn't…"

"I'm just kidding sweetie. You both have incredible abilities and I'm going to continue to protect you from anyone who wants to hurt you. Now, give me a hug and let's go back downstairs."

Emily and Gavin hugged Rebecca as hard as they could. They loved her and the fact that she wasn't going to go tattle on them made that bond even stronger.

"Now, before we go, you might want to clean off the sand on your clothes. It's a dead giveaway."

# 11
## Wednesday September 12, 2001

Basically Tuesday was a wash as the whole country shutdown as everyone watched the horrific events unfold. As Wednesday morning rolled around multiple news stations were still on the scene and speculations regarding who was responsible for the attacks was now the current focus.

With school cancelled for a second day in a row Sam and Bill left their families and headed to work. As usual Roberta had beaten them in and was manning the reception desk.

"What's the word?" Bill asked as they walked through the front door.

"Excuse me?" she replied.

"Has anything come up that we should be worried about?" Sam clarified.

"Oh. I'm afraid it's just business as usual around here."

"How're you holding up?" Sam asked.

"In one word, I'm angry," she stated.

Sam and Bill both nodded in agreement.

"If you want to take the day off please feel free to do so."

"I'd rather stay busy here," she retorted. "It'll keep my mind occupied."

"Thanks Roberta," Bill said. "We'll be in our office."

They left her behind and headed upstairs.

"So what are your thoughts on who's behind this?" Bill asked as they sat down.

"The U.S. has pissed off plenty of groups around the world, but my guess is that it's probably a faction from the Middle East."

"This is going to get ugly."

"Bet your ass it's going to get ugly."

# 12
## Wednesday September 12, 2001

Rebecca joined Julie, Kim and Laura in the kitchen as their children played in the next room. There was a sense of uneasiness that hung heavily over the country now, not to mention the raw images from the television that could not be easily dismissed from any of their minds. Although the tragedy didn't directly affect them, the repercussions from it most certainly would.

"My guess is that there's a group in the Middle East that planned and executed these attacks," Rebecca said.

"It's just unimaginable," Kim whispered softly as he sipped her coffee.

Julie spoke up. "How long do you think it'll be before Sam and Bill become directly involved in this conflict?"

"Oh sis, why'd you have to go there?"

"Come on Kim. You know you were thinking it."

Kim sighed. "Maybe. But that's not their job anymore. They're running things, not putting their own boots in to the mix."

"I hope you're right but you never know. We know our husbands and after this I think they'll be looking for some excuse to get involved in any type of payback."

"It's going to be interesting how this all plays out for our country," Rebecca added. "People want blood now and I don't blame them, I want it too."

"And that's the dangerous road we're on now," Laura said. "The attack was meant for us not to feel safe, and look at us huddled here together, it worked."

"True," Julie offered, "but as a group we've been fearful and worried well before yesterday's attacks."

"That's accurate," Kim said. "I mean, between the four of us sitting here drinking coffee, how many handguns are there between us?"

All four women took a moment, pulled out their Glocks and placed them on the table. It was the first time all of them had smiled since the attacks.

# 13
## Thursday September 13, 2001

With school back in session, and the kids safely dropped off, Sam and Bill skipped their morning run and drove straight to the office. It wasn't long before the two of them began to receive phones calls. They were told that the buzz around the Pentagon's water coolers was that going to war was only a matter of time. Their military contacts also wanted to know what SANDBOX could contribute to the upcoming campaign. Sam and Bill assured them that SANDBOX would participate, as long as their personnel wanted to take the contracts.

\* \* \*

Roberta buzzed their office intercom.

"What's up Roberta?" Sam inquired.

"A potential client just called in requesting some coverage for a lunch meeting today in Walnut Creek."

"You know we're tapped out on operators, right?"

"Of course I know that," she replied. "What I was thinking was how about the two of you taking this job?"

Sam and Bill, over the past four years, hadn't participated in many contracts due to a promise they had made to their wives. Julie and Kim wanted them out of harm's way even though that's what their company was obviously structured around. The battle had been waged between husbands and wives for years with the wives typically winning out.

Bill shrugged as he met Sam's eyes. "I can take a whipping from my wife if you can."

"So you're saying I get a beating from your wife and not mine?"

Bill cracked a smile. "You wish brother, you wish."

Sam grinned in return. "Roberta. We'll need the client's details and…"

"I have him on hold Sam. I'll transfer him to you."

"It's like you know us better than we do. Thanks Roberta."

* * *

"Thomas," Sam said over the mobile phone. "You busy?"

"You know me, just hanging around the house," Thomas replied as he paused the movie he was watching. "What's up?"

"Care to get out of the house and help Bill and me on a quick job?"

Thomas sat up on his couch, attentive. "What type of job?"

"It's just a routine protection contract, out in Walnut Creek, and we're short on operators. Think you can handle driving the Suburban while Bill and I do our thing?"

A smile appeared on Thomas' face. "You got it. How long do I have?"

"We'll be in your driveway in five. Business attire if any of your suits still fit."

"Very funny. See you in five."

Thomas ended the call and rushed upstairs as Laura trailed after him into the bedroom.

"Who was that?" she asked.

"Sam. They need a driver for a last minute client."

"You're going on a job with them?"

He nodded as he pulled one of his suits out of the closet.

"Is it going to be dangerous?"

"Sam said it was a routine job that just came up. That's all I know."

"I see." *Well, he's not lying.*

She watched as he quickly dressed and then looked himself over in the mirror.

"How do I look?"

"Excited," she replied as she straightened his tie. "And I'm glad to see you're getting off the couch and out of the house for a bit."

"Me too," he said as he slid a holster on his right belt and then a magazine holder to his left side.

"I thought you said it wasn't going to be dangerous?"

"Plan for the worst and hope for the best."

Laura smiled as they both heard Sam honk his horn.

"Well, be careful and don't have too much fun."

"Fun?" he replied. "This is all about work."

"Liar," she said with a grin.

"Alright, maybe it'll be a little fun," he said as he kissed her. "I've got to go. I'll see you later this afternoon."

\* \* \*

"Well well well," Bill said from the back seat as Thomas took over driving. "Look who decided to dress up and make time for us today. Looking good brother. Now, put this on," Bill said as he handed his friend an earpiece and microphone. Thomas did as he was told.

"Thanks," Thomas replied as he backed out of his driveway and headed towards the 101 freeway.

"No, thank you Thomas," Sam said from the passenger seat. "We appreciate it. Did Laura have an issue with you coming out with us?"

"Other than just wishing me luck, no, no issues."

"See," Bill said. "Why can't my wife be like that, or even your wife for that matter Sam?"

Sam chuckled. "Still harping on that after all these years? Just be grateful we get out in the field once and awhile."

The three of them wore identical suits, white shirts and black ties. All of them were armed with Glock 17 side arms and, if for any reason they needed additional firepower, they had a mini armory with them.

"So where are we headed?" Thomas asked.

Bill spoke up. "Take 101 to the San Rafael Bridge, south on eighty, east on twenty-four to the six-eighty split. We're going to pick our client, a Mr. Bernalillo, up from the Buchanan Airport. He chartered a flight from Las Vegas, now that the air ban has been lifted, and is coming in for a quick lunch meeting. He's a little nervous and doesn't expect anything to happen which is why he explained that he basically hired us for his own peace of mind."

"Sounds boring," Thomas said.

"Welcome to our world," Sam explained. "It's either boring or the bullets are flying. Take your pick but you should never look forward to the bullet side of the equation."

"Well, glad I could help."

Bill chuckled from the back seat. "Well, we figured this would be a milk run and it provided us the opportunity to get you dressed up and out of the house."

"Fuck you too," Thomas replied and smiled.

* * *

The three of them watched as the chartered plane landed and taxied over. An elderly gentleman exited the plane. Sam walked over and met Mr. Bernalillo as the man made his way towards them.

"It's a pleasure to meet you, Mr. Bernalillo," Sam said as he shook his hand. "My name is Sam Paige, and these are my associates, Bill Nicholson and Thomas Clark." Two additional handshakes were quickly taken care of.

"A pleasure gentlemen," Mr. Bernalillo replied. "However, I'm on a tight schedule so why don't we get going."

"Very well sir," Sam replied and opened up the right rear door of the Suburban for their client.

Once he was in Bill, Thomas and Sam entered the vehicle.

"Where to sir?" Sam asked without turning around from the front seat.

"There's this little restaurant off of North California Blvd in Walnut Creek."

He told Sam the name and Thomas nodded. He knew right where it was, nodded and put the Suburban in gear. He headed out towards the destination as Sam continued to question their client.

"Sir, how many people are you meeting?"

"Just one other. He's an old friend but it pays to be cautious."

"Cautious?" Sam inquired. "Are you expecting to be in any kind of danger?"

"No, no. I would have made the trip even if I hadn't procured your services Mr. Paige. However, the fact remains that I'd rather defuse any situation before anything potentially gets out of hand."

"That's s fairly cryptic answer, sir."

"It is what it is Mr. Paige. The question is, is that a problem for you?"

Sam bristled slightly in the front seat. "We'll be just fine sir, but thank you for asking."

Mr. Bernalillo smiled and sat back in his seat.

*  *  *

Ten minutes later Thomas pulled to the curb right outside the restaurant.

"Please drive around to the rear entrance," Mr. Bernalillo requested.

As Sam and Bill began to scan the area Thomas took the next two right turns and ended up behind the restaurant. Sam directed him to back into one of the parking spots and Thomas complied.

"Keep it running," Sam told Thomas who nodded in reply.

Bill and Sam exited the Suburban, performed a quick sweep of the area and then Bill opened the door for their client. With Sam in the lead the three of them entered the rear of the restaurant. Inside a few of the tables were occupied with large men in suits who flanked another table where a single elderly man, with white hair, sat. That elderly man stood up as they approached.

"Ahh, Sal, good to see you," his acquaintance said as the two men embraced.

"You too Tony. It's been a long time."

"Indeed it has. Too long." They pulled back from each other. "And who are these men with you?"

"Just a last minute insurance policy," Mr. Bernalillo stated.

"What? You don't trust me Sal? I'm hurt."

Mr. Bernalillo smiled and swept his arm around the room. "And you're going to try and convince me that these fine gentlemen are just here for the delicious salmon?"

Tony smiled. "Touché," he said and pointed to an open chair at his table. "Please."

Sal gave Sam and Bill a nod, turned back and sat down next to Tony. Sam and Bill moved away and each took up flanking positions against the three hired guns Tony had brought to the

82

meeting with him. Sam and Bill kept their faces blank and relaxed while they continued to observe the entire room and everyone in it.

Sam brought his hand up to his mouth. "Meeting has started. We have three potentials to deal with if something goes south. How's the outside look?"

"Clear," Thomas replied in Sam's ear. "No movement."

"Roger that. If anything changes then let us know immediately."

"Will do."

Outside Thomas swiveled his head continuously around as his eyes took in the environment around him. Sam and Bill had taught him well, passing off their knowledge to him through a variety of exercises over the years. Thomas soaked it up, just as much as he did when he went to the range to keep his skills current, and Sam and Bill were happy that their friend felt safer because of it.

Tony and Sal kept their voices low while they discussed whatever it was they needed to talk about. The three men with Tony continually eyeballed Sam and Bill throughout the meeting but the two of them couldn't care less. They knew they could handle themselves so they ignored the obvious ego looks and remained focused on the job at hand which was to protect their client.

\* \* \*

Thirty minutes later, as Sal and Tony were eating lunch, the atmosphere abruptly changed when Mr. Bernalillo rose from his chair and pounded his fist on the table. Both wine glasses toppled over. Sam and Bill promptly went on high alert.

"How dare you! I will not be forced out!"

"Sal, be reasonable. The offer is more than generous and I advise you to accept it."

"Go to hell," Sal replied as he turned to leave.

Sam and Bill began to move.

Tony stood up. "I'm afraid this is non-negotiable," he said as he made a motion to his men with a flick of his hand.

Sam and Bill both caught the signal and expeditiously pulled their handguns out just as the three men reached for their own.

"Don't," Sam warned them as he pointed his weapon at the closest man who had his hand inside his jacket.

Tony's face changed as the circumstances took a tangent.

Bill spoke into his left hand microphone as he moved closer to the exit, weapon up and pointed at the men who were frozen in mid draw. "We're coming out hot."

"Roger that," Thomas replied.

Sam kept his handgun trained on his opponents as he retrieved Mr. Bernalillo and pushed him towards the rear entrance.

Thomas pulled the Suburban out of its parking spot and right up to the rear door. Mr. Bernalillo appeared first, followed by Sam and Bill. All three quickly climbed into the Suburban.

"Go!" Sam commanded.

As Thomas shot forward Sam and Bill looked back and saw three large figures exit the restaurant with guns drawn. Thomas deftly took a left and raced away from the scene before any shots were fired in their direction.

"Thank you, Mr. Paige. That was excellent anticipation on your part."

"Just doing our job, sir. Are you alright?"

"Yes. I should have expected what the meeting was about and in hindsight I'm glad I hired you. Your reputation is well deserved."

"Thank you," Sam replied. "Should we take you back to the airport now Mr. Bernalillo?"

"Quite."

Once Mr. Bernalillo's plane departed Thomas took his earpiece out and handed the rest of the communication equipment back to Bill.

"Nice driving Thomas," Bill said.

"I see what you mean," Thomas replied. "Periods of boredom followed by potential gunfire."

Sam smiled. "Told you. And Bill's right, you did great."

"I can only imagine what it was like inside for you two."

"Just another day at the office," Bill said. "And this time no one got hurt."

## 14
## Thursday September 13, 2001

As students arrived that morning they were ushered into the school gym. Once the entire student population was seated in the bleachers the principal turned on the microphone and addressed them.

"Good morning. The events in New York City have affected all of us. However, it is my duty to continue doing my job, which is to ensure each and every one of you receive the very best education you can. Despite the horror that has befallen our great country, class must go on. Your teachers will be available, during recess periods, to talk with if you choose to. Our prayers and thoughts go out to those people who need it.

"Dismissed."

Gavin and Emily got up and began to make their way together towards their classrooms. Just as they were passing a section of modular schoolrooms they heard someone call out behind them.

"Hey freak!"

They stopped, turned around and came face to face with the same three girls that had accosted Emily a few days prior. Emily was unimpressed and didn't display an iota of fear.

"That's right, I'm talking to you."

The sixth grade bully stepped up while the other two held back.

"So who's this with you? Is he your protection? Ha! What a joke."

"What do you want?" Emily asked nonchalantly.

"Payback. I don't know how you did what you did but it ends now."

"You're mistaken," was all Emily said in return.

Gavin brought his leg up, bent at the knee, and brought his foot down as hard as he could on the girl's shoe. The large girl was unimpressed and lunged at him. Before Emily knew what she was doing she had cocked her fist and punched the girl in the face. The girl hit the ground hard, turned over, put a hand to her cheek and began to cry.

"You okay Gav?"

Her brother nodded in return. The two girls with her turned and ran as Emily bent down to talk with the bully.

"Are you done?"

"You'll...pay...for...this," the girl replied between gasps of air.

"Okay, I guess you're not done." She started to move her fingers towards the girl's face.

"No Em," Gavin reminded her. "Don't. You promised."

Emily looked over at her brother and stopped. She turned back and whispered in the bully's ear just as two teachers approached, brought by the other two girls.

"I'm not worth your time. Next time you come after me I won't be so forgiving."

"What's going on here?" one of the teacher asked.

Emily stood up and said. "She fell over and I was trying to help her up."

"Nuh uh," one of the other girls exclaimed. "You hit her."

"Is that right?" The teacher helped the sixth grade girl up and looked at her face. "Did she hit you?"

The bully thought it over and finally replied. "I tripped."

"I see," the teacher said as she sized up the large girl to Emily's much smaller frame. She quickly decided that nothing malicious had occurred. "In that case let me get you to the nurse to take a look at your face."

The bully looked over her shoulder one last time as she was led away to the nurse's office.

# 15
## Thursday September 13, 2001

Roberta closed her front door behind her, put her purse on the counter and made her way to the master bedroom. On the way she passed by a large collection of framed photos that filled both sides of the hallway. Pictures of her husband and two small boys started on one side. Her boys, Mike and Christopher, grew both taller and older as the pictures progressed, ranging from Halloween outfits to holiday celebrations. On the other side of the hallway there was a picture of Mike in uniform with his younger brother Christopher standing next to him. They both had smiles on their faces.

Roberta paused and put a hand up to touch the face of her son Mike that had been killed in Vietnam. The next few photos were just of her, her husband and Christopher, after their oldest son's death. Next on the wall was Christopher, all alone and proud as could be in uniform, after he enlisted. Roberta remembered the heated arguments they had had, but in the end Christopher wanted to honor his brother and disregarded his parent's wishes.

The last frame contained a folded American flag, the one she'd been given at Christopher's funeral. She's been told that his death had been a training accident. Her husband, beside himself, began to drink heavily. Two years later she filed for divorce and moved out as she attempted to put her own life back together. Seven years after Christopher's death she'd been presented with proof that Sam and Bill had been the ones responsible for her son's death and would she like a chance to make them pay. She had readily agreed and secured the executive admin position at the up and coming company known as SANDBOX.

Roberta stared lovingly at Christopher's flag and silently thought about her fifteen years of service working for Sam and Bill.

*I wanted them to pay for taking my son's life. For years I've deceived them, watched them get married and have children. As they grew I started to become an integral part of their lives. And for what?*

She sighed, continued down the hallway, through her bedroom and into the bathroom. She looked at herself in the mirror.

*Do I even have this vendetta anymore? Is it still alive? Do I even want revenge anymore?*

Roberta turned on the water, cupped her hands, leaned over and gently washed her face. She looked back her reflection, beads of water cascading down her face.

*I've done things; set things in motion that I never should have. I don't want to do this anymore, but what can I do? If I stop doing what they tell me then they'll expose me. And if I do then these last fifteen years will have been for nothing.*

Roberta struggled to look herself in the eyes.

*No, I'm not proud of what I've done or who I've become. I just don't want to do this anymore.*

\* \* \*

Rebecca Cross unlocked her front door to her small guest cottage, stepped inside and closed it behind her. She had enjoyed spending some time with the wives even though the conversation had been somewhat heavy. They had long ago accepted her as part of the family, and the children, especially Emily and Gavin, adored her. Rebecca knew she had passed whatever obstacles there might have been, from taking a grenade blast in Hawaii to rescuing Thomas and Emily in D.C. And she knew this because she had watched first hand as Emily worked on erasing Hobbes' memories right in front of her. They trusted her explicitly with their children's abilities and she made the decision right then that there was nothing more important than to protect them.

*   *   *

Hobbes entered his large San Francisco apartment and locked the door behind him. His life couldn't be better. Sam and Bill had stuck their necks and reputations out on the line when they hired him. He knew his buddy Calvin was currently in jail for assisting Victor Bannon in his illegal and unsanctioned activities. Hobbes knew he should be in jail as well but somehow had managed ending up in a senior roll at SANDBOX in charge of their entire computer network. The pay was great and the perks of interacting with Rebecca Cross from time to time weren't that bad either. He didn't know why he was so infatuated with her but he never gave that much thought. Of course, much of what he knew when he worked with Victor Bannon had been scrubbed from his mind, but he didn't need to know that.

Hobbes quickly ordered pizza and then settled down to a new video game he'd picked up the week before. Yes, life was good.

# 16
## Thursday September 13, 2001

Thomas, Laura, Emily and Gavin sat around the dinner table and the enjoyment of their meal had been dwarfed by the attack.

"We received a letter from the school today," Laura said.

Emily's eyes immediately darted to her mother and then over to Gavin.

"What about?" Emily asked.

"Apparently there's something the two of you haven't told us about."

Emily gulped and looked down at her food. *Here it comes, the bully episode.*

"What?" Gavin asked.

"They said you had a school gathering this morning in the auditorium and that they were making counselors and teachers available to talk to you about what happened in New York."

Emily sighed a breath a relief as Gavin nodded to his mother.

Laura continued. "Did either one of you have any questions or want to talk about it?"

"Are we going to war?" Gavin asked.

"I don't know Gav," Thomas replied.

"I think we should."

"And why do you think that?"

"Someone has to pay for what they did," Gavin said matter-of-factly.

"And why do you say that?"

"Because whoever's hurt us before has always got what's coming to them."

Thomas and Laura were stunned by their son's response. How often they forgot just how much violence their children had already been a party to in their young lives.

"I see," Thomas managed to say. "And what about you Em?"

"What about me?"

"Well, what do you think should happen?"

She shrugged. "I don't care."

"What do you mean you don't care?"

Emily laid her fork down on her plate and stood up. "I said I don't care. Stop badgering me!" And with that she left the table, headed down to her room and slammed the door behind her.

"What just happened?" Thomas asked somewhat confused.

"She's been very moody," Laura said with a sigh. "I'll try talking to her later."

* * *

Laura poked her head into Gavin's room and saw him tucked in under his covers with a couple of additions, Stir and Stickers. Stir's red eyes blinked a few times in her direction and then he settled back down. She closed the door, went next door to Emily's room, knocked gently and then headed inside. Her daughter was also in bed with her back towards the door.

"Hey Em. Are you awake?" Laura asked as she sat down on the edge of the bed.

"What do you want?"

"Well, we need to talk about you and your attitude. Your father and I are concerned about you."

"Why?" Emily replied without looking at her mother.

"It goes without saying that we love you very much. When we see you obviously hurting we want to help you."

"I'm fine."

"No, you're not fine. Fine stands for Fucked up, Insecure, Neurotic and Emotional. Now, please show me some courtesy by turning over and looking at me."

Emily reluctantly rolled over.

"Thank you."

"Whatever."

Laura grappled with the numerous responses inside her head as she tried to remain calm. She'd dealt with numerous patients in her past, and some of them had given her attitude as well, but her daughter just pushed her buttons so easily.

"Talk to me. What's going on?"

"What do you care? You'll just tell me I'm lying to you."

"I can't help the power I have no more than you can Em. I'm sorry you find it invasive but I can't turn it off. I only wish you never felt the need to lie to me. I thought we had a close relationship. Did I do something to make you stop trusting and talking to me?"

"No."

"Then what is it? Please Em, why not take a chance and just talk to me."

"What if I don't want to?"

"Well, from what I experienced in the past from the people I've helped, is that they don't want to talk about what's bothering them either."

Emily sat up. "Why not?"

"People tend to try and hide their pain thinking that if they don't talk about it, it'll just go away. The reality is that their pain only continues to build up inside."

"And those people that started talking to you about what's bothering them…what happened?"

"They got better. Now, I'm not saying talking about what's hurting you happens to be easy for anyone, because it's not, but it

97

does get easier and makes you feel better. That internal buildup, that pressure, is released and the weight on your shoulders feels lighter."

Emily contemplated what her mother had just said in silence and finally spoke up.

"I've been having nightmares."

Laura nodded. "Yes, I know. Do you know what they're about?"

"Everything."

"What do you mean?"

"I see everything. It's as if I'm there all over again."

"Where sweetie?"

Emily shivered slightly. "Explosions. Screaming. Fires. Gun shots. Blood." Tears began to stream down her cheeks. "I relive it over and over again."

"Oh Em, I had no idea."

Laura reached out, pulled her daughter close and held her tight.

"It's going to be okay. We're going to get through this together."

Laura internally berated herself for not catching the obvious signs that had been right in front of her. Her daughter had Post Traumatic Stress Disorder, or PTSD. *Her nightmares, irritability and quick to anger were classic symptoms that I should have caught on to sooner. What type of parent am I that I didn't see it?*

"We're going to get through this. You're going to be okay."

Laura kissed Emily on the forehead and lay down with her, holding her close from behind. Thirty minutes later Emily finally fell asleep and Laura slowly disentangled herself and left the room.

"There you are," Thomas said as Laura entered the bedroom. "I almost sent out a search party."

She sat down on the bed. "I know what's wrong with Em."

Thomas's giddiness turned serious. "What is it?"

"I should have seen the signs. I should have seen the signs and done something about it months ago. She has PTSD."

"Fuck. Are you sure?"

Laura nodded. "Pretty sure, since I treated vets with it before you and I even met. It's not as severe as it could be, but she's definitely been impacted from what she's been through."

"Poor kid. Hell, I don't even know how I've dealt with all that over the years. And she's just a kid, no wonder it's affected her so much. Is she going to be okay?"

"She will be in time and with my help."

"Good. But what about Gav? Why isn't he experiencing the same issues?"

"PTSD doesn't apply to everyone. I figure with Gav he's processed everything differently."

"Why?"

"Well, for starters he has used Stir as his tool to save us on two different occasions. My take is that he's processed those traumatic events very differently in his head than Em has."

Thomas nodded. "Maybe you're right. So where do we go with her from here?"

Laura scooted up into Thomas' arms. "It's going to take time and a whole lot of patience."

Thomas pulled her close and kissed her. "Thanks for figuring out what's wrong."

"You're welcome."

## 17
### Friday September 14, 2001

Sam, Bill and Thomas finally took the opportunity to run together Friday morning. With the stress of the week building up they all needed some time together, as well as the endorphin release. During their run they discussed how each of their families was handling the attack and subsequent fallout. Afterwards Sam and Bill headed to work while Thomas stayed home as usual.

Sam and Bill walked into SANDBOX and Roberta flagged them down.

"Please hold Colonel, they just walked in."

"What's going on?" Sam asked as they approached her desk.

"I've got a Colonel James on the phone. He says it's urgent that he speaks to the both of you."

"Alright. We'll take it in our office."

Sam and Bill headed off to the elevators while Roberta let the Colonel know it'd just be a minute. In their office they put the call on speaker.

"Colonel James?"

"Finally. Am I speaking directly with Sam Paige and Bill Nicholson?"

"Yes sir, you are."

"I'm calling from the Pentagon, or as you've seen on the news, what's left of it. I'm part of the investigation that's looking in to the New York attack; so gentlemen, I'll get right to the point."

"Yes, sir."

"The attacks on the twin towers may have been prevented. Right now everything's pretty chaotic, as you can imagine, but the bottom line is that our intelligence community fucked up."

Bill and Sam shared a glance as the Colonel continued.

"We're tracking down an immense amount of leads but it has come to our attention that the CIA and the FBI didn't share information between their two camps. Egos and pride got in the way and now thousands of our own people are dead because of it."

"Yes, sir. What do you need from us?"

"We have reasonable proof that Hamid Emal Habibi was somehow involved in the attacks. The file that I'm looking at right now says that the two of you worked with Hamid training Mujahideen rebels against the Soviets for nine months, starting in August of eighty-one."

It'd been a long time since either of them had heard Hamid's name or had even thought about training the rebels in Panjshir Valley two decades prior.

"Are you sure Colonel? Hamid was a standup guy the entire time we were with him and his people," Sam countered.

"At this point we're following down all leads. Besides, people and beliefs change in twenty years. Now, what me and my group need is for the two of you to fly out to Virginia so you can debrief us on anything and everything you know about Hamid."

"Alright. When do you want us?"

"Early next week."

"Will Monday work for you Colonel?"

"Perfect. Do you need transportation?"

"No. We've got that covered."

"Good. Badges will be ready for you at security when you arrive. I'll see you Monday."

"Yes, sir."

The line went dead and Sam and Bill were left with the fallout of what the Colonel had told them. They slowly sat down in each of their chairs.

Bill spoke up. "Do you really think Hamid had a hand in those attacks?"

"I don't know. The Colonel's right, people change. Twenty years is a long time and if fighting is all you know then anything's possible. He was an Afghan rebel fighting against the Soviets who had invaded his land. Who knows how or why he changed. All I know is that we're heading to the Pentagon on Monday morning and we have a shitload to get done before then."

Bill nodded. "I'll have Roberta make sure our plane is ready to go."

\* \* \*

Thomas stepped out of the shower, dressed and headed to his office. He hadn't figured out what he was going to do to keep his mind occupied for the day when the phone rang. The caller ID had an east coast prefix. He picked it up.

"Hello?"

"Please hold for the Director of Central Intelligence."

Thomas did a double take and his mind began to race. *It's been four years since we've even talked. What the hell is the DCI calling me about?*

The line clicked over and an old voice spoke in his ear. "Thomas Clark, this is Robert Duncan. I'm sure you remember me."

"Of course," Thomas replied. "You were the interim DCI that took over after Victor Bannon disappeared. Congratulations on filling his roll. What can I do for you?"

"I need to talk with you in person."

"Sir, it's been four years. What could you possible want to talk to me about?"

"I'm calling about the terrorist attacks that occurred in New York. There was a chance that they could have been prevented.

The country, just like you and your family are constantly in danger, but you know that already."

Immediately Thomas didn't like where this conversation was going. The hairs on the back of his neck stood up.

"I don't know what you're talking about."

"Yes, you do. I've spent the last four years doing my research and talking to people."

"About?"

"I don't want to get in to any details over the phone."

Thomas cringed. "Are you threatening me?"

"No, and my apologies if I came off that way. I actually want to protect you. I believe we can help each other in our country's time of need."

Thomas didn't like it. "And if I refuse?"

"I'm not like my predecessor. Black vans and helicopters aren't going to suddenly appear at your doorstep. All I ask is that you consider a face to face chat with me at your earliest convenience."

"I'll think about it."

"Thank you. I hope to see you soon."

Thomas hung up the phone and stared at it for what seemed like hours. His brain went in to overdrive and various scenarios began to unfold.

*At least now I have something new to worry about today.*

## 18
## Friday September 14, 2001

Friday night all three families got together for a group meal. Afterwards Rebecca hung out with the children while the six adults talked and drank out of earshot in the kitchen.

"You'll never believe who had the gall to call me today," Thomas said.

"Who?" Bill inquired.

"Robert Duncan."

"Who's Robert Duncan?" Kim asked.

"He's the Director of Central Intelligence," Bill replied.

"Seriously? Wow, what did he want?"

"He said he wants to protect me and my family."

"You can't trust him," Sam stated. "Just flat out, you can't trust him."

"I've have to agree with Sam," Bill added. "We've been down this road before and there's always an agenda, and it certainly doesn't have anything to do with protecting you, Laura or your kids."

"He alleged that he spent the last four years tracking down leads about us but he wouldn't be specific over the phone."

"He doesn't have shit," Sam concluded.

"Maybe, maybe not," Laura said, "but Thomas and I have already talked about this. We don't have a choice. We need to know what he knows or it'll drive us crazy."

"He asked to see me as soon as possible, that we'll be able to help our country. I booked a flight for Monday."

"You'll want to cancel that reservation," Sam said.

"Why?"

"Because you'll be coming with us."

Julie piped up. "What are you talking about Sam?"

"Apparently Thomas wasn't the only one to receive a phone call today. Bill and I talked with a Colonel from the Pentagon today. He's requested our presence."

"I don't understand. Whatever for?"

"Yeah," Kim added. "What the hell is going on?"

"I'm afraid we can't go in to the details."

"Why not?" Julie demanded.

"Because what he wants to talk about occurred twenty years ago. You know Bill and I don't talk about those days."

"And Kim and I are just supposed to be okay with you heading over to the Pentagon? You do realize it was hit by a plane earlier this week Sam, a fucking plane."

"Calm down Jules. We'll be fine."

"We'll I'm not okay. None of us are okay. Our country was attacked and I'm not okay."

Sam put down his beer and pulled Julie close. "It's going to be fine. We're in and out in one day. We'll be back Monday night."

"You promise?"

"I promise. This isn't about a job, this is just an informal information dump, I swear."

"But…"

"And we're taking the company jet so you can stop fretting about that aspect."

Julie relented. "Fine. Sorry. I'm just been so spun up and afraid."

"We all have," Kim added. "It's been an exhausting week."

"Well then, let's refill our glasses and try to forget all about it."

\* \* \*

# Saturday September 15, 2001

Laura curled up against Thomas' back as the glow of the morning light pried its way in through their bedroom's curtains. She knew he hadn't slept well the night before, worried over his impending meeting with the DCI and whatever ramifications that ensued from it. She was concerned as well but knew that she couldn't spend time thinking about something she couldn't control just yet.

*That probably will come later.*

Laura's plan for part of today was to spend some one on one time with Emily to combat her PTSD. Her daughter needed her more than ever, but more importantly Laura knew that if PTSD was left unchecked Emily's brash and unpredictable symptoms would only worsen.

"You awake?" Thomas asked.

Laura gently caressed his back. "I know you didn't sleep very well, if at all."

"I'm worried."

"I know."

"I've tried so hard to protect us for the past four years. I just don't know what I'd do if we were all at risk again. It's next to impossible to just disappear. What's left? Buy an island and turn it into an impregnable compound?"

"I'm sure it won't come to that."

Thomas rolled over and lightly kissed Laura. "Ugh, my brain hurts."

"Why don't you stay in bed until noon and we'll figure out a place to all go out to lunch. That'll help get your mind off all this."

"Maybe. I am a little tired."

"Try and get some sleep sweetie."

He rolled over on his back and within a few minutes began to drift off to sleep. Laura watched his breathing change and then got up to begin her day with Emily.

* * *

## Sunday September 16, 2001

Sam, Bill and Thomas crested the hill and jogged towards the bunker.

"So what's the Pentagon want to talk to you guys about?"

"We can't say much," Sam replied. "It was an old mission and they want our perspective on someone we used to know."

"Interesting."

"Not really," Bill said. "The government is on edge and reeling from the attacks. We're just doing our part."

"Your part? What does that mean?"

"Forget it," Sam said as he changed topics. "What about the DCI calling you out of nowhere and talking with you? Could he be anymore cryptic?"

"That's what I'm worried about. The past two nights I haven't been sleeping much at all."

"Well, you know we're here for you if you need us brother," Bill assured him.

"Thanks. I hope it doesn't come to that. The DCI doesn't understand the lengths I'll go to protect my family."

# 19
## Monday September 17, 2001

SANDBOX's Cessna Citation Encore taxied down one of San Francisco International Airport runways and took off into the sky headed for the east coast. Inside Sam, Bill and Thomas tried to relax as the two pilots navigated their way across the United States before the sun had even crested the horizon.

"Nervous?" Bill asked Thomas.

"That doesn't begin to describe what I'm going through."

"Just try and take it easy," Sam suggested. "Whatever happens, and if you need our help, you know we'll be there for you."

Thomas nodded. "I know, and thanks. It's just that I had practically convinced myself that it was all over. That my family's secret was safe and we'd be able to have a normal life."

"That's wishful thinking," Bill said offhandedly.

"What the hell do you mean by that?" Thomas snarled.

Bill held up his hands. "Chill brother. All I meant was that unless you move to the middle of nowhere your secret will eventually get out again."

"Not if I can help it."

Bill pressed the issue. "And how do you plan on guaranteeing your secret? If you haven't noticed your children are growing older. And even though they have remarkable abilities, you need to remember that they're still children, susceptible to hormones, peer pressure and teenage years. And while you think you have control over them now, rest assured that will change."

Thomas didn't reply but sent a scowl in Bill's direction as Sam took everything in.

"I don't want your world to turn upside down again, okay? That's all I'm saying."

"It sounds like you're saying much more than that," Thomas said as he maintained his anger.

Bill sighed. "Fine. Pretending to be a normal family isn't the answer you're looking for. What's your life style been like in the past four years? I'll tell you exactly what it's been. You've been constantly looking over your shoulder in fear that at any minute someone's going to come and take you and your family away. And I'm not saying you're wrong because I'd be doing the exact same thing if I was in your shoes. But look at what that stress, worry and anxiety has done to you. You're back to being a shut-in brother."

"You say it like I don't have a choice."

"Maybe. Maybe not. Here's what I do know. The world isn't ready for what you and your family can do, which by the way continues to blow my mind."

Thomas understood where Bill's heart was coming from but he was still irritated at his friend. He turned and looked at Sam.

"And where do you land with all of this?"

"Honestly?"

"It didn't stop Bill."

"Very well," Sam replied. "I think you're fucked."

That rattled Thomas. "Wait...what?"

"Bill's got a point. You're not a normal family but you're doing everything you can to be just that, and there's nothing wrong with that."

"But?"

"Except that one time when one of you makes the smallest mistake and it gets caught on camera. What happens then? Maybe nothing. Or maybe it'll start another shit storm of epic proportions."

Thomas sat back in his seat, somewhat deflated. "Are you saying I should just start up a circus freak show on the side or something? Put us all on display rather than hide and keep our secret? What the hell are you saying?"

"We're your best friends and you need to wake up. Life isn't going to get easier because you have these powers. It's going to get harder, as we've all unfortunately experienced four years ago."

"You guys are brutal, but you're still not telling me anything I don't already know. What will waking up get me? I'll tell you what, nothing. I have to keep my family safe and their abilities hidden or else all of this starts all over."

Sam put his hands up. "You're right Thomas. You're between a rock and hard place and it's easy for me to judge you without actually being in your shoes. Sorry."

"Damn right you're sorry," Thomas replied as he began to cool down.

"Aww," Bill said. "Look at the lover's spat."

"Eat a dick," Sam told him.

"And to think I hang out with you two."

"Yeah," Bill said, "but it's only because you love us."

Thomas cracked a small smile. "That's touching you asshole."

Sam spoke up. "And here I thought living with wives that want us out of harm's way was tough."

"No shit," Bill added.

"But in all honesty Thomas, I both envy and hate your situation."

"That's true," said Bill. "I mean, who else that I know can pretend to be Darth Vadar and choke a man using the Force from across the room. That's pretty cool."

Thomas started to breathe deeply and raised his hand towards his friend. Bill's smile faded as he clutched his throat.

"Hey now! I didn't say you should try it on me!"

111

Thomas dropped his arm and both he and Sam chuckled.

"Fucking hell. That's the last time I give any suggestion on how to abuse your power."

"Sorry brother," said Thomas as he apologized. "I couldn't resist. But I hear what you're both saying. Maybe it's time for a change. Maybe playing house isn't working anymore."

\* \* \*

Their jet landed at Ronald Reagan Washington International Airport earlier than expected. After procuring rental vehicles Sam and Bill made the quick drive to the Pentagon while Thomas drove north-west along George Washington Memorial Parkway towards the CIA.

\* \* \*

As Sam and Bill drove up they saw firsthand the damage that the plane had done to the building. It'd been a week since the attack and a multitude of engineers were hard at work to stabilize the damaged section. They parked, walked inside and checked in with security. After their identities were verified it wasn't long before Colonel James appeared and took them to one of the inner Pentagon layers.

The three men entered a secured room that contained a number of high ranking military officers as well as a handful of individuals dressed in suits. Colonel James closed the door and indicated to two open seats for Sam and Bill to occupy. He then walked to the opposite side and joined the other men at the table.

Colonel James cleared his throat and spoke up. "For the record please state your names."

"Sam Paige."

"Bill Nicholson."

"Thank you both for taking time out of your busy schedule to be here. Now, with that being said, our goal is to pick your brains on one Hamid Emal Habibi. What can you tell us about him?"

Sam and Bill shared a glance before Sam spoke up. "If you'll excuse me Colonel, is this an inquiry or a debrief?"

"Mr. Paige, you were invited here today, and agreed quite willingly, to provide us with information on Hamid. Is there a problem?"

"A little Colonel. We're feeling a bit ambushed here, as if we're on trial."

"Of course. Let me apologize that we didn't go around the room and introduce everyone. I'd also like to apologize that milk and cookies also weren't made available to you." His voice took a hard tone. "One week ago our country was attacked and we have a credible lead that names Hamid as one of the masterminds. You are not on trial. All we want is background information from the nine months you spent embedded with Hamid and his people, training them to fight the Soviets, twenty years ago in Afghanistan. Do I make myself clear?"

The other men in the room didn't flinch or make any movement whatsoever. Their eyes had remained focused on Sam and Bill the entire time.

"Crystal clear," Sam replied as he felt like he was back in the service. "Please proceed."

Colonel James relaxed a bit and began. "In August of eighty-one the two of you, along with ten other Special Forces members, arrived in Panjshir Valley, Afghanistan and began a training regiment with one Hamid Emal Habibi. Early on, during your nine months there, the village you were in was attacked by a Soviet Hind helicopter. In the ensuing attack two of your men..." The

Colonel paused as he looked through the file in front of him. "…a Lloyd Franklin and Kit Jones were killed."

"That's correct," Sam replied. "I'd also like to add that a number of the Mujahideen rebels were also killed."

"Of course," Colonel James stated without any real merit behind it. His eyes floated down to the file again as he continued. "Your reports, from twenty years ago, paint a clear picture that the training was very successful. Do you agree?"

Sam nodded. "I do."

"And you Mr. Nicholson. Do you concur?"

"The Afghan rebels were grossly outgunned. Hamid, and all of the men we trained, never once wanted to relinquish their land. They were fighting for their home and their tenacity was absolutely unparalleled."

"So you're saying they were radical?"

"Radical?" Bill asked. "I believe it's fairly common knowledge that anyone who fights against invaders for their own land isn't radical. That's just human nature."

"Thank you Mr. Nicholson. I believe you've just hit the nail on the head. We're done here."

Colonel James stood up as Sam and Bill shared a glance.

"Um…Colonel?"

"Yes Mr. Paige?"

"We flew all the way out here just to confirm a report I authored twenty years ago?"

"Is there a problem?" asked Colonel James.

"It seems pointless to have been a part of this process. What do you hope to gain from this feeble interview?"

"Mr. Paige. You did your job and we've done ours. Now, you'll have to excuse us. A Lieutenant will show you out through security. Thank you for your time."

*   *   *

Inside the CIA's lobby Thomas stared at the star, on the
Memorial Wall, that represented his father. He hadn't seen it for
nearly four years.

*Where are you pop? Why don't you come when Emily uses her
power?*

Thomas turned slightly as a man entered his peripheral vision
and he knew it was the DCI, Robert Duncan.

"I didn't think I'd ever come back here to see my father's star
again."

"Thank you for making the trip," Robert said as they shook
hands. "Perhaps we should take a walk someplace where there are
fewer eyes and ears."

The two of them stepped outside and began a meandering
stroll on a path that encircled the huge building.

"What are you after Mr. Duncan?" Thomas asked with an edge
in his voice.

"I understand your trepidations. I know you don't trust me or
the CIA at this point, and I don't blame you. Victor Bannon
abused his position of power and the atrocities that happened to
you, your daughter, as well as your family and friends, was
reprehensible."

Thomas didn't reply as they continued their walk.

"With that being said Mr. Clark, I'll get right to the point."

"Please do."

Victor, perhaps in his haste of performing his vanishing act,
left a folder in his private safe that I found when I took over as
interim Director. The file was labeled 'Project Zelda'."

"I've never heard of it," Thomas replied.

"Neither had I and that's because it was a conceptual plan. A
plan that I'm afraid you're all too familiar with. In it were the

details on harvesting your DNA, developing a serum and then using that serum on others to manifest super powers."

"Sounds like science fiction."

"I agree. But as I kept reading Victor had numerous referenced computer files that should have been in Victor's private archive."

*Shit.* "What kind of computer files?"

"Videos, interviews and that sort of thing."

"And you were able access these files?"

Robert shook his head. "The files had either been deleted or they never existed in the first place."

*Whew.* "I see."

"But I remained curious. A reoccurring name popped up in his file. A Dr. Yamato Takuma Matsushita."

Thomas cringed as he heard the name pronounced. That bastard had put him and Emily through hell and back in the bowels of Facility Thirteen. The DCI caught Thomas' reaction.

"So you know him."

"No comment."

"Very well," Robert replied. "With my curiosity peaked, and as time permitted, I began to personally track down any leads to both Project Zelda and what Victor Bannon had been covering up. As it turns out I was able to uncover that he used SANDBOX personnel, including your good friends Sam Paige and Bill Nicholson, to do his dirty work for him."

"They would never do anything illegal."

"I agree. SANDBOX has quite the reputation. But they would have been persuaded to do so IF they thought their families were being held against their will."

*Fuck. He knows too much.* "Get to your point."

Robert Duncan collected his thoughts before he spoke up. "I know about your children and what they can do."

116

Thomas didn't take the bait. "Like what? Finger painting?"

The DCI cracked a grin. "No, nothing so primitive. I'm aware that your daughter has the ability to manifest dead people out of thin air. I'm aware that she can control and manipulate people's wills just by her touch. Your son, well, he's something else entirely. He brought your friend's wife back from the dead, apparently quite literally, through a portal that I can only surmise travels to the other side. Extraordinary talent. Quite frankly, I didn't believe it until I saw the videos with my own eyes."

"Why tell me all this? Are you threatening me or my family?"

"No. I am nothing like Victor and I swear that no one else knows about this. As soon as I located the backup data drive, that Victor had hidden away and watched what as on it, I destroyed it."

"And I'm just supposed to believe that?"

"No, I don't suppose I would believe it either. However, wouldn't you and your family have been picked up by now?"

"Maybe. Maybe not. Regardless, you still haven't made your point."

"You're right, so here's my pitch. Wouldn't you like this world to be safe?"

"Who doesn't want that?"

"More people than I can imagine actually. I want you to help me."

"Help you how?"

"I want to re-open Project Zelda..."

"Fuck that shit!" Thomas cried out and then lowered his voice. "I'm not going back under the knife, nor am I going to subject my children to becoming guinea pigs."

The DCI put up his hands in surrender. "I apologize. I wasn't suggesting that. What I meant to say was that collaboration between us could help to make the world a safer place."

"The bottom line is that you want to use us."

"Work with, not use."

"And why would I even begin to think this thought process of yours sounds like a good idea?"

"Because maybe you're tired of looking over your shoulder. I mean, look at the lengths you went to cover up your children's abilities. I can only conclude that Hobbes had something to do with that, and I doubt you left his memories intact after the fact."

"You don't want to go down that path, sir."

"I imagine I wouldn't. And still to this day Victor Bannon hasn't resurfaced after miraculously disappearing four years ago."

"Imagine that," Thomas replied.

"I get it. You want to maintain your privacy and be a normal family. The bottom line is that I can't force you to do anything."

"I hope you don't."

"I didn't ask you out here to do that to you. I just want you to think about what your children can offer this world."

Thomas changed the flow of the conversation. "Why now? Why wait four years? What are you holding over my head if I don't agree?"

"Nothing, nothing at all. Until I saw the videos it all sounded like science fiction. But then I saw your children in action and I was amazed. The world is becoming unstable. I mean, a week ago the planes hit New York. The war has come to our doorstep. With your help we might be able to positively influence the direction the world is heading."

"With parlor tricks?"

"Your children's powers don't look like parlor tricks to me. The ability to change what people think or remember. To bring dead people back to life. It's incredible and mind blowing. All I want is a chance to make this world a better place."

"Sure. And all this coming from the Director of the CIA. Sounds too good to be true."

118

"I imagine it does. Is there anything I can do to make you believe I'm absolutely sincere?"

Thomas began to think it over. *I don't trust the CIA or the people who run it. They've always been after power and crush anyone in their way. But what if he's telling the truth? What if he really wants the world to be a better place and utilizing our powers to do so could be a very interesting endeavor.* Thomas shook his head. *That's crazy, what am I thinking. He's no different than Victor. I need to protect us from any and all threats. But how can I do that on my own? I've been trying and it's exhausting. Maybe Sam and Bill are right. Maybe it's time for a change.*

Thomas refocused on the DCI. "I'm going to make a phone call. I would like you to repeat what you've just told me."

"Who would I be talking to?"

"My wife."

Thomas pulled out his cell phone and dialed their home number. It rang a few times before Laura picked it up.

"Thomas?"

"Hi sweetie."

"Is everything alright? How was the meeting?"

"Everything's fine, for the most part. I'd like you to talk with Robert Duncan."

"The Director of Central Intelligence wants to talk to me?"

"Well, I'm insisting he does. Just do your thing."

"Okay."

Thomas handed his phone to the DCI.

"Mrs. Clark. This is Robert Duncan. Your husband has asked me to repeat what I've just told him."

"Go ahead," Laura replied.

Robert took two minutes as he told Laura about his plan for Project Zelda and to make the world a better place utilizing the children's powers. He also made it clear that his sincerity was on the level. When he was finished he handed the phone back to Thomas.

"Well?" Thomas asked his wife.

"Thomas, I don't like anything he had to say but he's not lying."

"Really? Not at all?"

"No. He definitely believes what he told me."

"Good. Thanks."

"I don't know what's going on but don't do anything without talking to me."

"I understand. I'll talk to you about this when I get home."

"Wait. You're going to do something, aren't you? I can tell."

"Now's not the time. I'll talk to you later. I love you."

He ended the call before Laura could reply and turned back towards Robert.

"So what was that all about?" inquired the DCI. "Some kind of test?"

"Yes, actually, and you passed. My wife says you were telling the truth."

Robert didn't get it. "I don't understand. How is that possible to do over the phone?"

"Sir, I'm taking a huge risk here and I already know my wife is going to be seriously pissed off at me. My children aren't the only ones with abilities."

The DCI's eyes widened. "What are you saying?"

"My wife knows when someone is lying."

"Bullshit. All records indicate that it's a genetic trait that stems from you."

"Dr. Matsushita created an early version of the serum. During our escape from Facility Thirteen I was stuck with one of the needles that I thought contained a sleep agent."

"Is that so?"

"And I pocketed what I thought was another one with the same drug. I was mistaken and I developed my own power. After my wife decided to inject the serum, she developed her own ability as well."

"Incredible. So you're saying you have a power, right here right now?"

"Yes."

"May I ask what is it?"

"Telekinesis."

"You have the ability to move things by just thinking about it?" A huge smile formed on his face. "That's incredible. How about a demonstration?"

"What? Here? People might see and I won't do that."

"You're right of course. I tell you what, how about just untying one of my shoe laces? No one will catch that."

Thomas pondered his request. *Oh, what the hell.* As the DCI watched his left shoelace quickly untied itself.

"Holy shit." He bent down and retied it before he stood back up. "Okay. I'm impressed. You know this changes things."

Thomas was instantly on guard. "What do you mean?"

"The serum was able to be created. And, on top of that, you and your wife have phenomenal abilities. I'm assuming from your demonstration that you're thinking about moving forward on creating the secret program with me?"

Things were suddenly moving very quickly. "I don't know. Maybe. I can't make a life changing decision like this without consulting my family."

"Of course, I understand. No pressure. I'm just thoroughly excited that all of this could become a reality. Thank you for trusting me."

"I still have my doubts."

"Good. Don't ever let your guard down, but I'm sure you know that lesson all too well."

"Yes, I do."

"Good. Well, I hope we can talk soon and see where this takes us. I also wanted to add that you and your family's level of participation are completely up to you. In fact, I don't think we should meet here again. I'll come to you and you'll call the shots. Security is paramount and I can't have this information leaking out. That would be disastrous."

Thomas liked what he heard. "Thank you."

"No, thank you Thomas," and extended his hand.

As they shook, and then went their separate ways, Thomas knew he had one hell of a hurdle to overcome and wasn't looking forward to the talk with Laura.

## 20
## Monday September 17, 2001

Sam, Bill and Thomas met back at the airport and boarded their private jet. Within minutes it had been cleared by the tower and was back in the air headed west towards California.

"So how'd your meeting with the Pentagon go?" Thomas asked.

"Apparently they just wanted to pick our brains," Bill replied. "But other than that you know we can't talk about it."

"Right. Sorry."

"The damage the plane caused to the Pentagon was pretty intense. Seeing the devastation in person rather than just images on television was a solemn experience."

"What about you?" Sam asked. "What did Robert Duncan want to talk to you about?"

Thomas turned his head away from his friends and stared out the plane's window. "He knows."

Sam and Bill shared a concerned look before Sam spoke up again. "What do you mean he knows?"

"He knows about my children and what they can do."

"Shit," Bill exclaimed. "What the hell? Did he threaten you?"

Thomas twisted back towards his friends and met their eyes. "No, actually. He wants to make the world a safer place and..."

Bill cut him off. "That sounds like complete bullshit brother. He's the head of the CIA. All he wants is power."

Thomas shook his head. "Initially I thought the same thing but I had him talk to Laura and she cleared him. He wasn't lying."

"He's faking it somehow."

"I have to agree with Bill," Sam said. "The DCI's good intentions seem unlikely. But besides all that, how did he come to figuring this all out? I thought we scrubbed any and all evidence both from the computer servers and from everyone's memories?"

Thomas told them about Project Zelda and a backup computer drive of Victor's that he'd hidden away that Robert had discovered.

"So what you're telling us," Sam said," is that he wants you to become part of a specialized task force or something?"

"Something like that," Thomas replied.

"And what would you and your ten and eight year old children be asked to do?" Sam pressed.

"That part of it is unclear at this time."

"You don't know?" Bill asked.

"No," Thomas answered.

"And you think this is a good idea brother, to just jump in bed with the CIA and pretend everything's suddenly going to be okay?"

Thomas lashed out. "Don't talk down to me like I'm an idiot. You don't have a fucking clue about the anguish I go through every day. The thought that my children are targets; that they could be taken from me and I'd never see them again weighs heavily on my shoulders. And the worst part is…the worst part is that I was the one that bestowed these abilities onto them. It's my fault they're in danger."

"Okay," Sam said in a soft tone. "Take it easy. All that Bill and I are trying to say is that you need to be extremely cautious, that's all."

"I know. Fuck. I'm scared to death but I don't know what else to do."

"I get it," Sam assured his friend. "You want what's best for your family as well as keeping them safe from potential harm. But coupling with the CIA is a risk no matter how you slice it."

"Are you sure this is what you want to do?" Bill asked.

"Sure? No. But now we're exposed again and that puts both my family and yours at risk."

"Well," Sam confidently said to Thomas, "whatever you do decide to do we've got your back."

"It doesn't sound like it."

"We are," Bill said. "Sorry about breathing down your throat. All I'm asking is that you think this through thoroughly. Have you talked with Laura about this yet?"

"No. She only heard what the DCI had to say over the phone."

Sam leaned back in his chair. "Well good luck convincing her."

"Tell me something I don't know."

\* \* \*

The jet landed at San Francisco International Airport and the three men, and both pilots exited. Soon afterward two fresh pilots boarded, refueled and headed off to rendezvous with the six SANDBOX personnel that had just completed a job in Saudi Arabia and were waiting for a ride home.

\* \* \*

Thomas walked in through the front door and Laura met him in the entryway. It was late at night and the kids were already asleep in bed.

"Hi."

"Hi back."

They embraced, kissed each other and Laura led him into the kitchen where she had something for him to eat already prepared.

"Thanks. I'm starving."

"Did you want a beer?" she asked.

"Maybe. Or maybe I should save it until after we talk," he said lightly.

Thomas sat down and Laura slid into a seat across from him.

Laura sighed. "Shit honey. What have you done?"

"You told me yourself that the DCI wasn't lying."

"Stop evading and talk to me. What did you do?"

Thomas had a hard time looking at his wife. "I told him about us."

"What?"

"I told him about our powers. He already knew about Emily and Gavin's."

Laura tried to keep calm. "Why the hell would you do that?"

"He knows everything. As much as we did to cover our tracks he found out everything anyway."

"I can't believe you told him. What did you agree to Thomas? What the hell were you thinking?"

Thomas lost it. "I just want us to be safe goddammit!"

"Safe? Are you kidding me? We'll be exposed all over again. I can't go through that again and neither can the kids."

"We're exposed already," Thomas began to explain. "The DCI did his research and found a hidden data stash. He's seen our children in action. If we become part of this Project Zelda then we'll be protected."

"You're lying to yourself. This is exactly what we've always fought against…and now you want to needlessly reveal what our children can do to the CIA? What's next, the world?"

"I…I…"

"What' going on in that skull of yours?"

Thomas lowered his head. "I don't know. I just know that we won't be able to hide our children's abilities from the world forever. They're getting older and we can't and won't be able to control them as they become teenagers. They're growing up and

126

have been making their own decisions about their powers for years. If they want to be a part of Project Zelda then it's up to them."

"No. No fucking way Thomas. They're just children. They're not old enough to make these kinds of life changing decisions. That's our job. Hell, they've been subjected to so many horrors already that I fear they'll never be normal. Emily has PTSD for Christ's sake. Do you want to have even more nightmares on top of what she's already been through?"

"No, of course not. I just need us to be safe."

"You don't feel safe here?"

Thomas shook his head. "I haven't felt safe in years, and how could I. For the past four years we've just been pretending that everything's fine and that all the shit that went down in D.C. and Hawaii never happened. Emily's not the only one that's having nightmares."

"Wait. You're having nightmares too?"

"Sometimes."

"And you didn't want to tell me because…?"

"Because I didn't want you to worry."

Laura relaxed and lowered her voice. "I'm sorry you've been having nightmares. And as much as I agree with you that we need to keep our family safe, we're not joining the CIA and putting our young children through that."

"But…"

"You need to hear me when I say 'no'. We'll figure this out together. No CIA. No deals. Promise me."

"Laura, we need to…"

"Thomas. We're a family and anything we do we decide together. Promise me that you won't make a deal behind my back."

He shifted uncomfortably in his chair.

"Thomas?  Promise me."

"Fine.  I promise."

"Good."  Laura got up, extracted a beer from the fridge and put it down in front of her husband.  "We'll figure this out together, but not tonight.  I'm heading to bed so I'll see you in a bit."

# 21
## Tuesday September 18, 2001

SANDBOX's private jet landed back at SFO, in the late afternoon, after it picked up six operators who had completed their Saudi Arabian mission and required a ride back home. Jessie, Mack, Corey, Randal, Ryan and Donnie departed the plane, with their gear, then bypassed Customs and headed back to the office. They dropped their gear at the front door and were greeted by Sam and Bill as they entered the building.

"Jessie," Sam said as he shook the team leader's hand. "Welcome back. How'd the protection detail pan out?"

"No complaints and nothing to report," Jessie replied. "It was a walk in the park."

Sam and Bill smiled. "Excellent. That's just what we wanted to hear. We're glad you and your team are back safely. Check in with Roberta and then we can sit down for the mission debrief after that."

"Roger that Sam."

After Jessie watched Sam and Bill walk away he made his way over to Roberta's desk as the other five operators lingered by the front door.

"Hello Jessie," she said as he approached.

Jessie took a serious tone. "We brought the latest shipment back with us."

Roberta, ever since she acquired her job at SANDBOX, had been working for General Aleman and the group known as The Organization. She had been shown proof that Sam and Bill were responsible for her son's death and she readily agreed to become a mole within SANDBOX over a decade prior. After Aleman was taken into custody she continued to receive instructions from a man who went by the name of Serpent. In the last four years, as SANDBOX grew in both reputation and region, Roberta used the company's resources to bring in drugs from around the world several times a year. And she made this happen through Jessie, and the other five operators, that she had been instructed to hire years before. Those six men had worked well together and frequently took jobs outside of the U.S. for this very reason, but their loyalty was bound to The Organization and that's who they ultimately received their orders from.

Roberta handed Jessie a folded piece of paper. "The procedure has changed. Call this number immediately."

"What's going on?"

"I wasn't told anything else."

"Shit. Okay." He turned and walked over to his men. "Something's off but I don't know what. Stow the gear and make sure the product is secured. Then come back here to debrief. We'll deal with this after that is taken care of."

\* \* \*

Jessie used a burner cell phone, one that he planned on using once and then destroying afterwards, and called the number he'd been given.

"Report," a voice he'd never heard commanded.

"Who am I conversing with?"

"Jessie. So many questions. You undoubtedly sound a little confused."

Jessie's face tightened. "Who is this?"

"Does it really matter? You have product that you need to deliver and I want to take it off your hands."

"Where's the person I typically network with?"

"Jessie. There's been a change in management."

130

"What? What does that mean?"

"It means that you'll be taking your orders from me now."

"And you are?"

"My name is General Robert Aleman."

Jessie was speechless for a few moments. "Sir, my apologies. I've only heard stories about you. I've been taking my orders from your father."

"I'm well aware of what you used to do, but he's no longer in the picture so you'll be reporting to me. Is that clear?"

"Clear, sir. What do you need me and my team to do?"

"The shipment you brought in today is the last one. I'm closing down the drug pipeline through SANDBOX."

"Yes, sir."

"I'll be in touch to let you know how and when I need your assistance."

"Very good, sir. We're at your disposal."

## 22
## Tuesday September 18, 2001

Thomas, Laura, Emily and Gavin had eaten quietly throughout dinner as they sat around the table. Everyone seemed lost in their own thought process.

"Sooo," Laura finally said, "how was school?"

Both of the children shrugged, clearly disinterested in engaging in any type of conversation.

"That good, eh?"

"Well," said Thomas, "I have something I'd like to talk about that's important."

Laura cut him off before he could continue. "However, your father and I aren't ready to talk about that with you quite yet." Laura shot him a death glare. "You two are dismissed. I want you to go and finish up your homework."

Emily and Gavin silently slinked out of their seats and headed down the hallway to their bedrooms. Laura watched them go before she unloaded on Thomas.

"What the hell?" she said in a hushed but displeased tone. "You can't just drop a bomb like that when we haven't come to a conclusion on how to proceed. This really pisses me off. What are you thinking?"

"You're right. I'm sorry. I wanted to see what they'd think about the idea."

"They're just kids; they're too young to understand the ramifications of what you're proposing. Don't do that again."

Thomas put his hands up. "I hear you." He got up from the table and walked away to his office.

\* \* \*

Later on that evening, after Emily's homework had been finished, she kept tossing and turning in bed. Sleep was tugging on her eyelids but she didn't want to close her eyes. The nightmares she'd been experiencing, even though her mother had started working through her PTSD issues with her, were bothersome to say the least. But as much as she resisted the sandman finally had his way and Emily drifted off to a fitful sleep.

Emily found herself in the back of a Suburban that barreled north up the Hawaiian highway towards the Marine Base.

Suddenly two vans blocked their progress as another two shot past and prevented their escape.

A barrage of deafening smacks stitched across the side of the Suburban as AK-47 rounds dug into the vehicle's armor plating and thick bullet proof windows.

Emily couldn't stop herself from screaming.

BOOM!

An explosion rocked one of the other Suburban's and a fire broke out.

Automatic gun fire illuminated the pre-dawn light and tore up the pavement along with everything else the bullets reached out and touched.

All she could do was keep screaming and screaming and screaming.

Emily awoke, awash in sweat and her mouth open in a frozen but silent scream. She wiped her forehead off with part of the bed sheet and collapsed back on her pillow.

She knew she'd never been in the Hawaiian attack because she'd been in D.C., with both her father and grandfather, during that horrific incident. No, she hadn't been there but it had been one of the memories she had wiped from Amanda, Craig, Sarah and Edward's minds. Inadvertently some of those memories

Emily had been asked to remove had remained in her head and now, years later, she had begun to feel firsthand what the other children had experienced.

* * *

With his bedroom door closed Gavin stepped through the portal and appeared on his private island. The never setting sun washed over his body and began to warm his skin.

"Hello Victor," he said as he passed the skeleton in the sand. "Don't get up on my account."

Gavin sat down in his usual spot and enjoyed the gently lapping of the ocean as it hit his feet and then receded away.

"Hello."

Gavin jumped at the sound of the voice behind him. He scrambled to his feet and turned to look at the man who had addressed him.

"Wait, I know you," Gavin said. "I met you before in Hawaii. You're Sam's dad. Do you want to sit down?"

"Thank you Gavin," the man replied and took a seat on the soft sand.

"What are you doing here? No one's come to visit me in a very long time."

The man who sat in the sand next to Gavin was none other than Ray Paige, Sam's father who had passed away while Sam and Bill were training rebels in Afghanistan.

"I was wondering if you could pass a message on to my son."

"To Uncle Sam? Sure, I can do that."

"Good. Thank you. Could you tell him that I miss him and that I'm very proud of whom he's become."

Gavin nodded.

"Also, before I go, your grandparent's, Michael and Betsy, wanted me to tell you that they miss you dearly."

Gavin's eyes opened wide and he got excited. "Why aren't they here? Why can't I see them?"

Ray shook his head. "I don't make the rules. We're all entombed in a network of guidelines and I was briefly able to bend one of them to come and see you."

"Oh. Well, tell them that I miss them too. We all do."

"You got it Gavin. Take care and thank you."

Ray stood up, walked towards the vast ocean and slowly disappeared into the distance.

# 23

# Wednesday September 19, 2001

After school on Wednesday Laura, Julia, Kim and Rebecca
took all six kids to Target to buy them their missing school
supplies. On the way there Gavin, amidst the normal banter that
was going on between the children, asked a question.

"Are we going to see Uncle Sam soon?"

"Maybe," Laura replied. "Why, what's up sweetie?"

"Nothing."

*That's a lie. I wonder what's going on?*

Before she could press the issue they had arrived at Target and
piled out of the Suburban. Gavin held Rebecca's hand as the
group entered the store.

Inside Target the small crowd made their way over to the
supply aisle and began to place items in the three carts based on
the list the teachers had recently sent home with each of their
children. Quickly the bottom of each cart was covered with
notebooks, coloring pens and a myriad of other objects. Rebecca
helped Gavin retrieve items that were too high for him to reach,
much to his delight.

"I can't believe the amount of stuff we're buying," Kim said
offhandedly.

"This is crazy," Julie responded. "And here I thought we were
already prepared."

"Apparently not," Laura said with a grin. "There are items on
this list we never had when we were young."

"Oh don't start that line of thought," Julie replied, "it'll only
make us feel older."

Five minutes, and three carts full of supplies later, everyone
began to make their way towards the checkout stands. Out of a

side aisle a blond haired woman, clearly not watching where she was going, walked right in front of Kim's cart. The woman noticed her mistake at the last second, tried to adjust but Kim's cart clipped her anyway. The blond tripped and fell to the floor. Kim immediately went to her side to help her up.

"I'm sorry. Are you okay?" Kim asked as she helped the woman to her feet.

"Thank you. I'm afraid that was my fault for getting in your way. Please, excuse me."

Laura's intuition immediately kicked in. *She's lying.* However, due to the fact that she was used to people lying whenever she heard anyone out in public, she dismissed the thought just as quickly as her ability had informed her about it.

The woman began to walk away, and as she did she turned back and said out loud, "General Aleman sends his regards."

Before any of the adults could register what she meant Kim started to wobble.

"Kim?" Julie asked. "Are you okay?"

A few seconds later Kim fell to her knees, flopped over on her back and began to convulse.

"Kim!" Julie cried out and rushed to her sister's side.

"Mommy! Mommy!" Tears instantly began to flow.

Rebecca looked at Laura and their eyes met. In that moment they both knew that their roles had suddenly reversed. Laura reached in her purse, pulled out her Glock and sprinted after the woman who had just exited the front entrance. White froth came out of Kim's mouth and rolled down the sides of her face. Rebecca went to Kim's side, whose eyes had already rolled into the back of her head, and took control of the situation.

"Julie, I need you to back up and take the kids with you."

"I'm not leaving my…"

"Do it!" she insisted.

Rebecca, with her background in battle trauma medicine, quickly figured out that Kim's condition was quickly deteriorating as Julie backed off and took the children with her.

"Mommy! Mommy! What's wrong with Mommy?"

A crowd had begun to form from the commotion. Rebecca took off her jacket, folded it up and placed it under Kim's head even though she had stopped convulsing and breathing.

*Shit, this is bad.*

She looked back over at Julie with a 'there's nothing I can do' expression on her face. It didn't take long before Gavin extracted himself from the group and plopped down next to Rebecca.

"I can help her."

"I know you can. Do your thing."

Julie and all the children watched as Gavin placed his hands on Kim's chest, closed his eyes and concentrated. Ten long seconds later Kim took her first ragged breath, rolled on her side and puked. Gavin moved away as Kim's eyes popped opened. Rebecca took a close look at them and was happy to see that both her appearance and demeanor had greatly improved.

"How're you feeling?" Rebecca asked.

"What...what the hell just happened?"

"Mommy! Mommy!" Sarah and Edward broke free from Julie and ran to their mother's side, tears streaming.

Kim managed to sit up, with Rebecca's help, and took them both in her arms and held them tight. "I'm okay. Mommy's going to be okay."

\* \* \*

Laura pulled her Glock 17 from her purse and rushed after the blond woman as Kim began to convulse on the store floor behind her. Store customers couldn't believe that a gun toting woman

139

came out of nowhere. A few of them began to panic, screamed and ducked down where they were or simply ran away from Laura as she rushed the front doors.

Outside Laura looked but didn't see the woman so she quickly scanned the area from left to right in an attempt to regain visual contact. A strange but familiar object caught her eye on top of a nearby trashcan. Laura took another look around, weapon at the ready, but didn't see the blond woman.

*Shit!*

She decided to put her gun back in her purse but kept her hand on it just in case as she walked over to the trash receptacle. There, on top, was a discarded blond wig.

*You've got to be kidding me.*

Laura took another look around, came up empty and rushed back inside. She made her way through the crowd that had gathered and saw that Kim was sitting up, both children in her arms with Rebecca and Gavin just off to one side.

*Oh boy.*

"How is she?" Laura asked Rebecca.

"Much better thanks to you know who. What about outside?"

Laura shook her head. "Vanished and she left her wig on the trash can."

"A wig? What the hell is going on?"

"No shit," Laura replied. "I don't know what's happened here but we all need to leave right now."

The urgency in her voice swiftly translated to Julie, Kim and the children and within seconds the group left their carts, and the mystified crowd behind, as they moved together towards the front doors.

"Get everyone in the two vehicles," Rebecca instructed. "We're going to SANDBOX."

140

Laura nodded as both of them worked in tandem to load everyone so they could flee the scene as quickly as possible. The two Suburban's raced out of the parking lot with whimpering and unsure children in tow. It wasn't until they were on the freeway that Laura called Thomas.

"Hey," he said, "are you still mad at me?"

"We were just attacked at Target."

It took Thomas a few moments to switch gears as his mind caught on to his wife's 'no shit' tone of voice. "What happened? Is everyone okay?"

"Everyone's fine now. Some woman pretended to get knocked down by one of our carts so Kim helped her up. As she walked away she said 'General Aleman sends his regards' or something like that. Seconds later Kim collapsed and began to convulse on the floor."

"Is Kim okay?"

"Yes, thanks to you know who."

"Oh shit."

"My thoughts exactly, amongst everything else that just happened to us."

"Where are you right now?"

"We're on our way to the office."

"Good. I'll meet you there."

Thomas grabbed his keys and jetted out of the house with Laura still on the line. He started up his vehicle and headed out.

"Give me a second. We need to patch in Sam and Bill on this shit."

Thomas put her on hold and called Sam's direct line at SANDBOX.

"Thomas. What's up?"

"Put me on speaker!"

Sam instantly put his game face on as Thomas' voice sent his mind into overdrive.

"Bill's on. Go."

"The women and children were just attacked at the Target they were shopping at."

"What the fuck?" Bill exclaimed, clearly unprepared for what Thomas had just told them.

"Laura's on the line and she can explain it."

"Sam? Bill?" she asked in a somewhat panicked voice.

"We can hear you. What happened?"

"A woman in a blond wig set us up. Long story short Kim collapsed and began to convulse soon after this woman touched her."

"Is Kim okay?" Bill immediately asked.

"Currently yes, as far as I can tell, thanks to you know who. The woman said something right before she walked away."

Sam and Bill shared a very nervous and uneasy glance as Laura continued.

"She said 'General Aleman sends his regards'."

"No fucking way," Bill instantly said.

Sam held up his hand and Bill closed his mouth. "Is everyone okay?"

"Yes," Laura replied. "I went after the woman while Rebecca tended to Kim. Whoever it was managed to get away. As soon as Kim was back on her feet we got the hell out of there."

"I want you all to come to SANDBOX right now."

"We're already on the way with two vehicles."

"How far out?" Sam inquired.

"Ten minutes."

"We'll see you then."

"Laura?" said Bill.

"What?"

"Thank you."

"You can thank you know who when we get there."

"Roger that."

Sam cut the line and they stared at each other. Bill was furious as his emotions rippled throughout his face. He finally opened his mouth.

"We should have killed that sonofabitch when we had the chance. He threatened our families once before and what, he's come back to finish the job?"

"Easy brother. I'm not saying you're wrong but we need to figure this out."

"Fuck easy. He went after my wife. She'd be dead right now if it wasn't for Gavin and his super powers."

"First thing's first. Let Roberta know that we'll be occupying the top floor nine minutes from now and tell her our family is in danger. We'll powwow as a group after we make sure Kim and everyone else is okay. Got it?"

Bill fought and reigned his emotions back in. "Got it."

* * *

Nine minutes later multiple vehicles converged in the SANDBOX parking lot. Sam and Bill, now wearing side arms, exited the building and brought their families inside. In a matter of minutes they had all taken up residency in the top floor suite.

Kim had completely bounced back to normal and Rebecca concluded that she'd be fine, but insisted that she get some rest. Roberta tended to the children's needs and emotions while the adults tried to get on the same page.

"How are you feeling babe?" Bill asked his wife as he handed her a glass of water.

"So much better. I don't remember much. I helped the woman up and right afterwards I lost my ability to stand up."

Bill squeezed his wife's hand.

"Let's go over it again," Sam said. "Julie, what happened?"

Julie answered. "A woman came out of a side aisle and got bumped by Kim's cart. She fell down and Kim went to help her up. She mumbled some apology and began to walk away, but then turned back and said something I don't remember."

"General Aleman sends his regards," Rebecca clarified.

"Yes," said Julie, "that was it. What the hell does that mean?"

"In a second," Sam replied. "What happened next?"

Julie continued. "My sister collapsed and the children began screaming. I didn't know what to do other than go to Kim's side. It was then that Rebecca told me to back off while Laura took off after the women."

"And then?" Sam pressed.

"And then…well….Rebecca looked at me like it was all over. Foam and whatever else was coming out of Kim's mouth. I think she'd stopped breathing.

Tears rolled down Julie's cheeks as she recalled the memory.

"I thought she was dead and that I'd lost her forever. But everything happened so quickly. Before I knew it Gavin had wiggled out of my grasp, placed his hands on her chest and blammo. She coughed, rolled over and puked all over the floor." Julie turned to Laura and Thomas. "Thank you. If he wasn't there to do what he does I don't know what I'd done if I'd lost my sister."

"You're welcome," Laura replied.

"It actually was the most remarkable thing to witness," Rebecca added. "I almost wish I could see him in action again."

Thomas interjected. "You might be able to because now we're exposed."

144

Sam caught on right away. "Thomas is right. Store security cameras must have the whole thing on tape."

"Oh shit," was their collective response.

"Not only that," Thomas continued, "all the kids also saw what our son did."

"You're right Thomas but let's deal with the external problem first," Sam said. "Bill, get Hobbes on the line and task him to retrieve that video before it gets a chance to go public."

Bill headed to another room to contact Hobbes.

"While that's happening I recommend that we stay here for the time being. It's the safest place for everyone to be while I figure this out."

"Don't you mean we?" Thomas asked.

"Not this time brother. I'm afraid this falls on Bill and I."

"Why?"

Sam looked around the table and met everyone's eyes individually before he continued. "General Aleman was a threat to us over a decade ago when Bill and I created SANDBOX. He wanted us to work for him."

"Work for him to do what exactly?"

"To use our company to move drugs," Sam simply stated. "And we told him to get lost. It was then that he threatened our families."

Julie's eyes opened wide. "I remember that day. You two came barreling into the house, guns drawn and bullet holes in your Kevlar vests."

Kim nodded. "I remember that as well."

Sam continued. "We tracked him down and put him away. Bill and I had no idea that he was still alive. Trust me when I say I'm going to get to the bottom of this. But, staying here I believe is the best option for the time being. Agreed?"

Everyone nodded, very unsure of who was after them and why.

"Good."

## 24
## Wednesday September 19, 2001

"Hobbes," Bill said, "I need you to pull the video footage from the local Target store's cameras ASAP."

"Okay," Hobbes replied. His office was filled with computers and a variety of equipment in various piles. He started typing away on his keyboard as he talked with Bill. "I should be able to do that as long as they're connected to the outside world, but since they're a national chain my guess is that they are. What's going on?"

"My wife was attacked at Target thirty minutes ago and I need that footage."

"Shit," Hobbes replied. "I'll take care of it."

"And when you have it make sure no one else has a copy."

"I understand. I'll permanently delete it once I have possession."

"Thanks Hobbes."

Hobbes hung up and worked his magic as he began to infiltrate Target's firewall.

\* \* \*

Bill walked back into the room and caught the gist of what Sam was telling everyone.

"We tracked him down and put him away. Bill and I had no idea that he was even alive. Trust me when I say I'm going to get to the bottom of this. But, staying here I believe is the best option for the time being. Agreed?"

Everyone nodded, very unsure of who was after them and why.

"Good."

Bill spoke up. "Hobbes is on the case. He should have possession of the video surveillance footage in no time."

"That's a start," Thomas replied.

Kim stood up. "I'm going to go be with my kids. I know they're terrified and they have every right to be."

"Babe," Bill started, "we need to talk about..."

"No," she replied firmly. "I know we agreed to purge our children's minds years ago but I don't know if I'm willing to put them through that again."

"They witnessed what Gavin can do. They're going to have questions."

"Then let them ask," she responded. "I don't have anything to hide."

"That's great. He saves you and you don't care if our kids talk and expose what he can do to the world."

Sam intervened. "Enough. This isn't getting us anywhere. We can discuss what happens later. Why don't Kim and Julie go check in on the kids, because all I know is that right now we have a much more pressing issue to figure out."

Julie and Kim left the table and headed into the family room while Sam, Bill, Thomas, Laura and Rebecca stayed behind.

Bill spoke up. "I want to apologize for my wife's remarks."

"Forget about it," Laura replied.

"No. This Aleman is our problem and he's targeted our families. Unfortunately, there's a chance you and your family could be exposed again Laura, and that's on us."

Thomas took the opportunity to speak. "I'd choose to expose us one hundred percent of the time if it meant Kim was saved by what our son can do."

Bill nodded. "Thanks brother. That means more than you know."

148

"The bottom line," Thomas said as he continued, "is that we're in this together and we'll deal with the fallout later."

Laura found Thomas' hand and squeezed it in support.

Sam spoke up. "I don't know if I can have you come along on this one Thomas."

"That's not your call Sam," he retorted. "You think I'm going to let my friends and their families get targeted and what, just sit back and watch?"

"You don't understand. This Aleman's not going to take any prisoners. He's playing for keeps."

"We're not going anywhere Sam," Laura told him. "You need all the help you can get."

"They're right," Bill admitted. "As much as I don't like it Sam, the Clark's do bring a certain advantage to this equation."

Sam knew he wasn't going to change their minds and relented. "Fine. Moving on." He turned to Bill. "We need to figure out why Aleman is out of prison and why."

"We could call General Franks and see what he has to say about it."

"Who's General Franks?" Rebecca asked.

"He's the one who paid us five million dollars to keep our mouths closed twelve years ago about Aleman's organization and how they had been using the military pipeline to smuggle drugs into the United States."

"Jesus Christ bro," Bill said. "That's classified intel."

"And look where keeping it a secret got us? Besides, everyone at this table is fully committed so bringing them up to speed is the right thing to do."

Bill closed his mouth as Sam continued.

"Let's try and get General Franks on the horn. Everyone else, take a break and make sure everyone eats something."

149

* * *

"This is General Franks."

Sam and Bill hovered over the speaker phone. "You're a hard man to get hold of General."

"I don't have time for games. Who is this?"

"General. This is Sam Paige and Bill Nicholson. You might remember us from twelve years ago."

There was an elongated pause before the General spoke again. "Shit."

"Shit is right General. I'll get right to the point. Our families have been targeted and the person who performed the attack said that 'General Aleman sends his regards'. Would you care to comment on that, sir?"

"Goddammit. I was hoping he'd just disappear and never resurface again. Apparently I was wrong."

"What are you saying?"

"You didn't hear this from me but we've been keeping Robert Aleman in a variety of black sites for the past decade. During his last transfer in Arizona the transport van he was in was ambushed and torched. Inside were four bodies which consisted of three guards and one prisoner. Initially we assumed that the job had gone sideways since the prisoner still had his restraints on. Until we performed the autopsies did we realize that we'd been setup. By that time the trail was long cold."

"And how long ago was this escape?"

"Four months ago."

"Four months!?" Bill exclaimed. "And you didn't think about calling to tell us?"

"No. You weren't a priority."

"What the hell does that mean?" Sam pressed.

"We put the men who ran The Organization under surveillance the moment we realized Aleman had escaped."

"These are the same men who most likely cut deals with you as to not embarrass the United States reputation?"

"No comment."

"I thought so."

General Franks continued. "Those men began to wind up dead, including Aleman's father."

"You're not instilling a high level of confidence here General," Sam stated. "But now that he's extracted his revenge on the people that remained free after his capture, it appears he's finally turned his attention back to us, the original two that are responsible for his disappearance in the first place."

"That would be my guess as well," General Franks said.

"And yet once these bodies began to pile up you still didn't call us."

"As you can imagine, we're all a little busy around the Pentagon as of late."

"That strangely sounds like damage control and yet another cover up General."

"Now you wait a damn minute. I will not be barked at…"

Sam cut him off. "We've been targeted General. We're not going to wait around as he kills our families. We're going to find Robert Aleman and finish this like we should have twelve years ago. Now, give us what you have on him."

"I can't do that."

"What the hell General? Why not?"

"I just can't."

"Wrong answer General."

The line went dead and Sam pounded his fist on the desk.

"That fucker just hung up on us," said Bill. "What the hell? Why would he be covering for Aleman?"

"I don't think he is. He's just used to covering his own ass and this is no exception."

They heard a knock on their office door.

"Come."

Hobbes opened it and held a dvd in his hand. "I got it."

Sam motioned for him to come over. "And this is the only copy?"

Hobbes shook his head. "No. I've got it digitalized on a server. This is a copy of that. But, I obliterated any trace of it off the store's recorder."

"Do you know if anyone there viewed it?"

"There's no way to tell."

"Damn. Then let me ask you this. Have you seen the footage?"

Hobbes looked back and forth between Sam and Bill before he answered. "I have."

Sam and Bill exchanged a look. "I see. Well, let's put this in and watch it."

Sam inserted the dvd into his computer and launched the simultaneous video feeds. It wasn't long before the three of them watched the events unfold.

It was obvious the blond woman had scoped out the group and made sure she got hit as she walked out of the aisle.

Kim went over, bent down and helped the woman back to her feet.

As the blond walked away she turned back and spoke. Moments later Kim collapsed and began to convulse.

"That son of a bitch," Bill whispered between clenched teeth. His hands curled in to fists.

Rebecca rushed to Kim's side as Laura pulled a gun out of her purse and rushed after the blond.

"Can I watch a particular feed in full screen?" Sam asked Hobbes.

"Sure. Double click on the one you want to focus on."

Sam enlarged one of the outside feeds and they all watched as the blond raced out of Target, removed and tossed her wig into the trash. A vehicle quickly pulled up. She got in and the vehicle pulled away just as Laura emerged from inside the store.

Sam reduced that screen and went back to the enlarged feed with Kim convulsing on the store's floor. She suddenly stopped moving altogether.

Bill put a hand to his face. "Fuck, this is tough to watch."

Gavin pulled away from Julie, and the other children, and knelt down by Kim's side. He placed his hands on her chest and closed his eyes.

"I don't understand what he's doing." Hobbes observed.

Ten excruciating seconds later Kim coughed, rolled over on her side and puked. Very soon thereafter she sat up on her own volition and embraced Sarah and Edward as they ran to her.

A crowd had begun to gather and they watched as Laura pushed her way through them, gathered them together and with help from Rebecca, got them all out of the store as quickly as possible.

The video ended as an outside camera caught two Suburban's racing off through the parking lot.

"That's it," Hobbes said. "But I still don't understand what happened."

"What do you think happened?" Sam asked.

"I...well...to be honest it looks like maybe your wife was poisoned or something."

"Go on," Bill said.

"And...well...it kind of looks like she stopped breathing."

"And?"

153

"And…somehow Gavin did something…"

"Something?"

Hobbes nervously looked back and forth between his two bosses. "You know, it's none of my business."

"It's okay Hobbes. Thank you for taking care of this issue for us. Now, we need your help with another pressing issue, the same issue that brought all our families here."

"The attack?"

Sam and Bill nodded. "We just hit a dead end with an old contact at the Pentagon. The man responsible for today's attack, and any future ones name is General Robert Aleman. Twelve years ago we put him away for drug trafficking, amongst other things. The government covered it up and…"

"And so did we," Bill added.

"That's true. My point is, when we took him down we recovered the General's briefcase. Naturally we turned that over for evidence, but not before we made copies of everything in it."

Hobbes eyes widened. "And you want me to comb through those and see if I can sniff out any leads on where he might be?"

Sam smiled. "Something exactly like that."

"I'm on it," Hobbes replied.

"Thank you."

"I'll take him down and dig that out of storage," Bill said. "Come on Hobbes."

\* \* \*

With everyone settled in and dinner prepared, Roberta took a quick break and headed back to her desk. During the initial arrival, and as Roberta watched over the children while the adults spoke, the children kept talking about how Gavin had done something to Kim. However, Emily and Gavin had kept to themselves off to one side, clearly uncomfortable.

Roberta had just sat down when the phone rang. She instinctively picked it up, even though it was well after hours, and answered it.

"Good evening, Sandbox Enterprises. How may I direct your call?"

"Give me an update," Robert Aleman said on the other end of the line.

A thin bead of sweat formed on Roberta's brow.

"I don't want to do this anymore. I'm out."

"You're in far too deep to ever get out my dear Roberta. I wouldn't want to expose you, but if I did I can't imagine how that would go down with your bosses, or their families. Now, I know you and my father worked together over the years, but truth be told he's not around anymore. And do you know why that is Roberta?"

"No...why?" she hesitantly asked.

"Because I killed him. He displeased me and I killed him."

"Oh my."

"Do you plan on displeasing me Roberta?"

"I...I..."

"I tell you what. Let's just continue our relationship and I'll forget you had a lapse in judgment. Now, give me my update."

Roberta struggled to resist but she was afraid of this man and what he would do. "The...the attack on Bill's wife failed."

"Interesting, even after you told me they'd be at that particular Target store. Very well, I'll be in touch."

## <u>25</u>
## Wednesday September 19, 2001

Sixty-two year old former General, Robert Aleman, ended the phone call with Roberta and had a disgusted look on his face. He paused for a second before he looked over at Anna Garland, the assassin who had killed a multitude of people for him over the years.

"How could you fail Anna? The woman is still alive."

"Impossible," she replied. "The female went down. There's no way she could have survived."

"And yet I just heard otherwise."

Her eyes inflamed. "That's impossible, insisted Anna. "She has to be dead."

General Aleman waved his hand dismissively in the air. "It doesn't matter now. Sam and Bill have been alerted, regardless of the outcome."

"Do you want me to try again?"

"No. I've decided to come at them from a different angle."

# 26

# Wednesday September 19, 2001

All six children had finally gone to bed a few hours prior, mostly reluctantly. As the clock finally struck midnight the adults continued to sit around and talk. Rebecca wasn't going to leave the children anytime soon and the adults knew it. Roberta also wanted to stay and help but Sam and Bill urged her to go home and get some much needed rest.

The tired group of adults turned their conversation towards Thomas and Laura as the realization that Kim would have died without Gavin's intervention became the new topic.

"I just wanted to thank you both again," Julie began, "for what your son did for Kim today."

"Yes, thank you," Kim added. "I don't remember much but after watching the video it's humbling for me to admit that I would have died if it wasn't for Gavin."

"You're welcome," Thomas replied.

"So do we get a discount now?" Bill enquired.

"What do you mean?" Laura asked.

"Well, save two sisters and get the third one for free?" he joked.

Kim punched her husband in the leg but everyone chuckled a little and that helped lighten the mood.

"But seriously," Bill said as he continued, "Gavin's one hell of a miracle worker."

"That he is."

"Speaking of Gavin," Sam added, "what are you two planning on telling the CIA?"

Thomas and Laura cautiously glanced at each other and then everyone knew an uncomfortable topic had just been broached. Julie and Kim, however, didn't know what Sam was referring to.

"Sorry. I didn't mean to put you both on the spot."

"No," Laura replied, "it's okay. Maybe we should take this opportunity and bring it all out into the light."

"Sweetie," Thomas began, "I don't know if that's such a good idea."

Julie cut in. "Um, what are you talking about?"

Laura stared at Thomas. "Go ahead. It's apparent Sam and Bill know so it's only fair that everyone else should be brought up to speed."

"Fine," Thomas said as he relented. "The director of the CIA, Robert Duncan, knows who and what my family can do."

"What he means to say is that he knows about our powers," Laura clarified.

"But how?" Julie asked.

"Yeah," said Kim. "How?"

"It doesn't matter now," Thomas replied. "What matters is that he wants to start up a special task force, for lack of better words, in an effort to make the world a better place."

"And use your kids towards that endeavor?"

"Yes."

Rebecca didn't like it. "I'm sorry for saying this, but that just sounds extremely shady, especially coming from the CIA."

"Agreed," Thomas said. "But Laura confirmed that everything the DCI said was on the level."

Kim turned to Laura. "Is that true?"

Laura nodded. "Yes unfortunately. He wasn't lying but that doesn't mean I didn't like what he was trying to sell us."

"So back to my original question," Sam said. "What are you two going to do?"

Thomas began to open his mouth but Laura answered for the both of them. "We don't know yet. Why are you so concerned Sam?"

"For the simple reason that all of our lives have become intertwined over the years. What you do affects us and vice versa. If you suddenly decide to run off with the CIA you realize there are implications."

"What implications?"

"Well, for starters, we'd miss you."

There were nods of agreement from around the room.

"Second, the people in this room are the only ones that know your secret. Who's to say they won't order you to have Emily erase our minds to protect that knowledge?"

"That's ridiculous Sam," Thomas snorted.

"Is it? Is it really? You're talking about the CIA, an entity larger than you or I could ever imagine. I could definitely see that happening."

Rebecca, Julie and Kim shifted uneasily in their seats.

"I wouldn't let that happen," Thomas assured the group.

Laura spoke up. "Okay, those are a couple of potential cons. What about the pros?"

"Protection," Thomas said immediately.

"Sure. What else?"

Seconds passed but no one else could come up with another pro to add to the list.

Thomas finally broke the silence. "Okay, I'll just come out and say it. I don't like the fact that the CIA knows about us. What I do know is that I don't feel like my family is safe, or ever will be. But, I think I would somehow feel safer if we cooperated with them."

"And right there is the conundrum my friend," Sam said. "Feeling safe and actually being safe are two different sides of the fence."

Laura agreed. "I'm afraid Sam's right. We don't completely know what we'd be getting ourselves or the children in to, and that's pretty scary to me. On top of that our children are only eight and ten years old. Do I relish the thought of them becoming intimately involved in our country's politics or whatever else the agenda is? The answer is no, they're just children."

"Children with amazing gifts," Bill said quietly.

"Let me ask you this then Bill," Laura shot back. "Would you expose your children if our roles were reversed?"

"I…um…I don't…"

"Uncle Sam?"

The conversation immediately halted as all heads swiveled towards Gavin who stood quietly in the doorway.

Rebecca stood up. "Hey kiddo, it's late. Let's get you back to bed."

"No."

Rebecca froze, unsure of how to reply.

"Uncle Sam, I need you to come with me."

Sam looked over at Thomas and Laura for advice but they only shrugged in return. Sam got up and walked over to Gavin.

"Alright little man. Back to bed."

The two of them walked down the hallway and entered one of the bedrooms.

"Climb back in bed and I'll pull the sheets up."

Gavin stood his ground. "I need you to come with me."

"I don't understand. Come with you where? We're already in your room."

Gavin reached out and took Sam's hand in his. A second later a portal appeared out of nowhere and flooded the room in bright light.

"What the hell…"

"Come," is all that Gavin said as he walked through and pulled Sam behind.

In an instant blinding sunlight assaulted Sam's eyes as it cascaded down from the sky. Gavin let Sam's hand go and stepped away. It took a few moments for Sam to adjust and when he did all he could do was stare in awe at his new surroundings. He took his time and looked around.

*Palm tree. Check.*

*Sand. Check.*

*Ocean. Check.*

*Skeleton. Skeleton!*

"Um, Gav. Where are we? Where did you take me?" he said as he stared at the bleached bones.

"The Other Place."

"Where…where is this place?"

"I don't know. Somewhere."

"I get that. But why? And is this who I think it is?" Sam said as he cocked his head towards the inert form in the sand.

Gavin nodded. "That's Victor Bannon."

"Huh. Well, I always wanted to know where he ended up. It looks like he didn't fair to well after we sent him here."

"Apparently not."

Sam turned back towards Gavin and then walked over to him. "Why did you bring me here?"

"It wasn't my idea."

"I don't understand."

A new voice emanated behind Sam. "Son?"

Sam spun around and came face to face with his dead father, Ray Paige.

*Holy shit.* "Dad? What's going on? I haven't seen you in four years, since that time that Emily made you briefly appear in Hawaii."

His father smiled. "I remember. You were scared to death."

Sam stepped forward and they embraced. "Dammit pop, I've missed you all these years. What are you doing here?"

"I asked this young man to bring you here."

"Why?"

"Because I have something that I need to tell you and I don't have much time to do it."

"I don't understand. What is this place? Why don't you have time?"

His father shook his head. "No questions. Things are already out of balance."

"Things? What things?"

"It doesn't matter son. Just listen to me. This might seem trivial to you but at your Ranger graduation, back at Fort Benning, I was wrong to tell you that I wasn't proud of you and that you had made a big mistake with your life."

"I…"

"I've watched you do so much good and I wanted to tell you that I'm so very proud of you. I love you son."

Sam was thunderstruck but his father's words held deep meaning for him. He remembered that day vividly and the fact that his father wanted to make amends for it now, and in this environment, wasn't lost on him.

"Thank you," Sam said. "That means more than you'll know."

His father smiled. "Good. Now, why don't we all sit down and enjoy each other's company for a bit."

As Sam took a seat he asked a question. "I hate to ask this, but what happened between you and mom? Why did you two get a divorce?"

"I'm sorry about that. It was all my fault. Her name was Eve and I made a mistake. My leaving had nothing to do with you."

"You cheated on mom?"

"Sam, I think it's better that we just leave the past the past. I'm sorry I hurt you and your mother."

"Fine." Sam looked out at the vast ocean as he struggled to forget what his father just told him. "I have to ask."

"What?"

"Where are we?"

Sam's father smiled. "There are things you're not ready to hear and I'm not allowed to talk about."

"Cryptic pop. What can you tell me?"

"I can tell you that time has no value here. Time is only a perception, a limitation. The universe has so much more in store for us."

Sam tried to wrap his head around that. "You're making my head hurt."

His father put his hand on Sam's back. "Then don't think. Let's just enjoy what little time we have together."

"But you just said time is…"

"Time still applies to the living, not the dead son." He looked over Victor's skeleton. "A clear example of that lies right over there."

\* \* \*

Sam walked back into the family room where everyone had been waiting for him. He had a faraway look on his face.

"So what did Gavin want?" Laura inquired.

165

Julie noticed something was off. "Are you okay honey?"

"I…I just spent the last two hours with my father."

"You were only gone for a minute, tops," Julie told him. "What are you talking about?"

Thomas and Laura looked at each other and then back at Sam.

"He took you to the island, didn't he?" Thomas asked.

Sam nodded as he sat back down.

"The island?" Kim queried. "What's that?"

"It's where Gavin used to go to get away; through the portal he can create. It's the same place he went when Julie died and it's the same place we banished Victor Bannon to. We told him he wasn't supposed to go there anymore."

"So much for that," Laura said. "No wonder he's been avoiding certain questions. He knows I'd pick up on his lies."

"It's okay," Sam said. "Please don't be mad at Gavin. My father wanted to tell me something and since I wouldn't bring him to me he made sure I came to him."

"This is all too much to wrap my head around sometimes," Kim said. "Powers and abilities."

"Tell me about it," Bill added. "You okay bro?"

"Actually yes," Sam replied. "But now I'm tired. I think we still have quite a bit to talk about but we also need our sleep. So let's table the CIA discussion for now because I don't know what tomorrow's going to bring, but whatever comes we need to be ready for it."

\* \* \*

Earlier in the evening, once Sam and Bill had handed their copies from Robert Aleman's briefcase off to Hobbes, he began a very detailed process of organizing it. First he made computer files for each of The Organization members based on the dated

166

information given to him. Once those were established he filled in the history of each man's life by adding huge amounts of raw data from various sources including phone and utility bills, mortgages, bank records, personal and business itineraries and travel. After that was compiled he tasked the computer to locate any patterns.

Hobbes cracked open a new Coca-Cola and began scrutinizing each piece of paper left as the computer crunched through the data. At four-thirty in the morning, tired and seeing double, the computer finally beeped that it had completed its job. Hobbes put down the current piece of paper he had been attempting to focus on and turned back to his computer screen. On it were numerous data points that overlapped each other throughout the previous twelve years.

For the next hour Hobbes scoured the records, working backwards from each individual's death up until SANDBOX came into existence in the late '80's. What he discovered was a plethora of evidence.

*Damn I'm good.*

Phone records crisscrossed the globe between various Organization members.

Spending more money than they each legally earned.

Property ownership.

Wire transfers.

Obvious payouts from one account to another.

*That's strange.* Hobbes turned his attention to a particular set of wire transfers that had occurred lately. What had caught his attention was the fact that the account in question hadn't wired money to this particular bank in twelve years. However, prior to that there had been a number of transfers, and just recently, activity had begun again in that specific account.

*Twelve years for an account to lay dormant and then come in to play again. Hmmm.*

Hobbes worked his computer magic and began sniffing around. Fifteen minutes later he had the identity of the wire recipient, one Anna Garland.

*If that's her real name. Although my guess is that it's probably an alias.*

Hobbes used a backdoor program he'd installed in the Department of Motor Vehicles on another occasion and began to search their database. It wasn't long before he got numerous hits on Anna Garland. But it wasn't until he browsed through the DMV license photos that he stumbled across a familiar face.

"Shut up," he said out loud.

There, on the computer screen staring him in the face, was the same woman who he'd seen attack Kim at the Target store.

"Oh, I'm good."

Hobbes looked at the clock and realized it was close to five-thirty in the morning.

*Shit.*

He decided against waking up Sam or Bill at this hour. He was extremely tired and knew he needed a fresh pair of eyes to continue working on this monumental task. Hobbes turned in his chair too quickly and ended up slamming the armrest into the side of his desk. The half empty can of Coke, that was precariously sitting halfway on and halfway off a coaster, was knocked loose and its contents spilled onto the documents that Hobbes had been pouring over.

"Shit! Nonononono!"

He righted the toppled can, raced to the bathroom to get a towel and once back began to blot the sugary liquid off the documents.

"Goddammit."

Although a few of the documents were damaged he managed to contain the spill quickly. After returning from the bathroom a second time, having rinsed out the towel for a final cleanup, he noticed something he hadn't seen before on one of the damaged documents. Out of the corner of his eye the word 'sandbox' had been scribbled. Naturally curious he extracted that particular piece of paper and scrutinized it. Most of the wording had been destroyed by the Coke but Hobbes was able to pick out a few that peaked his interest.

Sandbox.

Bill.

Sam.

Informant.

July, 1986

*What the hell? Informant?*

Hobbes turned to his computer and imputed a date range that started at 1986 through the present. He then backtracked and added everyone that had been hired by SANDBOX in the first two years. The list was relatively short and it didn't take long for the computer to crunch. Hobbes wasn't happy with the results.

"Oh shit on me."

He changed the parameters to include all SANDBOX hires to date and reran the search. When it was done Hobbes was left with correlating phone records, bank accounts, patterns of oversea visits that also corresponded with sizeable employee payouts.

"This does not bode well."

At the center of the data one name perpetually popped out. Roberta Constance.

## 27
## Thursday September 20, 2001

Early the next morning, during breakfast, all six children began to whine that they'd rather be at school than stay in the SANDBOX suite. At first their parents chalked it up to cabin fever, but the kids kept at it throughout the meal and by the time dishes were being washed the parent's resolve had reached its inevitable limit.

"Enough already," Bill said as he finally gave in. "Sarah. Edward. Go get ready for school."

His kids ran off down the hall to get dressed.

"Dad," whined Amanda, Sam's daughter, "it's not fair that they get to go and we have to stay here."

"You're right, it's not fair. But that's how life is Amanda, it's not fair. My job is to keep you safe and I can do that by making sure your butt stays right here."

His thirteen year old had grown into quite a handful and she wasn't about to back down. "For how long? You haven't told us anything and we're just supposed to do what you say? This isn't the military dad and you can't keep me out of school. That's illegal."

Julie, Kim and Laura tried to stifle their smiles and hid them behind their coffee mugs. Sam stared down his daughter who met his eyes and didn't budge an inch.

"Fine. I don't like it, but fine."

Amanda's attitude changed immediately and she smiled. "Thank you daddy."

"Go on, get, before I change my mind."

Amanda and Craig headed back to their rooms to also get ready for school.

171

"You softy," Bill joked.

"Oh please, you gave in well before I did," Sam retorted.

"That's true. But I know when a battle can't be won. You're a little thick when it comes to the obvious." Bill smiled.

Julie spoke up. "I think it's cute that he tried to put up a fight against our daughter. She's as stubborn as he is."

"Hey now."

"Don't worry Sam," Laura said, "it's not the last time you two will butt horns."

"Gee thanks. I'm just worried about their safety. Why are you letting Emily and Gavin go to school without a fight?"

"That's an easy one Sam," Thomas replied. "They can take care of themselves."

"But just like that? No arguments?"

"Well, I still have a few tricks up my sleeve and I need to go back to the house and feed Stickers before the kids disown me."

Laura gave Thomas a 'what the hell are you talking about' look but let it go.

Rebecca stepped in and interjected. "Listen, I'd be more than happy to take a couple of operators and make sure the kids get to their schools safely."

"Do you think this is a good idea, letting them out of our sight?"

"I'll watch out for them," Rebecca assured them.

"Fine. Jessie and his team are back in town. Call him and get two of his men over here ASAP, on my orders."

"Roger that Sam," Rebecca replied.

*  *  *

Two Suburban's left SANDBOX in tandem. The first one contained Emily, Gavin, Rebecca and Ryan, who was one of

172

Jessie's men and was behind the wheel. The trailing vehicle was driven by Donnie, another of Jessie's men, as well as Amanda, Craig, Sarah and Edward. All three operators carried Glock 17 side arms along with extra magazines to keep a low profile.

Two miles later, as the surrounding area turned residential, the two Suburban's drove around a blind corner and managed to stop before they hit a stalled truck that had blocked the road. A man had just lifted the hood of his truck as the two Suburban's rolled to a halt ten feet away from his car. He looked up with an apologetic look and then back down at his engine.

"Stay here," Rebecca said to Ryan. "I'm going to check this out."

Rebecca exited the Suburban, looked around and then walked over to the man.

"What seems to be the problem?"

"I don't know. It just up and died on me." The man took a closer look at Rebecca's face. "Oh wow, that's quite a scar you have Miss."

Rebecca unconsciously traced the scar from her right eye down her cheek, the one she'd received back in Hawaii years before.

Suddenly, from out of the woods to her right, a man with an assault rifle pointed at her appeared. She swiveled her head and stared down the long barrel of the weapon that was twenty feet away. She tensed and began to reach for her weapon.

"Don't make any sudden moves," said the man she'd been talking to as he produced a handgun and pressed it firmly up against her left temple.

*Shit!* Rebecca froze as the second man slowly approached and began to bark orders.

"Get the kids out of the vehicles!"

*  *  *

Gavin and Emily, in the first suburban, saw the man appear out of the woods and then watched as the man Rebecca was talking to put a gun to her head.

"REBECCA!" Gavin shouted.

"Get the kids out of the vehicles!"

Ryan, their driver, pulled his handgun, got out and opened the back door. He pointed the weapon at the two kids. "Out."

In the second suburban Donnie did the same thing to the other four children.

*  *  *

Rebecca couldn't comprehend why Ryan or Donnie were complying with the two abductors.

"What the fuck are you doing Ryan?"

"Shut up Rebecca."

"Are you with these men? What the hell?"

"This is bigger than you can imagine," Ryan responded. "Now shut up."

In a matter of seconds all six children had been pulled from the two vehicles. All of them were crying except for Emily and Gavin. The man with the assault rifle slung his weapon and produced a tranquilizer gun from behind his back. He pulled additional darts from his pocket and walked over to the children. He pointed the gun at Sarah and pulled the trigger. The dart hit her in the chest and she collapsed. The other kids screamed as he reloaded.

"What the fuck are you doing? Leave them alone!" Rebecca yelled.

Emily took the opportunity, reached out and grabbed Ryan's left wrist. He stiffened as she took control of him.

"Save them," she commanded.

Ryan instantly swiveled towards Donnie and raised his weapon, much to Donnie's and everyone else's surprise. Ryan's gun bucked as he put a round right into Donnie's skull. Wide-eyed, Donnie fell backwards onto the pavement and his gun clattered out of his dead hand.

As Donnie toppled over Rebecca made a desperate move for her own weapon.

A dart appeared in Gavin's chest and he began to fall to the ground before he could summon Stir to help them all.

Ryan began to traverse his weapon around.

The first man didn't understand why Ryan had turned on them, but couldn't help but notice Rebecca making a move. He pulled the trigger once and then swung his handgun around and shot Ryan in the head just as Ryan aligned his sights on his cohort, who had just reloaded his tranquilizer gun again.

Ryan's arm was yanked out of Emily's hand as his dead body tumbled to the ground.

A second later Emily felt a sharp pain in her chest and barely had time to look down at the protruding dart before she lost consciousness and landed next to her brother's inert body.

Craig, Edward and Amanda were all screaming bloody murder, but their cries lessoned as each one of them, in turn, was tranquilized.

"Fuck. What the fuck was that?" asked the first man as he slammed the truck's hood.

"Shit if I know," replied the second. "Let's get these kids in the truck and get out of here before anyone else shows up."

"What about the bodies?"

"Leave'em. Our orders were to collect the six children and get out without any complications. Those bodies are just that, complications."

## 28
## Thursday September 20, 2001

Twenty minutes later Roberta answered the main SANDBOX line and transferred the call to Sam and Bill's office.

"Who's calling Roberta?" Sam asked.

"It's the police. A Detective Sinclair."

"What does he want?"

"He wouldn't say."

"Fine. Put him through."

Sam placed the phone on speaker as the call was routed.

"This is Sam Paige."

"Mr. Paige. This is Detective Sinclair with the Marin PD."

"What can I do for you Detective?"

"I'm afraid I'm calling you from the scene of a dreadful crime scene."

Sam and Bill immediately changed gears internally and gave the Detective their full attention.

"Explain," Sam said.

"I have two empty Suburban's, registered to your company, that contain a number of children's backpacks. I also have two dead bodies, both with fatal head wounds, and another was in critical condition and on the way to the hospital."

Sam gripped the side of his desk with enough force that his knuckles turned white. "Are any of them children?"

"No sir. All three are adults; two males and one female."

"Fuck me," Bill whispered.

"You said that one of the them is female?"

"I did."

"Does she have a scar underneath her right eye?"

"I don't know. She's on route to the hospital as we speak."

"She's alive?"

"She's in critical condition with a head wound."

Bill lowered his head as the news began to sink in. They had just lost two operators.

"Mr. Paige? Are you still there?"

Sam tried to regain his composure. "Yes. I'm still here."

"The main reason I'm calling is that, at least to me and my partner, this scene has the distinct feel of an abduction."

"Give me one second Detective." Sam placed him on hold and looked at Bill. "Call the fucking school right now and see if the kids ever arrived."

Bill used his own phone and called the school. Two minutes later he learned that their kids were unaccounted for. He shook his head solemnly at Sam who in turn gritted his teeth as he took the Detective off hold.

"Detective. We just called the school and our kids never arrived. At this point we have to assume they've been taken hostage."

"I'm sorry Mr. Paige. We're putting out an APB and we'll do what we can from here but I think it's best if we got the FBI involved."

"Agreed."

"I'll be in touch."

"Thank you Detective."

Sam hung up the phone and then tried to fling it violently across the room but the phone cord stopped its trajectory just short of slamming into the far wall. It landed on the office floor in a tangled mess.

"It's Aleman," Bill managed to spit out between clenched teeth. "He has our kids and he killed two of our own."

Sam's eyes were wild. "I'm going to fucking kill that bastard when I get my hands on him."

"You and me both."

"I'm going to rip him limb from goddamn limb."

"And I'll be right there with you, but right now we have to go tell everyone what went down."

"Shit," Sam said and then nodded. "Let's go."

The two headed back up to the suite. When they stepped out of the elevator Julie, Kim, Laura and Thomas knew right away from their behavior that something wasn't right. They all stood up as the two walked over to them.

"What is it?" Julie asked, panic beginning to set in.

"There's been an incident and…"

"It's our kid's, right?" interrupted Kim. "Something happened to our kids."

Sam and Bill nodded their heads and both sisters burst into tears.

Thomas took over the conversation. "What happened?"

"Rebecca's in critical condition and on her way to the hospital," Sam told him.

"Oh fuck."

Laura managed to barely sit down before she slumped over to put her head into her hands. Her tears flowed fast and furiously. Thomas put an arm around his wife while Julie and Kim were left speechless until Sam continued.

"The two other men that were with her are dead."

"What about our kids!?" Julie screamed at him. "What about our kids!?"

"They're missing. Taken."

"Taken! Someone took our kids!"

Kim lost it and collapsed to the floor. Bill rushed to her side to help comfort her. Sam tried to pull Julie towards him but she slapped him in the face.

"This is your fault! They're gone because of you!"

179

Kim shrugged Bill off her as well. "Get away from me and go get my babies back!"

* * *

Five minutes later Thomas, Laura, Sam and Bill stood in the kitchen while Julie and Kim clung to each other in the other room for support.

"What else do you know?" Thomas asked his two friends.

"The Detective at the scene said that both Suburban's still had school bags in them."

Laura winced at the thought. She wished she would have gone with them. *Maybe things would have turned out differently. Maybe I could have prevented this.*

"He also said that all two of our people died from single shots to the head," Sam added.

Thomas put his right hand on her head. "This is this guy Aleman again, isn't it? He has our kids."

Sam and Bill nodded. "That's a safe assumption. Twelve years ago he told us he'd go after our families but we were stupid enough to think he wouldn't go after our children. Who knows where they are right now."

"I can help with that," Thomas said.

Laura pulled away from his shoulder. "How?"

"I hate to admit this sweetie but I've implanted GPS chips in nearly all of their clothing ever since we moved back to Marin."

Laura was shocked. "But...but why didn't you tell me you've been doing that?"

"I don't know."

"Bullshit. That's a lie."

"Fine. I thought you'd think I'd gone overboard with my paranoia, okay."

She kissed him and then pulled back. "Paranoid to the end but I know you're just looking out for them so I get it. But now they need our help. What do we do?"

"I need a computer."

Sam and Bill grabbed Thomas and hurried him out of the kitchen and towards the elevator.

*   *   *

Hobbes was rudely awakened as four people simultaneously roused him from his few hours of sleep, if that. They were all yelling at him, talking over each other in an attempt to be heard.

"One at a time!" he managed to get out and everyone shut their mouths. "What is it? What's going on?"

Sam spoke up. "Long story short, we have operators down and our six kids have been kidnapped."

Hobbes's adrenaline immediately kicked in and he was suddenly wide awake.

"Shit. What do you need me to do?"

Thomas produced codes he kept in his wallet and handed them over to Hobbes. "Go to their website and start plugging these codes in."

Hobbes took the paper and started in on the task. "It's going to take a bit. There are a lot of codes here."

"My kids have a lot of clothes."

The four hovered over Hobbes as he worked before he asked them politely to give him some space.

"I need about twenty minutes to enter all these codes Mr. Clark."

"Thank you Hobbes. If I was at home they'd be in the system already, but since I'm not we figured you could work your magic."

"I understand." Hobbes turned to Sam. "When you get a minute I need to talk to you."

"Not now Hobbes. I'm sure the FBI will be arriving shortly and quite frankly we won't be able to leave once you locate our kids with the GPS trackers."

"I don't understand," Hobbes replied. "Why wouldn't you tell them the children's location?"

"Because I'm not going to trust our children's lives to an FBI raid, especially when Robert Aleman has them."

Hobbes' phone line beeped and he put it on speaker. "Yes?"

"It's Roberta. Are they with you?"

"We're here Roberta," Bill replied.

"The FBI just arrived."

"We'll be right there."

Hobbes ended the call and went back to work.

"Finish up here," Sam instructed him, "and let us know when you have a positive location."

"Yes, sir."

\*　\*　\*

"I'm Special Agent John Hartin," he said as he shook Sam, Bill, Laura and Thomas' hands.

"Why don't we get you and your team setup in our main conference room," Sam replied.

"Perfect." He and his team followed Sam with their equipment to the meeting room. "Have you been contacted yet?"

Sam shook his head as the other agents began setting up their various machines.

"What makes you believe your children have been taken hostage?"

Bill lost it. "Are you kidding me? We've got two dead operators, one in critical condition and six missing children. You do the fucking math! Do you have any other obvious questions you'd care to ask you prick?"

The tension in the conference room immediately elevated and Sam made sure he stepped between Special Agent Hartin and Bill.

"My apologies Mr. Nicholson. I take it from the nature of your work that you've naturally acquired a number of enemies over the years."

"More than likely," Sam answered as he took over the conversation.

"Right. Well, do you have an idea who might have been behind your children's abduction?"

"We have a pretty good idea. A General Robert Aleman."

Special Agent Hartin cocked his head to one side. "A general?"

"Former general. This piece of work threatened our families twelve years ago before we put him away. Apparently he has a long memory and has come back to finish the job."

"I'm sorry to hear that. Why don't we finish setting up here and we'll go from there."

"Thank you," Sam replied as he forced Bill out of the room.

"That guy's a fucking asshole and…"

Sam cut him off. "Keep it together and go check on Hobbes. You're not the only one who had their kids taken."

Bill opened and closed his mouth. In a few seconds his attitude changed. "Sorry. I'll go see what Hobbes is up to."

"We'll go with him," Laura told Sam.

\* \* \*

As Bill, Thomas and Laura entered Hobbes' office he looked up and smiled.

"I found them."

They all came around and looked at the computer screen together. A large overlay of the San Francisco Bay Area was up on his screen. Hundreds of dots were clustered in one area and a few were in a completely different location.

"That's your house," Hobbes said as he pointed to the huge cluster. "And these should be where your children are."

Thomas and Bill slapped Hobbes on the back and Laura bent down and kissed him on the cheek.

"Good job Hobbes," Bill praised, "and way to be one hell of a paranoid motherfucker Thomas."

"It's what I do."

"Print that location out, I want a address."

"You got it," Hobbes replied.

"Let's go tell Sam."

"Hey," Hobbes said as they started to leave. "Have any of you seen Rebecca today?"

The three of them looked at each other and then lowered their heads.

"Hobbes, I...uh...don't know how to tell you this but..."

"What?"

"Rebecca was injured during the attack. She's at the hospital right now."

Hobbes' face instantly dropped and tears formed in the corners of his eyes. "No. Don't tell me she was one of the three..."

Bill slowly nodded.

"Oh shit. Shitshitshit. Is she going to be okay?"

"I don't know. It's too early to say. I'm sorry Hobbes."

"Me too," he finally managed to say. "Um,...I'll...I'll get the location of those trackers to you right away."

The three of them left Hobbes behind and rejoined Sam and the FBI hostage team back in the conference room. As they walked in the phone began to ring.

## 29
## Thursday September 20, 2001

Special Agent Hartin let the phone ring as his team enabled both the digital recorder and tracing equipment. At the end of the third ring he motioned to Sam who pressed the speaker button.

"Hello?"

"Daddy daddy!"

The adults recoiled as they heard their children crying for them in the background, their children's voices full of panic. The shrieks stopped as everyone heard a door close over the phone. Bill held onto Kim and Julie while Thomas and Laura stood close to Sam.

"Do I have your attention now?" Robert Aleman asked.

"Yes," Sam replied through gritted teeth.

"I see that you have involved the FBI. Please say hello to them for me."

"What do you want?"

"I see. You get right to the point, don't you Sam. What do I want you ask? It's simple. I want you to suffer like I've suffered for the past twelve years. I had everything and you TOOK it all away."

"You made a huge mistake coming after our families."

"I made a huge mistake? I MADE A HUGE MISTAKE? Ha! Sam Paige, your pain is just beginning."

"Fuck you Aleman you gutless piece of shit."

"I tell you what Sam, what if I take the life of one of your children right now just to prove my point?"

Laura spoke. "Oh shit. He's not lying. He's going to do it."

Julie began to sob in Bill's arms. "Nooooo!"

"You sonofabitch."

"But to be fair I'll let you decide which one lives. Tick tock. So tell me, which one will it be, Amanda or Craig?"

Julie began to scream as Bill held her back. "YOU BASTARD! YOU BASTARD! THEY'RE JUST CHILDREN!"

"Ahhh, a pleasure to make your acquaintance Julie," Aleman said coolly. "There's nothing like a mother's love to bring out the best in a situation. Now, you both have a tough decision to make. Tick tock."

"LEAVE THEM ALONE! THEY'VE DONE NOTHING TO YOU!"

"Well, since you can't make a choice I'll have to take both their lives. Then I can start on Bill's children."

It was Kim's turn to partially collapse as her knees weakened.

"Don't you dare touch them," Sam warned him.

"Please Sam, that's an idle threat and we both know it. The fact is that I own you, plain and simple. You need to understand and remember that."

"Fuck you."

"Now, stay by the phone so I can tell you what I've done to your children."

The call ended and the conference room immediately erupted. FBI agents began conversing while Julie and Kim remained severely hysterical.

"Did you get the trace?" Agent Hartin asked.

The agent working the trace shook his head.

Julie kept repeating the same statement over and over. "My children!? My children!? My children!?"

Sam tried to calm her down but she was too far gone.

Kim, on the other hand, had grown quiet and her eyes focused on something unseen far in the distance. Bill tried to talk to her but she had become unresponsive.

A female FBI medic quickly came over and insisted that the best course of action would be to sedate the two of them.

Thomas and Laura took the opportunity to race back to Hobbes' office as Sam and Bill took their wives back to the top floor suite and put them in bed.

Hobbes looked up as the two entered his office.

"I have the address where the GPS trackers are," he said as he handed it over to Thomas.

"Are they still in the same location?"

Hobbes pointed at his screen as Thomas and Laura came around to look.

"Right there."

Right as Hobbes pointed the blips ceased to exist and disappeared entirely from the screen.

"What the hell?" Thomas said, somewhat startled. "What just happened?"

"I…I don't know. It's possible the trackers have been either shielded or…"

"Or what Hobbes?" Laura pressed.

"Or they've been discovered and destroyed."

## 30
## Thursday September 20, 2001

Amanda, Craig, Sarah, Edward, Emily and Gavin sat huddled together on a stained mattress. The room they had been locked in had no windows. A small skylight in the ceiling barely illuminated the dingy surroundings they had all been locked in.

The six of them had begun to wake up from the tranquilizer. Soon all but Emily and Gavin had started sobbing as the memories of the abduction began to fill their minds. However, Em and Gav had unfortunately been in situations like this before and, even though they were frightened, they waited for their chance to turn the tables on their captors.

"Gav, I think I saw something you're not going to like before they took us."

"What? What are you talking about?"

"I don't know how to say this…but I think Becca's dead."

Gavin lowered his head. "Are you sure?"

Emily slowly shook her head back and forth. "No."

"Okay. Maybe there's a chance she's okay."

"Maybe."

The large steel door to the room clanged loudly as the lock was disengaged. Moments later it swung inward and a man holding a gun and a phone entered. He pointed it right at them, sweeping it back and forth as the children's screams of fear became louder and louder.

"Your father is about to pick up the phone Amanda. Why don't you make sure he hears you?"

"Daddy! Daddy!"

Robert Aleman pulled the steel door closed behind him and reengaged the lock, leaving the six children alone again. Emily and Gavin tried to calm the others down but they were whimpering and close to becoming catatonic.

"Take it easy," Emily said as she stroked Amanda's hair. "It's going to be okay."

"Hey Edward, I need you to calm down. We're going to get out of here."

It took a minute for the two Clark kids to focus the other four children.

"We have to get out of here on our own," said Gavin.

"H..how?" Craig asked as he pointed at the steel door. "That's the only way in and that man has a gun."

"I know you're scared," Emily assured them all, "and so are we, but we don't have a choice. He's going to come back in here and kill us. I saw it in his face."

Their sobs briefly rose again until Gavin grabbed two of their hands.

"Everyone hold hands, we're getting out of here."

"Wh…why?" Sarah said between gasps.

"Just do it," Emily ordered as she took Sarah's hand in hers.

Before any more questions could be asked there was a flash of light and a shimmering portal appeared in the darkened room. The four children instantly jumped, lost their grips and backed away.

"What it that?" Edward asked.

"Take my hand," Gavin repeated. "We have to get out of here."

"No…no way!"

"Keep your voice down," Emily said, "and do what Gavin says. Or do you want to stay here and never go home again?"

That comment urged them to comply and soon everyone was holding hands with Emily in the lead and Gavin taking up the rear.

"We're going to walk through the portal."

"I don't want to."

"I'm scared."

Gavin nodded to his sister and with a firm grip on Sarah's hand she walked through the portal first and practically dragged the group behind her as Gavin continually urged them to move forward. Five seconds later they were all through and the portal vanished.

Ten seconds after that Robert Aleman reopened the door, pistol in hand looking for one of Sam's children to put a bullet in. He stopped short and a very confused look appeared on his face.

"WHERE THE FUCK ARE THEY!?"

The room was small and there was nowhere for six children to hide.

"FUCK!"

* * *

Ten minutes later the phone rang and Sam waited until Special Agent Hartin gave him the sign to answer it as Bill stood by and listened. Thomas and Laura still hadn't come back from Hobbes' office.

"They're all dead Sam," Aleman told him. "You couldn't decide who to choose so I killed them all. All six. Do you hear me Sam?"

"You're full of shit. You can't be that heartless."

"Awh…poor Sam and Bill. You two have no more mouths to feed. I think I'm going to cry."

Everyone in the room, FBI included, were silent as they contemplated what Robert Aleman had just said. Sam and Bill didn't want to believe it was true.

"Are you still there? I haven't misplaced your attention have I?"

"Fuck you," Bill managed to finally say. "We're going to find you, and then we're going to kill you."

"That's the spirit! Of course you're welcome to try but know that I'm just getting warmed up."

The line went dead.

"Trace?" Special Agent Hartin asked.

"No sir."

"Goddammit."

Bill grabbed Sam's arm. "You don't think he…"

"I don't know. Laura wasn't here to confirm what he told us. If he hurt our kids nothing's going to stop me from ripping him limb from fucking limb."

"You and me both brother. Let's go find Thomas and Laura and figure out our next move before we end up losing it."

* * *

"Anything?"

"No sir. No trace of the children outside at all."

General Aleman turned to the few men that he had with him.

"Time to abandon this location. Pack everything up and then burn this place."

"Yes sir."

He turned around and checked the small room he had them locked up in again.

*How the hell did you all escape? Shit. Well, at least Anna will finish up what was started earlier.*

# 31
## The Other Place

Gavin's portal closed behind them and all six children collapsed in the warm sand. It took them some time to wrap their heads around the fact that they were in one place one instant and now they were suddenly somewhere else.

"Good job Gav," Emily said as she praised her brother.

"Thanks."

Thirteen year old Amanda suddenly bellowed. "EEWWW!"

The others turned and immediately saw what she was pointing at, Victor's skeleton.

"It's okay, it's okay," Gavin reassured everyone. "He can't hurt you. Relax."

The children stood, put their hands up to their foreheads to block out the sun and looked out over the vast horizon. After looking around they realized they were on a small tropical island.

"Where...where are we?" Edward, Bill's nine year old son, finally asked.

"I don't know," Gavin replied.

"What do you mean you don't know?"

"Well, I come to this place to be alone."

"How did you do that Gavin?" Sarah asked as she interjected.

"Magic."

"Hmph," she replied in disbelief.

"Magic?" Edward replied. "That's cool."

"It's not cool," Sarah insisted. "He's lying."

"Then how do you explain where we are sis?" Edward said matter-of-factly.

"I...I can't."

"Then who cares. Gavin and Emily saved us from whoever that person was with the gun. I don't care how we got here. Do you?"

Sarah didn't respond. Sam's kids, Amanda and Craig, came over after they finished a quick circuit of the small island.

"Thank you," Amanda said. "I was scared out of my mind but this place has really calmed me down. Where are we?"

"Yeah," added Craig. "What is this place?"

"It's just my special place."

"How did you do that portal thing?"

"Magic."

Craig smiled. "That's awesome. Scary but awesome."

"Anyway," Gavin continued, "this is my special place. I come here when I want to be alone. Sometimes I even get to talk to people."

"Who?" Sarah asked. "Like that skeleton over there?"

"No," a new voice said behind them, "he means someone like me."

The children jumped and cautiously turned around.

"Hi Ray," Gavin said.

"Hello again Gavin."

"Um, who are you and where did you come from?" Amanda asked.

"I'm your father's father. In other words Amanda, I'm your grandfather," Ray explained.

"Wait. How do you know my name?"

"This place is peculiar like that my dear."

"What's my name then?" Craig demanded.

"It's Craig, and I've been watching the two of you grow up for many years now."

Amanda and Craig looked at each other and then back at their grandfather.

"I don't understand. We've never met you. Our dad's father is dead."

Ray nodded his head. "I know. I died before either of you were born."

"This sounds crazy," Sarah said. "Are you sure we're all not dreaming or something?"

Emily reached out and pinched Sarah's arm.

"Ouch!"

"You're not dreaming," Emily said. "This is all happening so just stop with all the questions." She turned back to her brother. "This is your show Gav."

Gavin looked up at Ray. "What are you doing here?"

"At the moment I'm looking out for you."

"What do you mean? We're safe on my island."

"No, you're not. Gavin, you shouldn't have brought them here."

"We didn't have a choice," Emily said.

"True. That was a tight situation you were all in. Still, you've endangered everyone by coming here in such numbers."

"What does that mean?" Gavin asked. "And even if I took them back we'd just appear in the same place. On top of that no matter how much time we spend here it'll only count as mere moments back in the real world."

"The real world?" tested Amanda. "If we're not in the real world then where the heck are we?"

"Quiet," Emily ordered.

Ray spoke up. "Gavin, you won't necessarily appear in the same location."

"I've been here too many times," Gavin responded. "It's always the same."

"Like I said, not necessarily."

"Okay. What does that mean?"

197

"Typically," Ray began, "as you've discovered, this island is used as your beacon. No matter where you created the portal in the real world you always end up here, correct?"

Gavin nodded. "Right."

"What you don't know is that you can visit another island, and that island is tied to someplace completely different."

Gavin's eyes sparkled. "That makes sense, buttttttt I don't see any other islands."

"No, you won't. They're far away from here."

Craig interjected. "So how are we supposed to get there?"

"Why not take the boat?" said Ray.

"What boat? I've been around this island and there isn't a..."

Ray stepped aside and behind him, pulled up onto the shore, was a boat.

Craig and the others were dumbfounded. "How did you do that?"

"Magic."

"Told you," Gavin said with a smile.

Ray motioned for them to get onboard. "Hurry children. I need to get you out of here."

With everyone in the boat Ray pushed it off the sand and then climbed in as it gently left the island's shores.

"Why?" Gavin asked Ray. "Why do we need to get out of here?"

"Others might be attracted to your presence, especially since there are so many of you here at once."

"I've always been safe on my island."

"I don't doubt it Gavin, but your existence is masked because of your ability. Emily and the others are like beacons in the night and trust me when I say that they know you're here."

"Who will?"

"Let's just say that you wouldn't want them to find you and leave it at that for now."

The small boat, with all seven inside, lifted itself out of the water a few inches and then propelled away from the island at lightning speed. The children couldn't believe how fast they were travelling and that the boat they were in was actually flying. The warm wind whipped their hair and smiles actually appeared on their faces.

"Wow!"

"This is neat!"

"Awesome!"

Gavin turned and faced Ray.

"Thanks for your help," Gavin said.

"Thank you for bringing my son to see me. That was a rare moment that I'll never be able to fully repay, let alone forget."

In the distance they collectively spotted another island. Edward was the first to yell out about it.

"I see it! I see it!"

The boat rapidly approached, then slowed down and eventually stopped, hovering over the water fifty feet from its shores. The boat dropped back into the water but didn't move closer to the island. Gavin looked back at Ray who had stood up and was looking at something off in the distance.

"Hurry children. Over the side and into the water. Swim!"

Emily and Gavin didn't hesitate and within seconds the other four had jumped in after them. The water was warm and they all began to swim towards the island.

"Hurry! Go!" Ray urged from the boat.

Ten feet from the shore the children were able to stand up, walk out of the surf and onto the sandy beach. Gavin turned around and waved to Ray.

"Thank you!"

"Go and don't look back!"

Gavin turned, made the portal and together, holding hands, they all stepped through.

# 32
## Thursday September 20, 2001

"Fuck you," Bill managed to finally say. "We're going to find you, and then we're going to kill you."

"That's the spirit! Of course you're welcome to try, but know that I'm just getting warmed up."

The line went dead.

"Trace?" Special Agent Hartin asked.

"No sir."

"Goddammit."

Bill grabbed Sam's arm. "You don't think he…"

"I don't know. Laura wasn't here to confirm what he told us. If he hurt our kids nothing's going to stop me from ripping him limb from fucking limb."

"You and me both brother. Let's go find Thomas and Laura and figure out our next move before we end up losing it."

Sam and Bill raced out of the conference room and headed to Hobbes' office where they found Thomas, Laura and Hobbes yelling at the computer screen.

"What do you mean the GPS trackers were found and destroyed?"

"I only said it was a possibility."

"But all of them at the same time? Laura hesitantly asked.

"What's going on?" Sam asked with an edge.

"The trackers went offline all at once."

Thomas and Laura then noticed that their jaws were clenched and they had a wild look behind their eyes.

"That might explain…"

"Shit," Laura said. "What is it? What happened?"

"I...I don't know how to say this but...," Sam started to say until Bill put a hand on his friend's shoulder.

"I got this brother." Bill took a deep breath. "There's a possibility that Aleman killed our children."

"WHAT!?" Thomas shouted.

"NoNoNoNoNo," Laura repeated over and over as she fell to her knees. "Impossible. That's impossible. They have to be okay, they just have to be. I can't go through that again. Not like Alcatraz. I can't go through that again."

Thomas bent down, placed his wife's head on his shoulder and then put his arms around her as she struggled to take the information in. He looked up at Sam and Bill.

"Tell us what happened."

"We didn't hear anything. He only told us he killed them."

"Do you believe that he's telling the truth?"

Sam and Bill didn't want to answer Thomas' question. Doubt was already creeping into their minds.

"Maybe he did do it," Thomas said as Laura sobbed into his shoulder. "All the GPS trackers stopped transmitting a short while ago."

"That doesn't prove anything," Sam replied as he grasped at straws.

"Shit!" Hobbes exclaimed. "Holy fucking shit!"

His sudden outburst cut the sniveling off as all four of them instantly focused on Hobbes.

"What? What is it?" Bill asked.

"The signals are back!"

They piled around behind Hobbes and looked over his shoulder. There on the screen the missing trackers had reappeared.

"Hobbes, they're not in the same location," Thomas observed.

"No, they're not. In fact this doesn't make any sense to me at all."

Laura wiped her tears away. "Where the fuck are those signals coming from now? Where are my kids?"

Hobbes turned and looked over his shoulder at everyone. "They're right on top of us…outside."

\* \* \*

The portal vanished behind them and the six children started to shiver a bit from the abrupt temperature change. Water dripped from their bodies and sand littered the floor as it flicked off their feet and clothing.

"Where are we?" one of them asked.

"I don't know," Gavin replied.

They were in a dark enclosure but as their eyes became for accustomed to the low light Emily figured it out.

"I think we're in the motor pool."

"Oh yeah," Amanda said. "That's perfect. Thanks Gavin."

"Yeah," Craig added, "thanks Gavin. I can't wait to tell everyone how we got here."

"That boat ride was crazy awesome," Edward said.

"Wait," Emily said.

"What is it?" Sarah asked her.

"Line up first."

"I don't understand. Why?"

Before any of the other kids could say another word Emily quickly touched each one and spoke a single word."

"Sleep."

\* \* \*

It wasn't long before a parade of FBI agents and most of their parents located the children in the company motor pool. The lights were quickly turned on and they found the six huddled together, wet and sandy, but very much alive. Tears freely flowed down Sam, Bill, Thomas and Laura's faces as they cradled their babies in their arms frantically asking if they were okay. Blankets were produced and within minutes they had transported them back into SANDBOX and up to the suite.

"How did you get here?" one of the agents asked them after they had been examined by medical personnel and each given a thumbs up.

"I don't know."

"Where are we?"

"How did we get here?"

"Why was I wet?"

A few minutes later protective parents stepped in, told the FBI that it was obvious the children didn't remember anything and to back off. They complied.

"We'll be in touch," Special Agent Hartin told Sam on the way out. "I'm extremely happy with this outcome."

"You and me both."

Thirty minutes later, with the FBI packed up and heading out, Julie and Kim woke up and were absolutely overjoyed that their children were back safe and sound. More tears were had by all and during this time Thomas and Laura took Emily and Gavin to another room and closed the door behind them.

"What really happened?" Laura asked them.

Emily and Gavin walked their parents through the ambush, being shot with tranquilizer darts, waking up in a dark room with a man waving a gun at them, to deciding to use the portal to escape.

"Are you mad at me?" Gavin asked.

"No, of course not sweetie. We're so happy you're both in one piece."

"What I don't understand is how you ended up somewhere different?" Thomas asked.

"I told Ray the same thing."

"Ray?"

"Sam's dad. He helped us."

Thomas and Laura exchanged a glance.

"I'll go grab Sam and Bill for the rest of this," Laura said.

"Good idea."

A minute later Laura, Sam and Bill came back.

"Start over," Laura told her kids.

* * *

"…and then your father was really worried about something that was coming for us so he told us to hurry. We swam to the new island, I made the portal and we all went through it."

"And appeared in the motor pool," Sam said.

Gavin and Emily nodded in agreement.

"Well," said Bill, "that explains the water and the sand."

"Not to mention how the GPS trackers jumped from one location to another so quickly."

"What do you mean trackers?" Emily asked.

"We'll go in to that later sweetie."

"First thing's first," Sam said. "Thank you very much, both of you. You have no idea what this means to us."

"What he said," Bill added. "You two are amazing."

Emily and Gavin smiled from ear to ear.

"Welcome," Gavin replied.

"But I have another question," Sam said. "Why can't our kids remember what happened?"

Emily had a hard time looking Sam in the eyes. "I'm sorry Uncle Sam. That's my fault. They couldn't wait to tell everyone what happened and…"

"It's okay," Sam assured her. "What you did was smart thinking, and that goes for both of you. Very smart thinking. You should be very proud of yourselves."

"Thanks," Emily said.

"I hate to ask this of you Em, but maybe I could thank my father as well, you know, in person."

Emily nodded. "K."

Sam extended his hand and Emily touched it. Nothing happened. A confused look washed over her face and she tried to summon Ray a second time; a third. Nothing.

"I don't know what's wrong."

"What's it mean?" Sam asked. "It's the same thing that happened with your father, Michael, right Thomas?"

Thomas nodded. "We don't understand why and it's been years now."

Sam withdrew his hand. "That's okay. I know he's watching me right now so thank you pop for saving them all today. Thank you."

Sam and Bill started to head towards the bedroom door when Gavin asked a question.

"Is Becca dead?"

They all looked down at Gavin and Emily. Their eyes were wide and full of hope.

"No," Sam replied. "She's in the hospital."

"I hope she gets better," Gavin said softly.

"Me too," Emily added.

"Can we go and see her?" Gavin asked. "I can help her."

"Maybe tomorrow," Laura replied as she pulled her son and daughter close to her.

At the abduction sight a quick thinking police officer immediately ascertained that Rebecca Cross was barely holding onto life, even with such a brutal head wound. He called for an ambulance that, within minutes, retrieved Rebecca from the scene and then transferred her to a medical helicopter that rushed her to the hospital. Rebecca's heart had stopped beating on the way down to the ICU wing.

"She's coding!" one of the nurses exclaimed and hit a button.

Across the hospital wing the intercom blasted out an automated warning. "CODE BLUE ICU. CODE BLUE ICU."

"Bring me the crash cart dammit!"

The bandage that had been applied to Rebecca's head had bled through. Her face was pale and the tips of her fingernails were already blue indicating that her blood levels were well below normal.

The crash cart was hastily wheeled into the room as a multitude of medical personnel went to work on her immediately.

"Charge to two-hundred."

"Someone go and secure bags of A-Negative. If this works we're going to need them."

"Come on people, she needs our help."

"CLEAR!"

The doctor placed the paddles on Rebecca's chest and depressed the button. Her body rose up as it enveloped the electric charge and fell back down. There was no change to her heartbeat; it was still flat-lined.

"Charge to two-fifty."

"CLEAR!"

Her body arched again and a feint blip appeared on the monitor; then another and another.

"She's back. We need to stabilize her as much as possible before we can assess the extent of her injuries. Start the IV drip and where the hell is that blood I asked for?"

*  *  *

Hours later Rebecca had been thoroughly examined by a leading brain surgeon. As he poured over the x-rays he knew her prognosis was dire. The bullet had entered downward through her left temple and had sufficiently damaged everything in its path before it lodged itself next to her brain stem. He couldn't fathom how she was still alive or whether she'd even survive the surgery to remove it.

Before any steps could be taken, Rebecca's heart kept beating but she stopped breathing. A part of her brain had stopped sending the signal for the lungs to operate properly and she was quickly placed on a ventilator.

*  *  *

It was late when the telephone in the suite rang.

"This is Sam Paige."

"Mr. Paige. This is Doctor Holmes and I'm one of the doctors caring for Rebecca Cross. I apologize for the hour of this call but I understand that she has listed you as her emergency contact."

Sam sat up on the couch as the other adults looked on in earnest, especially Emily and Gavin. The other four children were already in bed. "Yes sir. How is she? We haven't heard a thing."

Dr. Holmes paused. "I'm afraid she's in pretty bad shape. She was shot in the head and part of her brain function has shut down. Currently we have her on a ventilator."

Sam's face instantly changed when he heard the bad news and Emily and Gavin picked up on it immediately. "Doc, I'm going to put you on speakerphone." Sam pushed a button and then cradled the handset. "Go ahead."

"As I was saying," the doctor continued, "we have her on a ventilator but it's been touch and go ever since she arrived."

"I need to save her," Gavin said out loud as he stood up.

"I'm afraid it would take a miracle for her to pull through," Dr. Holmes said.

Sam quickly picked up the phone and disengaged the speaker function. "What are her chances she'll survive?"

Dr. Holmes hesitated.

"Give it to me straight doc," Sam urged.

"At this point it's only a matter of time before her body completely shuts down. Yes, I could remove the bullet in her head, even though the process is complicated and delicate, but the best case scenario is that she would be on a ventilator for the rest of her life. That's the best case and I say that without any idea of how her brain would actually recover. In all likelihood she'll never recover and remain on life support indefinitely."

"Thank you doctor. What do you need from me?"

"Quite frankly, a decision."

"I understand. Give me a minute."

Sam placed his hand over the receiver, relayed Rebecca's dire status to everyone else and the doctor's request.

Gavin pulled away from his mother. "I can save her. What are we waiting for? Let's go!"

Thomas and Laura shared a glance. "It's not that easy. The exposure is too high."

Emily couldn't believe what she'd just heard her father say. "But this is Becca we're talking about. We have to do something!"

Gavin was adamant as well. "Fine, if you don't want to go and save her then I'll go all by myself." He turned and made a portal but before he could step through Laura grabbed his arm.

"Let's go see Rebecca, but we're going to do it as quietly as possible."

Gavin disengaged the portal and smiled.

\*　\*　\*

In the hospital's ICU wing an assassin, Anna Garland dressed as a nurse, peered through the glass at her next target.

*I haven't taken out someone who hasn't been able to fight back before. Hmmm, this should be interesting.*

Due to the early morning hour the ICU wing was staffed lighter than usual. For Anna it had been child's play to bypass the hospital's security, access the records and determine what room Rebecca was being kept in.

Anna moved to the door and let herself into Rebecca's room. The ventilator machine rhythmically moved her chest up and down. Her eyes were closed and her head was wrapped in fresh dressings. An IV tube ran down her side and into the top of her hand. Anna closed the distance and took a moment to observe her victim and choose a course of action.

*This will be easier than I anticipated.*

Anna lifted her left arm and pushed the off button on the machine that supplied oxygen. She then turned off the alarm that was attached to Rebecca's vitals. Thirty seconds passed before Rebecca began to convulse, her body starving for air.

Anna smiled as Rebecca's heartbeat flat-lined.

210

*　*　*

*Where am I?*

*What's happening?*

*Who is that?*

Rebecca looked over and saw herself laying in the hospital bed, a tube coming out of her mouth and a nurse looking over her.

*What's going on?  Why is she smiling?*

The nurse turned and left the room.

At the end of the hallway the elevator doors opened and Rebecca watched as Thomas, Laura, Sam, Gavin and Emily made their way to the nurses station.  The nurse picked up the phone and made a call.

*Why are they here?  Are they here to see me?*

Rebecca looked down at her own hands. *They seem real.*  She walked over to the mirror on the wall and was shocked at her own reflection. *It's me, but it's not me.*  Rebecca took her right hand and traced the scar on her face like she had done a thousand times before.  But this time when her fingers ran down her cheek there was no scar to trace.  It was gone.

Rebecca was still confused but it was starting to fade as she put the pieces together.

*Am I dea...*

"What the hell!?"

The door to the room flung open as Dr. Holmes realized that Rebecca's machines had been disabled.  The family stood outside and watched through the window as he hastily checked Rebecca's vitals.  His shoulders slumped.  He turned around and slowly shook his head from side to side.

"I can save her!  I can save her!"

Laura bent down and hugged her son. "It's too late Gav. She's gone."

It was at that moment when both Emily and Gavin finally broke down as the entire day washed over them in one huge torrent of emotion. Thomas and Laura took and held their children close as all of then openly wept together as a family.

Rebecca pressed her hands against the glass and watched her adoptive family weep for her passing. It was at that moment that absolute clarity of her situation washed over her.

*Don't be sad Gav. I love you and I'll always be with and watch over you.*

## 33
## Friday September 21, 2001

After a night of restless sleep, due to the fact that the children spent it in their parent's bed, getting up in the morning hadn't been an easy job. Slowly but surely they all got out of bed and filtered into the common kitchen. Once the kids were out eating breakfast Sam and Bill told their wives the story of how the children had escaped and the reasoning for their memory loss. Julie and Kim were very grateful to have their kids back safe and sound and found themselves in the debt of Emily and Gavin once again. And naturally, for the foreseeable future, sending any of the children to school was out of the question.

"Morning," Thomas said as he greeted Sam, Bill, Julie and Kim.

"Hey brother," Bill replied.

The six children were off in the family room watching cartoons. Sam and Bill peeked in on them and then sat down at the table, both looking exhausted. Julie and Kim took the time to hug both Thomas and Laura.

"Thank you."

"You're welcome," Laura told them. "But we didn't do anything."

"You've done more than you know," Julie said. "We heard what happened and your kids have good heads on their shoulders."

"They kept it together when even we couldn't," Kim added referring to herself and Julie's necessity to be tranquilized.

"I was on the verge of needing a shot myself," Laura replied, "so there's no need to beat yourself up."

Kim and Julie smiled.

"Anyway, where do we go from here?" Julie asked.

"We won't be safe until he's dead," said Sam. "It's as simple as that."

Bill nodded. "Sam's right. We have to take the fight to Aleman."

"But we have to find him first."

"And how do we do that?" Laura asked.

"Good question," Sam replied.

"I'm feeling cooped up and my heart hurts," said Bill. "Do you guys want to go out for a quick run so I can clear my head?"

"Sure," Sam said.

"Okay," Thomas added.

"You're going to leave?" Kim asked her husband.

"Don't worry, you'll be safe here and we'll be back before you know it."

\* \* \*

Ten minutes later the three men had jogged a good distance away from SANDBOX and talked amongst themselves.

"What the hell are we supposed to do?" Thomas asked his friends. "I mean, this Aleman guy has us all in his sights. We already lost Rebecca."

"We're sorry about that Thomas," Sam said. "Had we known that Robert Aleman had escaped from custody we would have been much more proactive. Now we're on the defensive and…"

"And that's not a situation we're used to, nor do we enjoy," Bill said as he finished Sam's sentence.

"So what's the plan then?" Thomas inquired.

Sam and Bill shared a glance as the trio continued to run down the road.

"We're still figuring that part out."

"So we're just supposed to stay at SANDBOX and never leave?"

"No, of course not."

Thomas wasn't finished. "He's attacked us twice now so my guess is he's not even close to being finished. Maybe we should be thinking about what his next potential move will be?"

Sam's cell phone rang so they all stopped running so he could answer it.

"Hello?"

"Sam, it's Roberta. I need you to get back to the office."

"What's going on?"

"The FBI are here."

"Okay. Do they have new information to share with us?"

"No. They're here with a search warrant."

\* \* \*

Sam, Bill and Thomas got back to SANDBOX as quickly as they could and were met with a contingent of FBI agents both outside and in the lobby.

"What's going on here?" Sam asked as they walked in. "Who's in charge?"

A familiar face approached them. He was the head of San Francisco FBI branch and had served them a search warrant before when Victor Bannon had Hobbes plant incriminating evidence about Nikolay Dmitriev in SANDBOX's computers four years prior.

"Hello Sam. Bill."

"What brings you back to my neck of the woods Agent Packard?" Sam asked defensively.

"I'm glad you asked," he said as he handed over a search warrant. "SANDBOX is being indicted for both drug smuggling and money laundering."

Sam and Bill laughed. "That's preposterous. Someone's pulling your leg Agent Packard."

"Perhaps, but the evidence I've personally seen indicates otherwise."

"Bullshit. Whatever you've seen is clearly a fabrication."

"This is what's going to happen Mr. Paige. You and Mr. Nicholson are currently not under arrest. However, we're conducting this search whether you like it or not."

"But…"

"Furthermore, we've frozen your personal and company assets. Your office is to be evacuated and shutdown pending this investigation. All outstanding contracts are hereby terminated and you will bring your people home."

"This is outrageous. We've done nothing of the sort and yet here you are shutting our business down? How dare you!"

"This came down from above and this is happening right now." Agent Packard motioned with his hand and a dozen agents went to work. "Now, if you're telling me you're not willing to comply then I'll be left with no choice other than to detain the two of you."

Thomas put his hand under Sam's right arm and began to pull him away. "Come on Sam. You have a family to look after. Keep your mouth shut and let him do his job."

"Listen to your business partner Mr. Paige."

The three of them walked away as the agents began to do their jobs.

"What the hell is going on?"

"Shit if I know brother. Things just got a hell of a lot worse."

Sam didn't like any of it. "If these allegations stick then we're dead in the water. This is our reputation at stake; our company. What the fuck is happening?"

\* \* \*

Before long additional agents arrived and began carting out boxes of records and equipment. The men had gone back up to the suite, explained the situation and packed up their families. Meanwhile, Roberta was extremely busy terminating contracts and leaving messages that all operations were to cease and to come home immediately. An agent closely monitored her work.

*All of this is going to come back to me. They're going to find out what I've been doing. I'm being thrown under the bus. What should I do?*

\* \* \*

"Can I help you?" was the first thing Hobbes asked when four agents entered his office.

"We require access to the servers and you will provide that to us right now."

"I don't understand. What the hell is going on?"

The agent speaking produced the search order and waived in in front of Hobbes' face.

"No more questions. Comply or we'll have you removed."

*What the hell?*

"O…okay. What do you need?"

\* \* \*

"Aleman has to be behind this," Bill said.

"No shit. I don't believe in coincidences. What I don't understand is how he made any of this stick."

"I don't understand that either. What I do know is that he's flushing us out in to the open."

Sam nodded. "We need to be on guard."

Thomas walked over and joined them. "What's the plan?"

"Reconvene back at my house for the time being. I've got four operators that are back in town and I'll have them watch over everyone. In terms of paying them…"

"Forget it," Thomas said. "I've got it. Whatever you need."

"Thanks."

Sam left the group and headed over to Roberta who was still at her desk.

"Roberta, I need Jessie, Mack, Corey and Randal activated immediately and sent to my house."

She nodded in compliance and picked up the phone. Hobbes appeared from the hallway and walked by the family members and a bunch of FBI agents as he bee-lined to Sam.

"What's the prognosis Hobbes?"

"They're after something, that's for sure."

"I don't get it."

"Yeah," Hobbes replied as he stole a quick look towards Roberta. "Listen Sam, can I talk with you?"

"Can it wait? This hasn't been the best day."

"Um, not really. This is actually pretty important."

Sam sighed. "Fine. They're forcing us out so we're all headed back to my house. Unless you have someplace else that's safer to go to why don't we talk there?"

"Sure. Okay."

Sam turned back to Roberta who had just hung up the phone.

"Roberta, this has turned in to one hell of a shitty day. I'd rather not split us all up, especially in the light of what's happened.

If you're done here then let's all head out together so we can figure out our next steps."

## 34
## Friday September 21, 2001

Former General, Robert Aleman, was extremely happy with the results as he watched the events at SANDBOX unfold through high powered binoculars. Six heavily armed men formed a protective circle around the General on the hilltop as he watched FBI agents wheel out carton after carton of evidence they had confiscated.

Twenty minutes later he finally watched as Sam, Bill and the rest of the family leave the confines of their office, get into vehicles and head out.

*Excellent. I know they didn't see that coming. SANDBOX is crippled, and so is whatever future they thought they had. Now it's time for them all to die.*

Robert Aleman lowered his binoculars and motioned to his men that it was time to leave.

## 35
## Friday September 21, 2001

The four SANDBOX operators, Jessie, Mack, Corey and Randal were at Sam's house when the families pulled up. They were each armed with MP5's and side arms. Three of the four immediately took positions between the vehicles and the street while they constantly scanned the area for any signs of trouble. Jessie, the team leader, walked over as Sam disembarked and shook his hand.

"Glad you and the rest of your team are here Jessie."

"Thanks Sam. So, what's the sitrep?"

The other adults hustled the children inside the house while Sam remained outside. Roberta cautiously glanced at Jessie, quickly met his gaze, and then hurried inside the house with everyone else.

"SANDBOX just got shutdown," Sam answered.

"What are you talking about? I don't understand."

"That makes two of us. The FBI came up with some trumped up allegations that my company has been smuggling drugs and laundering money. It's an insane notion."

"shit," Jessie answered. "That doesn't make any sense."

"I know. Anyway, thanks for showing up and looking after us. I appreciate it."

"No problem boss."

"And before I forget, I wanted to say sorry about Ryan and Donnie."

Jessie nodded his head. "Yeah, they were good operators. I was sorry to hear about them and about Rebecca Cross. Such a terrible loss for us all."

223

"Yes, it was. We'll get the bastard that did it. Anyway, keep an eye out and stay safe out here."

"Roger that Sam."

* * *

Roberta corralled the children in the family room as the adults convened in the kitchen. Julie, Kim and Laura went about preparing lunch for everyone while Bill, Thomas and Hobbes tried to pitch in wherever they'd let them. It wasn't long until Gavin came in and proceeded to get his father's attention.

"What about Stickers? It's been a few days. He has to be starving."

Thomas' eyes widened. "You're right. I forgot. Tell you what, I'm going to walk down to our house right now and take care of him, okay?"

Gavin smiled and nodded.

"Okay, good. Why don't you head back in and play with the others and I'll be right back."

Thomas went to the front door and opened it just as Sam approached it from the outside.

"What's up?" Sam asked.

"I'll be right back. Heading down to feed our extremely pissed off cat. I can only imagine where we'll find his presents."

Sam chuckled. "Fun times. You're armed right?"

Thomas patted the side of his hip. "Always."

"Good. I'll go with you."

"Suit yourself," Thomas said as he closed the door behind him.

With a nod to Jessie the two of them walked from Sam's house and over to Thomas' front door. He unlocked it and let them in. As Thomas closed the door Stickers came out of nowhere meowing loudly. Thomas bent down and scooped him up.

"I'm sorry Stickers. We didn't mean to forget about you."

In no time Thomas opened a can of cat food, emptied the entire contents onto a small plate and put it down on the floor. Stickers wasted no time to devour it.

Sam smiled as he watched the cat eat. "And portions of our normal life keep marching on, doesn't it?"

Thomas threw the empty cat can in the garbage, turned and looked at Sam. "What the hell Sam?"

"What?"

"Drug smuggling?"

Sam put his hands up. "I'm as confused about the allegations as you are. You know me and you know there's no way I'm involved in what they're saying."

"It's not that Sam, trust me. But this is some serious shit. Nothing like this gets made up unless there's some truth to it."

"Maybe, but I think this is just another tactic to force us out into the open."

"And what if there actually is some truth to all this? What then?"

"I don't know. Right now I can't think about that with Aleman out there wanting to put a bullet in all of us. My company, rather, our company is the last thing on my mind."

Thomas softened. "I'm sorry this is happening to you."

"It's happening to all of us."

"Well," said Thomas, "whatever happens I want you to know that Laura and I are here for you."

Sam nodded. "Thanks. Speaking of help, and since all my assets are frozen, you wouldn't happen to have a twenty you could spot me? I need to buy Top Ramen to feed my family because apparently that's all I can afford at the moment."

Sam smiled and Thomas grinned in return. "You're an asshole."

"Yeah, that's me. Anyway, let's head back."

*　*　*

Lunch was being served as Thomas and Sam walked in. Hot dogs had been heated up for everyone and a quick buffet style created to accommodate individual condiment tastes. Shortly thereafter, once everyone had a plate, the kids headed back to the family room while adults sat down at the large kitchen table together.

"Good hot dogs ladies," Hobbes said. "Thank you."

"You're welcome," Julie responded. "Now, before we get on some bullshit meaningless topic that takes the focus away from what transpired this morning, let me ask this. What the hell is going on?"

"I have the same question as my sister," Kim added. "The FBI raids the building with a search warrant and tells us that the company is being shut down on charges of drug smuggling and money laundering. Explain how any of that makes one iota of sense."

Everyone's eyes darted around as Kim's words hung over the table.

"Umm…," Hobbes began to say, "I think I may be able to shed some light on what's happening."

They all stopped eating and looked at Hobbes. Sam spoke up first.

"What do you mean you might be able to shed some light? What are you talking about?"

"Do you have a laptop I can use?" Hobbes asked.

Sam gave him a strange look, decided against something and instead got up and retrieved his laptop. He returned and handed it to Hobbes, who in turn opened it up and turned it on. From underneath his shirt, tucked into the back of his pants, he produced a slim dvd case.

"What's that?" Bill asked.

"As you know the FBI confiscated and impounded everything this morning. The other day, after you guys gave me the copies of General Aleman's briefcase from twelve years ago, I began to enter that information into a database. I ended up working all night as I dug through history of each of the members from The Organization."

"Get to the point," Sam pressed.

"Right. Long story short I was able to piece together a substantial list of information which includes phone and bank records, burn it to dvd and smuggled it out of the office."

Sam and Bill looked at each other and then back at Hobbes. "What are you trying to tell us?"

"Umm, well, that's where it gets tricky. I'm not really good at confrontation."

"I still don't understand the point you're trying to make," Sam said. "Out with it, right now."

Hobbes gulped and took a deep breath. "Alright. My research indicates that…, well…, that Roberta is involved."

All heads immediately turned and stared at Roberta who pushed back her chair and stood up from the table.

"That's ridiculous. I have been nothing but loyal to Sam and Bill."

"You're lying," Laura told her.

Everyone at the table, except Hobbes and Roberta, knew that Laura's ability was on to something.

"How dare you question me," Roberta said in defiance. "I've worked for Sam and Bill for well over a decade and would never do anything to betray them."

"You're still lying Roberta."

"No, I am not."

Sam stood up. "Take a seat Roberta while we figure this all out."

Roberta sat back down while Hobbes removed the dvd from its case and inserted it into the laptop. He tapped a few keys and information appeared on the screen. He handed it over to Sam and Bill who tried to make sense of it.

"From the correlated data you can clearly see that there are years of wire transfers that have been deposited into her account. Looking at the data even closer I found a pattern of phone numbers. Shortly after receiving a call from a specific number the wire transfer would occur. Delving even closer I was also able to discover that she made money transfers to other SANDBOX personnel around the same time frame."

Sam was furious. "And where did those specific phone numbers originate to Roberta from?"

"They came from the man known as Serpent, Robert Aleman's now deceased father."

Everyone couldn't believe what they'd just heard and jumped as Sam slammed his fist hard down on the table.

"What the hell does all this mean Roberta? We've trusted you since the beginning. What the fuck have you brought down on my family?"

Roberta's eyes filled with water and tears quickly spilled down her cheeks. "You killed my son!"

"I did what?" Sam replied absolutely confused.

"Both of you," she said as she pointed her finger back and forth between him and Bill. "Both of you killed my son."

"We've killed plenty of bad guys, but we don't even know your son."

"That's bullshit," Roberta said. "The military told me he died in a training exercise, but it wasn't until years later that I was told he was killed while on a mission with the both of you. That person told me you killed him."

Sam and Bill were clearly confused.

"I don't understand," Sam stated. "Back up so we can figure this out. What's your son's name?"

"Like you don't know," she replied through tears.

"What's your son's name goddammit?"

"Christopher Jones. Back in the days, in Special Forces, everyone called him Kit. Kit Jones."

"Holy fucking shit," Bill exclaimed as the realization hit him and Sam at the same time. "Kit Jones. Afghanistan."

"That was your son?"

Roberta nodded.

"But his last name was Jones, not Constance like yours."

"Jones was my married name. Kit thought that Christopher was too long a name and he shortened it long before he joined the military. But none of that matters now because you killed him."

"What are you talking about?" Julie probed. "What happened in Afghanistan?"

Sam and Bill shared another glance and shrugged.

"Fuck it," Bill said. "In eighty-one Sam and I were sent, with a small team, to train Mujahideen rebels in their fight against the Soviets. We were there for nine months. However, early in our training there was a Hind attack."

"What's a Hind?" Kim asked.

"Right. Sorry. A Hind is a Soviet attack helicopter designed to rain death on a battlefield from the sky. Basically it's loaded with a shitload of guns and rockets. Anyway, this damn Hind came over the ridge and began to obliterate the village we were in. In the aftermath a number of the villagers were dead along with two of our own."

Sam sat down and leaned back in his chair. "It was the first time I had lost anyone under my command and, trust me when I say this Roberta, it was a horrible feeling."

"I don't believe you. You killed him!"

Sam shook his head. "We didn't kill him. It was just bad luck."

"You were lied to," Bill added. "You've been used since the very beginning."

"No."

"It's true."

Roberta shook her head in disbelief as she tried to wrap her mind around the thought that for fifteen years she'd been working under the idea that Sam and Bill were responsible for her son's death. That she had continued to keep the flame of revenge alive within her when all along it may have been a lie.

"I'm guessing that whoever told you this lie also helped you obtain the Executive Admin position?"

Roberta nodded.

"And that individual wanted to keep you close to us?"

Again Roberta nodded.

"For what purpose?"

"Revenge," she barely managed to say. "I wanted to hurt both of you as badly as I'd been hurt. But as the years went by, and as I became a part of this family, I realized I didn't want to do it anymore."

"So why did you?"

"Because I was constantly reminded that I had more to lose than The Organization would. They knew my life had become intertwined with SANDBOX and exposing what I had done was more than I knew I could handle. I'm sorry."

"We trusted you with our children!" Julie screamed. "And here you were stabbing us in the back the entire time!"

Kim was furious but couldn't find the words.

Laura stood up and pointed her finger at Roberta. "All this time. All this time and you pretended to be on our side, as part of our family and part of our hearts. You should be ashamed."

Sam took his turn. "We trusted you with our business. We trusted you with our family. We trusted you with our lives. You can imagine that I'm having a really difficult time with all this Roberta."

"I'm sorry. I'm a horrible person for wanting to hurt you like I did. I was blinded by such hatred and rage. All I wanted was revenge for my son who had been taken away from me. I lost my husband to drinking because of his death. My entire life was upended."

Hobbes opened his mouth. "The data doesn't lie so I also know this. General Aleman has been incarcerated for the past twelve years. From his own notes I learned that it was his idea to use SANDBOX as his method of continuing a small portion of his drug trade. The members of The Organization, most noticeably his father, codename Serpent, took his son's idea and ran with it. Roberta has probably been run by that man for the last twelve years, but now that they're all dead my guess is that Aleman has been the one that's been contacting her as of late."

"Well?" asked Sam.

Roberta nodded. "It's been a different voice but he knew all the protocols."

"So what you're telling us is that you've been using my company's assets to help The Organization all this time?"

She nodded.

"Goddammit! No wonder we're under indictment. We're totally fucked and because of you this company is going to fall apart. Bill and I are guilty without even knowing it."

231

"Shit on me," Bill said. "This is bad. If people working for us have been smuggling drugs for the past decade or so, and they can prove it, then yes…we're screwed."

"Wait," Kim said. "Does that mean you could be going to jail?"

"It's a possibility, and with our money frozen we can't put up much of a legal fight."

"Don't ever worry about the money part of this equation," Thomas assured them.

Quiet tears slid down Kim and Julie's faces. The cold reality began to hit them as the extent of the damage began to sink in.

Hobbes took the laptop back, punched a few more keys and new information appeared on the screen.

"This is video from Target, of the woman who attacked Kim."

"Why are you showing this to us?" Kim asked.

"The woman's name is Anna Garland. As it turns out she's been responsible for quite a few assassinations. Her traditional method of killing is by applying a toxin directly to the skin."

"How does she do that? All she did was touch me with her hand."

"She probably used a thin membrane to cover her skin and the toxin was applied to that. And contact, however brief, would immediately transfer the poison."

"That's sick."

Hobbes continued. "My search came up dry on her when Aleman was incarcerated. But, since he got out she's been busy. My guess is that Aleman had her take out the remaining members of The Organization and stepped in to run it all on his own."

Bill shook his head in disbelief. "Anna's as crazy as he is."

"It would appear so," Sam said in agreement.

"And, if we can locate her, then we can find him. Shit. All I know is that Kim would have died if it wasn't for Gavin."

Roberta and Hobbes perked up at Bill's comment.

"What does that mean?" he asked.

"It's complicated," Laura said.

"So what do we do now?" Bill said as he changed the subject. "What do we do with her?" as he pointed at Roberta.

Thomas spoke up. "Laura. Why don't we start with the truth and go from there. Maybe Emily can shed some much needed light on this situation."

"No," Sam said immediately. "Think of the exposure."

"We're well past that at this point Sam," Laura replied. "We're all in danger now."

Laura returned with Emily and Gavin and then closed the door to the kitchen behind her.

"Roberta. How would you like to talk to your son?"

"I don't understand. What are you saying?"

"I don't know if it'll work," Emily whispered to her mother.

"Go ahead Em."

Roberta or Hobbes had no idea what was going on as Emily walked around the table and over to Roberta.

"It's okay," Emily said. "This is going to be very strange for you."

"What? What does that mean?"

Emily reached out and touched Roberta's hand. Instantly Kit, her son, appeared. Roberta panicked, fell out of her chair and she began to backpedal until she hit the wall. Her son approached her slowly. Hobbes froze in his seat, eyes wide open, and didn't move a muscle.

"Hi mom. It's me."

"No. No. This isn't happening."

Kit bent down and gently touched his mother's cheek with the tips of his fingers. At first she tried to recoil but her curiosity soon took over.  She opened her eyes and stared into her dead son's eyes.

"Kit?"

"Yes.  It's me."

"Ho...how?"

He smiled.  "Magic.  May I help you up?"

His mother nodded and Kit helped her to her feet.  He took that moment to hug her and she returned it with a tremendous amount of ferocity.  They finally pulled away from each other and she returned to her chair.

"I am at a loss for words," Roberta said.  "How is this possible?"

"That's not important right now," Kit told her.  "I'm here to tell you what happened in Afghanistan.  The Soviet Hind surprised us all and was able to get a good first pass on the village before we could mount a proper defense.  On its second pass is when I was killed, along with Lloyd Franklin.  It wasn't Sam or Bill's fault mom, it really wasn't."

Roberta began to cry.

"I'm sorry to say this but you've been used.  I've watched over you for the last twenty years, seeing the pain you were in and only wanting to take it all away from you."

Roberta lowered her head.  "I'm so ashamed of what I've done.  I'm so sorry.  Please forgive me.  I know there's nothing I can ever do to make this right.  I betrayed my family and I've betrayed yours.  And now, experiencing the closure that Emily has given me, I can completely understand why you protect your children so much.  I'm sorry."

"Goodbye mom," Kit said.  "I have to go now."

Roberta stood up and hugged her son again.  "Thank you Christopher.  I love you."

"I love you too."

And with that he vanished.  Roberta stumbled to regain her footing and eventually sat down again, emotionally exhausted.

"What the hell just happened?" Hobbes incredulously asked.

"Welcome to the club," Laura said.

"The club?"

Laura waved her hand dismissively.  "It's a joke but right now's not the time."

Hobbes could only nod in return.

"So putting aside Roberta for the time being," Thomas began, "what's the plan?"

"Well," Sam replied, "SANDBOX is effectively shut down. We've been told not to leave town, and if that's not enough, we have a madman after us."

"There's more to it than that," Bill said.  "Hobbes, you said Roberta was making wire transfers to other SANDBOX personnel, which I can only assume are the ones that have been smuggling drugs under our noses."

Hobbes nodded, still very unsure how someone dead could suddenly appear and disappear.

"Okay.  On top of everything that Sam just said we can add the fact that some of our own personnel have been working for Aleman."

"Great, just great," Julie said.

"Out of the pot and into the fire," Kim added.

"It gets worse," Roberta managed to say.

"What?" Sam asked.  "Is there something else you haven't told us?"

"The four men that are outside that are guarding us right now."

"What about them?"

"Those are all that's left of the six that I've been working with."

"Fucking hell," said Bill.

Sam turned to Laura. "Well?"

"She's telling the truth."

"The joke continues to be on us then."

## 36
## Friday September 21, 2001

After Jessie explained to his remaining three operators what Sam had told him they stopped watching the street for impending attacks, turned around and now made sure no one left the house. Jessie took a phone out of his pocket and made a call.

"Report."

"All three families have congregated in Sam's house, including Hobbes and Roberta, sir."

"And their children are with them?"

"Yes sir."

*I still don't know how they escaped.* "Keep them contained. I'm on my way with five additional men. It ends today."

"Sir. What happened to my other two men? Did you have them killed during the abduction?"

"If you're asking whether I sacrificed them then the answer is no. I don't know what happened when the children were being taken. But that doesn't matter. What matters is all of this ends right now and then you and your team get paid and disappear. Understood?"

"Roger that sir."

## 37
## Friday September 21, 2001

"So you're telling me that the four operators outside have been working for The Organization this whole time?"

Roberta nodded her head.

"Shit," Sam replied. He looked over at Bill. "It's time to go on the offensive."

"Roger that."

"What's that mean?" Kim asked.

"It means we're not going to idly sit around and let them take us out." Sam pointed at Thomas as he stood up. "You're with us. The rest of you grab the kids and come to the master bedroom."

Everyone got up from the table. Hobbes and the women went to the family room and began to gather the other four children while Sam, Bill and Thomas headed directly to the master bedroom. Once there Sam entered his large walk-in closet door, pushed a hidden button and a shelving unit that held clothes made an audible click. He pushed the unit backwards and it seamlessly glided open to expose a large hidden space. Inside were quite a number of small arms, ammunition and other equipment.

The three men entered the hidden room and Sam handed a Kevlar vest to each of his friends who immediately put them on. Sam followed suit.

"Our men," Bill began before he corrected himself, "...I mean the men outside are armed with side arms and MP Fives."

Sam nodded. "I saw. The last thing we want is to endanger our neighbors, so we'll fight fire with fire."

From one of his weapons rack Sam picked up two MP5SD 9mm sub-machine guns and handed them over to Bill and Thomas. These were the exact same models as the men outside had except they had suppressors, which made for a much quieter report when the weapon was fired. He also gave them three thirty round magazines each, which they stuffed in their back pockets, and then he armed himself.

As the three emerged from the hidden armory they saw the worried faces of their wives and children as they entered the bedroom.

"Inside, all of you. Arm yourselves and wait."

"What's going on?" Sarah asked.

"It's time for daddy to go to work sweetie," Bill replied. "Just stay with your mother and everything will be alright."

Thomas moved to Laura and kissed her. He then bent down and whispered to Emily and Gavin.

"Keep everyone safe, okay?"

They both nodded.

Thomas smiled. "Good. I love you both."

"I love you too," they said in unison.

He stood up and spoke softly in Laura's ear. "Keep an eye on Roberta. She can't be trusted."

Laura nodded. "Be safe."

"Always."

The group filed into the closet and received quick kisses from Sam and Bill on the way in. Sam pulled the shelving unit closed behind him and then shut the closet door.

\* \* \*

A dim light remained on inside the armory as Kim, Laura and Julie extracted Glock 17's from another weapons rack, inserted full magazines into them and racked the slides. The children were anxious, aside from Emily and Gavin, and huddled on the floor together. Roberta began to walk over to them but Julie stepped in her way.

"Don't even think about it."

"I…"

"You're a traitor. And even if you had doubts about what you were doing years ago you should have come clean about it then, but you didn't. Now look at the position we're in. SANDBOX is under indictment and my husband's reputation will most likely be ruined. All his work; the years of sweat, blood and tears and for what? Nothing."

Julie raised her weapon up and pointed it at Roberta but Laura came over and gently placed her hand on Julie's arm.

"Not here. Not like this. And definitely not in front of your children. They need you now so why don't you go take care of them, okay?"

Julie met Laura's eyes and the fire in her own died down a little. She lowered her weapon, gave Roberta one final look of disgust and went to tend to her children.

"Thanks," Roberta told Laura.

"She's right you know. We brought you into our lives. We've counted on you for years, so don't act surprised now that you're suddenly short on friends." Laura paused. "You do anything out of the ordinary and I won't hesitate to put a bullet in you."

Roberta's eyes went wide and all she could do was nod.

"Now sit down and keep quiet. Our men are out there risking their lives when they shouldn't even be in this position."

As Roberta slunk to the floor Gavin got his mother's attention.

"What is it Gav?"

"Can I bring Stir out?"

"No Stir unless I say so."

"K."

* * *

"You up for this Thomas?" Bill asked as the three walked back towards the front of the house, weapons loaded and ready to go.

"I'll do whatever it takes to keep my family safe so stop worrying about me and let's just get this unpleasantness over with."

"Understood. What's the plan?"

"I'm going to call Jessie and tell him that Roberta just collapsed and we need to take her to the hospital immediately," Sam explained.

"You think they'll believe it?"

"Who cares. As long as it brings one or two of them to the front door where we can control the situation."

"This is going to get messy."

"Tell me something I don't know," Sam replied as he pulled his cell out.

The trio ended up in the kitchen and looked out the front window. A couple of the operators had their weapons up and were closing in.

"Uh, Sam," Thomas said. "This doesn't look good."

Bill pulled both Thomas and Sam to the floor as the front windows of the house imploded. Bullet holes stitched across the kitchen and family room walls as the house was continuously pummeled by round after round of automatic gunfire.

"Fuck me!" Bill screamed as broken glass and bits of sheetrock cascaded down on them.

There was a lull as the four operators dropped their spent magazines and quickly reloaded their weapons with fresh ones.

Sam made sure he had Bill and Thomas' attention before he motioned for them to stay low and move back down the hallway from where they came. Thomas went first, followed by Bill as

242

Sam guarded their back. As Sam began to move the front door was kicked in and two of the operators entered. One of them caught Sam's movement and opened fire, barely missing Sam's legs as he scrambled on hands and knees through the shattered glass and debris that littered the floor.

"Got movement in the kitchen!" one of them yelled.

Two more appeared through the front door as the original two made their way towards the kitchen, weapons at the ready.

In the hallway Thomas had entered the first available door which happened to be a small bathroom while Bill had continued down the hallway. Just as Thomas had turned around gunfire erupted and Sam skidded past Thomas's position as bullets tore up the kitchen floor where he'd just been.

Thomas poked a portion of his head into the hallway just as a barrel, from around the kitchen door, came in to view. A barrage of gunfire from it erupted and Thomas managed to pull his head back faster than he ever thought possible.

Round after round tore up the hallway floor, walls and ceiling as an entire thirty round magazine was expended in to the hallway.

From down the hallway, where Bill and Sam had gone, more automatic gunfire pounded the air.

Thomas felt like he was drenched in blood and wiped his forehead. He looked down at his own sweat that had rapidly formed. He refocused his attention on the kitchen hallway as he heard the sounds of crunching glass as it was walked on.

More gunfire from another part of the house.

Thomas readied his weapon. His back was against the bathroom's far wall. He was in a sitting position, legs out in front of him.

Crunch.

Thomas saw a shadow appear against the hallway wall. The man was closing in on his position. The front of a weapon slowly appeared, and as the man turned to fill the bathroom with hot lead Thomas squeezed his own trigger.

The man's eyes opened wide as five rounds stitched a bloody line up his torso with the final one exiting the back of the operator's neck. He pitched back against the far wall and collapsed with a gurgling sound as his heart continued to pump out blood through the ragged tear in his neck.

Before Thomas could react another operator began to fire at the bathroom's doorway, walking the bullets across the floor as he moved in on Thomas.

Dozens of bathroom tiles exploded and showered Thomas in debris, who had little choice but to protect his face with his free arm or risk serious injury, his weapon now pointed away from the doorway.

The operator emptied his magazine, let it swing loose on its sling and pulled his side arm. He stepped into the bathroom and pointed right at Thomas.

Thomas blinked and looked up at the man just as the trigger was pulled. The round exploded next to Thomas' head as he used his power to forcefully shoved his attacker back against the far wall. The man's side arm was ripped from his grasp so quickly that his index finger broke in the process. His legs didn't touch the ground as he remained pinned helplessly up against the wall.

The operator's eyes couldn't fully comprehend what was happening to him. "What are y.."

\* \* \*

Bill kept low and moved as fast as he could as Thomas ducked into the bathroom. He reached the end of the hallway, where it branched to the master bedroom as well as the family room, and bobbed right.

244

Bill squared up on the wall as automatic gunfire, from where he'd just came from, tore up the floor. Sam skidded down the hallway and joined Bill just as the entire hallway filled with bullets.

Bill quickly peeked into the family room and saw two men just inside the front door. He brought his weapon up and came out shooting. One of the operators toppled backwards. Bill dived for cover behind a couch as the remaining one unloaded a barrage of return fire that punched numerous holes in the couch.

It was Sam's turn to move out of the hallway. He came out weapon up and squeezed his trigger. A multitude of suppressed rounds ripped through the operator's chest and arms. The entryway turned crimson as blood spray colored the white walls.

Before Sam or Bill could turn around another full magazine was emptied back down the hallway where Thomas was.

Sam twisted around and took the few steps towards the hallway while Bill got to his feet to verify the two men at the front door were indeed out of play.

A single gunshot rang out.

Sam turned the corner and witnessed the operator being flung high against the wall. The man's side arm was yanked violently from his hand and the sound of his finger breaking in the process was quite audible.

"What are y…"

Sam quickly put two bullets in the man's brain but the operator continued to hang there like a limp puppet. Sam had already seen the second body on the hallway floor, outside the bathroom, and yelled to compensate for his loss of hearing.

"Thomas!"

No response.

"Thomas! Bill, I've got two down in the hallway!"

"I've got two in here!" Bill yelled back. "Coming through the kitchen!"

Sam watched as Bill appeared at the end of the hallway.

"Thomas!"

Nothing.

Sam motioned to Bill. "Cover the front while I check Thomas' condition!"

Bill nodded, turned and watched the front as Sam made his way down the destroyed hallway to the door.

"Thomas! I'm coming in!"

Sam did a quick peek around the bathroom entryway and saw Thomas getting to his feet. He came in and helped his friend up.

"You okay?"

Thomas nodded. "I almost bought it that time," as he looked back at the bullet hole that embedded itself in the wall next to where his head had been.

Sam turned and checked on the other downed operator and easily determined he was dead.

"I'm going to go check on the family," Sam said down the hallway towards the kitchen where Bill was at.

"Hurry up. I hear sirens in the distance."

"Fuck."

\*    \*    \*

General Aleman's two vehicles slowed to a halt a hundred feet down the street.

"Goddammit. Those idiots didn't wait, probably pissed off that two of their team were killed when I had the children taken."

Two police cars were outside Sam's house and from the sounds of it many more had been frantically called in and were no more than thirty seconds out. Aleman watched the scene for two minutes as the entire area filled with uniformed officers.

"We should go sir," one of his men said.

"Not quite yet."

From out of the bullet ridden house two officers marched Sam and Bill outside, who had already been handcuffed. It was at that moment when Sam and Robert Aleman locked eyes in the distance.

"Now we can go."

## 38
## Friday September 21, 2001

Special Agent Greg Packard, the lead San Francisco FBI agent in charge, closed the interrogation room door behind, pulled back the free chair and sat down across from Sam and Bill. They had been taken to the San Francisco FBI office and detained. Both of their hands were on the table and secured with long chained handcuffs through steel rings, which gave their hands limited mobility. A video camera in an upper corner covered the entire room.

"Where are our families?" Bill asked with a worried look on his face. "Tell me they're safe?"

"They're fine," Agent Packard replied. "All of them are here in a holding area."

Relief washed over Sam and Bill.

"Now, just this morning I served you a search warrant for drug trafficking. But now you're in my custody because of a massive firefight that occurred at your house between you and your own men." Agent Packard shifted his body. "I've been at this job for a long time, but you clearly have my attention now. What the hell is going on?"

"You wouldn't believe us even if we told you," Sam replied.

"Try me."

"Very well. Twelve years ago General Robert Aleman asked us to join his organization to smuggle drugs into the United States. We refused so he threatened both us and our families. We were able to capture and turn him over to the authorities. Little did we know that just a few months ago he managed to escape and decided to make good on his old promises.

249

"However, what we didn't know was that Roberta, our Executive Admin we hired when we started SANDBOX, had actually been employed by Aleman's father. She's the one who's apparently been coordinating the drug smuggling we've been charged with. On top of that Aleman, since his escape, has neutralized his father and all other members of the group he used to work for and has now apparently concentrated his focus on us."

"I see. I'm aware of the kidnapping of your children, but what about the firefight at your house?"

"Those men…"

"You mean the men that are in your employment."

Sam nodded. "We just learned from Roberta that those four men work for Aleman. We defended ourselves. It's as simple as that."

"Nothing about what you just said sounds simple Mr. Paige. In fact, your story sounds pretty farfetched and very convenient. It's downright amazing for me to believe that both of you would have zero knowledge of nefarious activities, that you say have been going on for years, occurring right under your noses."

"I'm telling you the truth. Call General Franks at the Pentagon to confirm what I'm telling you. Robert Aleman is behind all of this. He's out to ruin me, which has already started, and to kill both of us and our families."

Agent Packard leaned back in his chair and eyeballed both of them. "Maybe you're telling the truth and maybe you're not. But, the fact remains that you're under indictment AND you shot up your neighborhood. The charges against you are serious which means for the time being I'm holding you and your family right here at my facility."

"This is bullshit," Bill spat out. "We're being setup."

Agent Packard got up from his chair. "Is there anything else I can do for you?"

"We want to see our families," Sam instantly requested.

"That's out of the question right now."

"Why not?"

"Protocol. Is there anything else?"

"What about a lawyer?"

* * *

Thomas, Laura, Julie, Kim, Roberta, Hobbes and the six children tried to relax in a large holding room that was locked and with a guard stationed outside the door. Water bottles and sandwiches had been brought in and left on the table. A small but enclosed bathroom was located in the back corner of the room. Kim and Julie's children stayed next to their mothers while Emily and Gavin meandered around the room as Thomas and Laura whispered to each other.

"What do you think they did with Sam and Bill?"

"Since we haven't seen them since the house I have to assume they've been segregated," Thomas replied, "most likely so they can talk to them."

"You mean interrogate."

"Probably. How often are you charged with drug smuggling and then end up involved in a gun battle in the same day? I think it's safe to say they're not going to be joining us."

"And yet they didn't detain you and you were involved in that same firefight."

"Yeah. That part I don't understand. Although I'm sure they'll pull me out of here to question me, and all of us, soon enough."

Laura put a hand on her husband's arm. "Was it bad?"

"Going against the four men?"

Laura nodded.

"Yeah. That wasn't fun but I did what I had to do. I'd do it all over again to protect you and our kids."

"I know. I believe you."

"Used your powers right there?"

"No. Woman intuition. You're a good man Thomas and the hand our family has been dealt has taken us to hell and back."

"That it has."

"But we're in this together and that's all that matters. I know you look out for us, more than I ever knew. I didn't realize how worried you've really been until just recently. And now I see how much that worry has really taken its toll on you."

Thomas squeezed her hand. "We just need to figure this situation out. Now Roberta and Hobbes know about our secret but now's not the time or place to ask Emily to wipe them."

"I'm not sure that's a good idea. I discovered that most of her nightmares came from other people's memories."

"What? How?"

"She told me about the attack in Hawaii as if she was there. She described it in detail."

"But she wasn't there. She was with me in D.C."

Laura nodded. "I know. Those memories are from the other children after she wiped them. I can't explain it. When she took their memories some of them remained behind in her."

"Shit. The poor thing. No wonder she has PTSD. I don't think I could take reliving something like that over and over again in my head without cracking."

"I'm working with her and we'll get through it. All I'm saying is that we need to look out for her well-being moving forward."

"The CIA offer. That's what you mean, right?"

"Yes," Laura replied. "We can't make any blind decisions about our future without considering all the ramifications."

"Food for thought." Thomas looked around. "But right now we need to figure out our next move, especially since we haven't been charged with anything."

*　*　*

Two hours later the door to the interrogation room opened once again.

"Your lawyer's here," the agent said.

A sharply dressed middle-aged woman walked in and the agent closed the door behind her.

"My name is Grace Fraser." She sat down across from Sam and Bill.

"I'm Sam Paige and this is Bill Nicholson."

"Nice to meet you," she replied as she extended her hand towards Sam.

Sam, despite the relatively short handcuff chains, was about to shake her hand when Bill violently used his body to shove the table against the woman. It hit her in the mid-section and she was propelled back in her chair.

"What the fuck?" Sam snapped.

"It's her! It's Anna Garland! It's the bitch that tried to kill my wife!"

Anna's face instantly turned to a sneer as she recovered. In a second she had launched herself across the table in an effort to touch one of them with her right hand. Sam jerked his hands back and she barely missed him.

Bill pulled up on his chains as Sam pulled back and one leg of the heavy table lifted off the floor.

Anna swiped at Sam again but Bill jerked the table towards him, the handcuffs biting into his wrists, and Sam was dragged with it.

"Help me goddammit!" Bill yelled as he began to lift the heavy table again.

As Anna lunged for the third time Sam finally found his footing and helped Bill reposition the table so they kept it between them and her. She missed again.

"There's nothing you can do," she spat. "You're both dead."

As Sam and Bill dragged the heavy table around the room together, blood trickling from their handcuff abrasions, they had little choice but try to anticipate the next move Anna would make.

The interrogation room burst open and an agent, with his weapon drawn, entered the room.

"They're attacking me!" Anna screamed.

"Come to me ma'am," he motioned.

As the agent tried to comprehend what had happened in the room Anna moved towards him.

"Watch out!" Sam yelled at the agent.

Anna brushed her right hand against his face. She smiled and a look of confusion instantly washed over him.

"No!" Bill yelled.

Two seconds later the agent's gun slipped out of his hand and he collapsed to the floor, barely able to keep himself up. Tears of blood ran out of his eyes and he began to violently gasp. He fell to his side and grabbed his throat with both of his hands. It was then that blood spewed out of his mouth like a fountain and covered the floor. A few seconds after that he stopped moving altogether.

Anna turned back towards her targets and kicked the door closed. "Some of my best work. Did you know that I also ended Rebecca's life while she lay there helpless in the hospital?"

"You killed Rebecca?" Sam sneered.

Anna nodded. "Now, who's next?"

She came at them full force, right hand extended, but lost her footing in the fresh blood. Anna stumbled and went down hard.

Sam and Bill upended the table using all their strength, twisted and then brought the edge down hard on her exposed legs. One of them snapped and she screamed.

"Hands!" Bill yelled "Get her hands!"

Sam and Bill, blood coming from their own wounds, pulled the heavy table up her body until they were both able to grab her wrists. Sam managed to grab her left hand while Bill grabbed her right with powerful grips. Anna lay immobile, a heavy table pinning her down while the two men restrained her arms as she struggled through the pain.

The room had been destroyed and blood was everywhere. Anna screamed again and fists began to pound on the outside of the door.

"Where's Aleman!?" Sam bellowed.

"Go to hell!"

The pounding on the door became louder.

"Where is he!?"

Sweat ran down the sides of Anna's face but she refused to talk. Sam and Bill were out of time and they knew it.

"This is for Rebecca!"

As the door ruptured inward Bill forced Anna's right hand towards her face.

"NOOOO!" she barely had time to scream out before her own poison found a new home.

Anna struggled to break free of their grips to no avail as her own toxin began to race through her blood stream. Her eyes were awash in panic as she felt the first symptoms hit her. She coughed and a blood bubble formed between her lips.

"Freeze!" multiple agents yelled as they entered, guns up and pointed at the two men.

Sam and Bill quickly dropped her wrists, stood and moved as far away from Anna as possible, dragging the table with them.

"What the fuck happened in here…" Agent Packard began to say from the doorway but the jet of blood that burst forth from Anna's throat cut him off. He quickly turned and puked in the hallway.

"Good riddance bitch," Bill whispered.

*  *  *

Twenty minutes later Sam and Bill found themselves in another room and their wrists had been bandaged. Their clothing had blood on it but that didn't bother them. They both knew they were extremely lucky to be alive. They had told Agent Packard not to touch her hands as they were removed from the room. They hoped he had listened.

The cell door opened and Sam and Bill, no longer in handcuffs, sat on the cell bench and watched Agent Packard enter.

"I just watched the interrogation room video. Who is she?"

"Her name is Anna Garland and she's a professional assassin," Sam replied.

Agent Packard rubbed his head. "You're not kidding are you?"

"Do you usually let anyone into your building under the guise of being a lawyer, or just assassin's?" Bill quipped.

"She had the proper documents," Agent Packard shot back.

"So do all professionals," Sam replied. "Do you believe us now?"

"You're telling me that this General Aleman sent her to kill you?"

"He sent her to finish the job with Rebecca Cross. She admitted as much before she died. But Aleman's got a hard-on for us," Bill said, "if you haven't noticed. By the way, we're sorry about your agent. That's just a horrible way to go."

256

Agent Packard nodded. "Listen, I'm starting to believe you and this conspiracy theory you have."

"But?"

"But I still have to do my job."

"Agreed," Sam told him. "This issue affects both of us right now. We want to protect our families and now you want this guy for the death of one of your own. However, we're all in danger and, no offense, but this facility was just breached. We're on your side, I promise you, but right now we have to think of the bigger picture."

"What are you proposing?"

"Take us to SANDBOX. Put us in the top floor and guard us there."

"My superiors would have my head if I did that. What about a hotel instead?"

Sam and Bill shook their heads. "A hotel isn't going to cut it. That's worse than here, sorry to say. What just occurred back there did actually happened. An agent of yours was killed by an assassin that was trying to take us out. You need us alive and contained for multiple reasons now. What better place than our own? Our wives and our children are at risk too. Do the right thing Agent Packard. Please."

Agent Packard pointed his finger at Sam. "You'd better not be bullshitting me."

"No sir. Not when it comes to my family."

Agent Packard pulled a radio from his belt and spoke into it. "Prep the families. We're leaving in ten minutes."

## 39
## Friday September 21, 2001

"What do you mean Anna's dead?" Robert Aleman said in disbelief to his contact over the phone. "She can't be dead, not my Anna."

"I'm afraid it's true sir," the man on the other end confirmed.

Aleman clenched his teeth. "How did she die?"

"It's too early for full confirmation but…"

"Just tell me what you've heard goddammit."

"Yes sir. What was relayed to me was that she died from some sort of fatal toxin. Apparently her death was quite bloody, sir. When she died Anna was in the interrogation room with Paige and Nicholson."

"Anything else?"

"Yes sir. An FBI agent that burst in on them was also killed in the same manner. They're going to come after you now."

"Let them come. What about Paige and Nicholson?"

"They left the FBI facility hours ago and were headed back to SANDBOX under guard."

"Thank you. That will be all."

Robert Aleman quietly pressed the end button on his mobile phone and put it back in his pocket. His plans for revenge had been derailed due to various circumstances, but Anna was dead now because of him, and he knew it.

*My dear, sweet Anna. You served me faithfully for decades, killing those that were a threat to The Organization. I shouldn't have sent you to exterminate the two men that I should have taken care of twelve years ago. Instead I fled, was caught and was locked away; forgotten. With your death I will no longer stand idly by. I will now undertake what I've yearned to do for the last*

259

*twelve years, to kill Sam Paige and Bill Nicholson myself. To hell with the plan! They're going to pay for your death in blood Anna, and I'm going to collect in full.*

# 40

# Friday September 21, 2001

The families had been removed from the FBI facility and transported, under guard, to SANDBOX. After they arrived the top floor suite was searched and all weapons were collected before they were allowed inside. Sam and Agent Packard remained in the lobby while everyone crowded into the elevator and headed up to the suite.

"Don't make me regret this," Agent Packard said to Sam on his way out.

"And yet you leave us defenseless. What the hell do you think we're going to do, attack your agents?"

"I've taken enough heat allowing you to camp out in your own building rather than holding you at my facility. This isn't an ideal situation for either of us, given the fact that you were attacked inside my building and an agent of mine died on my watch. Now, if I also armed you, well, say goodbye to my career. Besides, I've got eight agents watching out for you and my task force will find Robert Aleman long before he thinks it's a good idea to come knocking on your door Sam."

"You don't know him like I do Agent Packard. He's not going to just give up and call it quits. This man is fanatical, and probably even more so, now that we took his assassin out of play."

"Sam, you will stay put and do it with a smile. Let us do our job."

Sam had hit a brick wall with Agent Packard and let it go. "Fine. What about something to eat? It's been a long day already and dinner time is only a few hours away. We've got some snack items but nothing else in stock."

"I'll send a food truck around in a few hours with meals for everyone, including my people, okay?"

"Thank you."

"Also, later this evening I'll send eight more agents to replace the ones that I'm leaving here."

"Understood."

"Is there anything else you need Sam?"

"Only for this nightmare to be over."

"I hear you. We'll do our best to locate Aleman and take him out of play."

"Good luck."

"Yeah, I think I'll need it."

Sam watched Agent Packard as he left SANDBOX, get in his vehicle with two other agents and depart. Eight other agents remained to both protect the families and to prevent them from leaving. Four were posted in the lobby, two in the stairwell and two in the suite itself.

"Sir."

Sam turned to face the FBI agent who had addressed him and saw that the agent was politely ushering him towards the elevator. Sam nodded, took one last look at the parking lot and then rejoined his family on the top floor.

* * *

It'd been six hours since the families had been taken from the FBI facility in San Francisco and brought back to SANDBOX. Seven o'clock had come and gone and still the food truck hadn't arrived as promised. As eight-thirty rolled around everyone had become grumpy, especially the children. As it turned out, fruit roll-ups and mixed nuts don't constitute a meal.

At a quarter to nine the truck finally arrived. The agent's ear pieces, that were with the families in the suite, came to life and informed them that the food was being offloaded and to come down and retrieve it. They acknowledged the radio call and headed down in the elevator to the main lobby. The two other agents, from the stairwell, also turned up in the lobby as the food from the catering truck was being unpacked in the large conference room. The truck started up and left the parking lot as Sam, Bill and Thomas watched it drive away from one of the top floor windows. The elevator dinged a minute later and the two agents got off carrying a ton of food and headed to the kitchen to drop it off.

"Dinner's here kids."

"About time," Emily said, "I'm starving."

"Me too," Gavin added.

"We'll be downstairs eating Mr. Paige," said one of the agents. "Our replacements should be here within the hour."

"Understood," Sam replied.

The kids ran to the kitchen as Julie, Kim and Laura took over and began to dole out plate after plate of delicious smelling food. Roberta and Hobbes received their plates and sat down beside the rest of the family. It wasn't long before the only sound was everyone scarfing down their meal. As stomachs began to fill up the bellyaching, from the kids, began to subside but was soon replaced by curious minds.

"What does the FBI want with us?" Amanda asked her father. "We have a right to know what's going on."

"Well, it's complicated," Sam told his daughter.

"Try harder daddy. We're not dumb. None of this makes any sense in my head and the rest of us kids don't understand why no one will tell us anything."

Sam looked uncomfortably around the table at the other adults, as well as the children, looked to him for an answer. He sighed, wiped his mouth with his napkin and gently placed it down beside his plate.

"You want the truth?" Sam asked his daughter.

Amanda nodded.

"Alright, I can deal with that and I believe you can too sweetie." Sam looked over at the Clarks. "And how does that grab you Thomas? Laura? Is it time for the truth? Our children used to know everything back in Hawaii, but things happened that had to be wiped away, so to speak. Maybe it's time for the truth to come out again?"

Thomas and Laura looked at each other.

"What'ya think?" she asked Thomas.

"It's more exposure and it puts them all at risk buttttt….they did used to know and it made life so much easier that they did. I'm tired of hiding it from our family."

Laura nodded. "I agree. Keeping this secret has become much more of a burden than we ever anticipated."

Amanda, Craig, Sarah and Edward knew the adults were talking in riddles on purpose.

"What secret?" Amanda pressed. "And how did we know something and then not know it?"

Roberta and Hobbes were confused as well but remained quiet as they took it all in.

Laura turned and addressed the two wives. "What about you Julie? Kim?"

Kim spoke up first. "At this point I don't know what to think. Whether I want to acknowledge it or not, the fact is that we're all in the crosshairs, and we've been in the crosshairs for years."

"Kim…" Bill tried to speak but was cut off as his wife continued.

264

"If it was just us," Kim said as she motioned to the adults, "then maybe I could handle this better. But we all have children and this isn't the first time they've been placed in harm's way. I'm tired of being afraid for their safety, and ours."

Bill took Kim's hand in his as Julie took a turn.

"Kim's right. We've been through hell and back but we've been through it together, as a family. Have I been a nervous wreck since my sister nearly died at Target? Absolutely. But my world changed four years ago when I was shown what Emily and Gavin could do."

The children still didn't understand.

"What can Emily and Gavin do?" Amanda asked. "Why are you talking in riddles?"

"Patience young lady," Sam told her. "If my guess is correct you're about to have your mind blown wide open."

Amanda gave her father a 'whatever' look but stopped asking questions.

Julie picked up where she had stopped. "As I was saying, our lives, collectively, have been through the ringer. I know the decision we made for our children was the right one at the time. They were too young to live with that much horror in their heads. But now we can't protect them as much as we'd like to anymore, and they'll begin to have their own lives as they grow older. So why not let the cat out of the bag now and see where the chips fall."

Thomas looked at his son and daughter.

"Gav? Em? Thoughts?"

"Amanda, Sarah, Craig and Edward knew about us before," Emily explained. "I still think that taking their memories was the right thing to do but I'm tired of hiding the truth from them."

"Me too," Gavin added. "And Stir's upset about it as well."

"What's a Stir?" Craig asked.

265

"Took our memories?" Sarah asked. "That doesn't even make any sense. What kind of creepy things are you all talking about?"

"Take it easy sweetheart," Bill said to his daughter.

"So we're all in agreement then?" Sam asked.

A round of nods came from the adults and from Emily and Gavin. Laura stood up and began to clear the table. Kim and Julie quickly joined in as the conversation continued.

"Okay then," Sam said as he looked at each of the four children and then switched his gaze over to Roberta and then Hobbes. "You're all in for one heck of a bedtime story. The first rule is that what you're about to see and hear does not leave this room. The second rule is not to get scared or angry. We will answer all of your questions until you understand why we did what we did. I want you to promise me or this doesn't go one step further."

"I promise," Sarah said.

"I promise," Edward said.

"I promise," Amanda said.

"I promise," Craig said.

"I don't know what's going on but I'm intrigued. I promise," Hobbes replied.

"I've already experienced something I can't even begin to explain today," Roberta said. "I promise."

"Good," Sam told them all. "Now the story we're about to unveil to you is going to sound crazy but every bit of it is true. On top of that you're going to see things that might make you jump, but I promise you that nothing is going to hurt you." Sam paused as he got a read on his children. They were engaged but skeptical of what was about to come. "Thomas, I think it's only right that you kick this all off."

All eyes turned to Thomas.

266

"I think it'll be easier if we start with the truth. Emily, Gavin, Laura and I have special abilities."

"Like magic powers?" Craig asked.

"They're lying," Amanda stated, "and I don't want to be lied to." She stood up. "Why would you..."

Before everyone's eyes Amanda's body lifted off the floor and rose into the air.

"Holy shit..." she managed to say as she floated over the table.

Roberta, Hobbes and the other three children scooted their chairs back as if Amanda was possessed. Her body did a flip in the air and then was gently lowered back down to her seat.

"THAT WAS AWESOME!" she exclaimed with a huge smile on her face. "I want to do that again."

"How did you do that?"

"I'm next. I'm next."

"Wow."

Roberta and Hobbes just sat there with open mouths and disbelief once again on their face. They thought they had seen everything already when Emily brought Roberta's son back. They all scooted their chairs back in as Thomas continued.

"Do I have your attention now?" Thomas asked.

The children all vigorously nodded their heads together in unison.

"Okay then. I just did that to Amanda. It's called telekinesis and it allows me to manipulate things."

"Like the force?" Craig asked.

"Yes actually, something along those lines. Laura has the ability to tell when people are lying. Emily can make people do what she wants by touching them. She can also summon relatives that have passed away, here to our reality. And she can remove memories from people's heads."

"Is that what you meant earlier?" Amanda asked. "Did Emily take a memory of mine?"

Thomas nodded. "She did, but we'll get to that in due time, okay?"

"Okay." Amanda sat back and listened intently.

"Gavin has the ability to heal, summon portals to another reality and summon a little pet with red eyes he calls Stir."

"A pet?" Edward asked anxiously. "My dad won't let us have a pet. Can we see him? Can we see Stir?"

"Go ahead Gav," Thomas said. "Give them what they want."

Gavin smiled and was ecstatic that he could once again share Stir with the other children. They all loved him before but for the last four years he had to keep him a secret and he didn't like it.

"Don't be scared," Gavin told everyone.

Before another word could be spoken a small, smoke encompassed form with red eyes appeared on the table.

"His name's Stir," Gavin reminded them.

Stir wasted no time to make his way over to Edward. Hobbes and Roberta's mouths seemed to open even wider.

"Woah," Edward said as Stir came over. But instead of moving away he leaned forward. "Can I touch him?"

"Sure. He's the best. All of you loved playing with him in Hawaii."

"We did? I don't remember."

"I know," Gavin told him.

The other three children got up from their chairs and crowded behind Edward. They all took turns petting Stir and in no time he began to purr.

"He feels so weird. I like it."

"Yeah, it's like petting thick smoke or something. I don't know how else to describe it."

"Wow Stir, you're awesome."

Stir thumped his tail loudly on the table in appreciation. A few minutes later the children returned to their seats. Stir decided to lie down next to Gavin as Thomas continued the story.

"So just to make sure, you all believe we have special abilities now?"

There was another round of communal nods.

"How'd you get them?" Sarah asked.

"That's a great question. Eleven years ago, back in nineteen ninety, I was experimented on without my knowledge. It was during that time when I met Laura. What I didn't know is that when she and I decided to have children I passed on a genetic anomaly to them."

"What's that?" Craig asked.

"Good point. I just got too technical."

"Basically it means that Emily and Gavin have had their abilities from birth," Laura told them.

"Oh. Okay."

"Thanks babe," Thomas said and Laura smiled.

Sarah wasn't satisfied. "But that only explains Gavin and Emily. How did you get your power?"

"You're absolutely right. Laura and I got ours four years ago, and we'll get to that part shortly. Anyway it wasn't until four years ago that Em and Gav began to exhibit the first signs that they had these extraordinary gifts. It was then that some bad men took them from us."

"You were taken?" Sarah asked Emily with a twinge of concern mixed with sadness.

"Yes," Emily replied.

"That's horrible. What happened?"

"Do you remember when daddy got shot in the leg?" Bill asked.

Sarah nodded.

"Well, that happened when Uncle Sam, Thomas and I went to rescue them. We moved to Hawaii shortly thereafter."

"Hawaii was beautiful and fun," Amanda said.

"And sunny," Edward said.

"And sandy," Craig added.

"But I can't remember why we left," Sarah remarked.

"You're right, I don't remember either."

"We were targeted," Sam explained. "Bad men wanted to hurt you so you tried to escape. There was…"

Julie held up her hand and stopped Sam. "They need to hear this from me."

"What?" Amanda asked. "What happened mom?"

Julie let out a deep breath before she continued. "It was early in the morning and we were all woken up, rushed outside and put into vehicles. On our way to the Marine base we were attacked."

The children looked around with confused looks on their faces.

"I don't remember any of this."

"I know, but let me finish so you understand why."

Her daughter nodded.

"Bullets slammed against the exterior of the vehicles. They were loud, really loud. There were explosions. All of you were screaming and crying, Kim and I included. The only one of us here that really had their shit together, pardon my language, was Laura. Anyway, I lost my nerve during it all, left the vehicle in a blind rage and shot one of the men who attacked us."

"You…you shot someone mom?"

Julie nodded. "To save and protect you. But here's the worst part of the story. I was shot."

"No."

"Actually I died on that highway. It was Gavin who brought me back to life."

Everyone who hadn't known the story was stunned.

"You were dead and Gavin brought you back to life." Craig repeated.

Julie continued. "My eyes changed to black that day, when before they were always brown. And, to top it all off, I had amnesia and didn't know who any of you were."

"I don't remember any of this. Why don't I know what you're talking about?"

It was Kim's turn. "Because we decided to take your memories of that moment, and more, away from you. We chose to remove that ugliness from your heads so you wouldn't have to live with it every day."

"Oh. There's more?"

Kim nodded. "With Roberta's help we were able to escape Hawaii and shake off any pursuers that were still after us. During that time Laura helped Julie regain her memory. But that was short lived when the yacht we were all on was boarded and we were taken hostage."

"Seriously?" Sarah questioned. "Where were dad and Uncle Sam during all of this?"

"They were being forced to do jobs for the same man that took us hostage. Your father and Uncle Sam were led to believe that if they didn't we'd be killed."

"And Uncle Thomas?"

"And now we get to the part of the story that will answer one of your earlier questions," Thomas responded. "Emily and I had been taken and experimented on in a secret underground facility in Washington D.C."

"Why?"

"They wanted to extrapolate…"

"To extrapawhat?"

"Sorry. They wanted to figure out a way to recreate my genetic trait so they could have other people develop abilities. It was during our escape that I was injected with an untested sample that they had created. I hooked back up with your father and Sam and we came to rescue all of you. It was then, under duress, that I discovered my ability."

"And Auntie Laura?"

"I ended up with a second syringe and Laura decided to use it, which is where she got her ability from."

"So you must have taken some of those memories from me as well," said Hobbes as he put two and two together.

Thomas nodded. "We had to protect our children from anyone who knew of their abilities that Emily had worked her magic on."

"I get it," Hobbes replied. "All of this is crazy but I believe you. I probably would have done the same thing if I was in your shoes."

Amanda spoke up again. "So why are the FBI guarding us daddy?"

"We've been targeted again. Twelve years ago, before any of you were born, Bill and I were threatened by a man called Robert Aleman. We caught him and put him away. Well, as it turns out, a few months ago he escaped and is trying to make good on the promise he made all those years ago."

"There's more to it though," Bill said. "Our company has been charged with drug smuggling. But there's a catch. It's actually been happening behind our backs for years."

"How? Why?"

"The how is unimportant for now. We believe the reason it happened was to discredit us. Robert Aleman had plans to ruin us from the beginning if we chose not to go along with him. Well, it worked. Right now SANDBOX, Sam and I are under indictment."

"What's that mean?"

"It means they're going through our entire company piece by piece looking for evidence to use against us."

Sarah got out of her chair, rushed over to her father and climbed into his lap. "Does that mean they're going to take you away?"

"I don't know sweetie. I just don't know."

Sarah wrapped her arms around his neck and hugged him.

"How did any of this happen?" Amanda pressed.

An uncomfortable silence came over the room.

"It was my fault dear," Roberta admitted.

"No. How? You've always been there for us, ever since I can remember. I don't understand."

Roberta lowered her head. "I made a deal with the devil a long time ago and he came to collect. Ultimately I was wrong and in doing so I hurt your family."

"Is that why that lady hurt Auntie Kim at Target?"

"It's my fault; it's all my fault. I'm the one to blame. I should have said no to them years ago but I was blinded by revenge. I know the truth now and I know I can never make it right. Emily showed me the truth. I'm so sorry."

The children had a hard time processing the fact that Roberta wasn't the nice, sweet lady they all knew anymore. They were visibly shaken and didn't know what to do.

"But I'm afraid we're not done with the truth quite yet," Sam said. "Yesterday all of you were kidnapped, taken by force on your way to school."

Sam saw multiple blank faces staring back at him.

"Robert Aleman had all six of you in his grasp and was about to kill you. Emily and Gavin rescued you by taking you through his portal. Afterwards Emily quickly erased that horrible encounter from each of your memories."

"Portal?" Craig asked.

There was a quick flash of light as Gavin created his portal. No one was expecting it and a number of them jumped.

"Wow."

"Neato."

He made it disappear.

"So this man wants to hurt us?" Amanda inquired.

"Yes," Sam answered. "And he almost succeeded this afternoon which is why I requested that we be taken back here so we could watch out for each other."

"Like one big family?"

Sam smiled. "Like one big family."

Hobbes hesitantly raised his hand.

"What's on your mind Hobbes?" Bill asked him.

"Now that I know the truth, and thank you for trusting me with it, but what's the plan for our future? Am I going to be out of a job or something?"

"You bring up a valid point," Sam told him. "I don't know what's going to happen to SANDBOX quite frankly. I know we'll fight to clear our names and get back to business, but those waters seem pretty muddy at the moment. As for your job I think it's safe to say you're not going anywhere. Thomas, Laura and the kids, on the other hand, might be. Isn't that right Thomas?"

"Dammit Sam," Thomas exclaimed. "That was a…"

"Secret?" Sam said as he finished the sentence. "It's a night of sharing so why not put all your cards on the table Thomas?"

Emily and Gavin also looked at their parents with some confusion. Thomas rubbed his head with reluctance and didn't answer.

"Daddy?" Emily eventually prodded. "What is it?"

"Fine," he breathed out. "Here's the deal. The new director of the CIA wants to start up a new division, a secret branch."

"What's that have to do with you?" Kim asked.

"He wants my family, and our abilities, to spearhead that division."

274

"That's crazy," Julie said. "Why would you even consider an offer like that after everything you've been through with the CIA already?"

Laura spoke up. "The offer is actually legitimate."

"Laura, you know about this?" Kim inquired.

"I do, but I am as skeptical about it as all of your faces clearly indicate. Thomas feels he's between a rock and a hard place. We've been put through some seriously harsh situations over the years because our children have unique gifts. Yes, the CIA on two separate occasions have been behind the abduction of our children. Does that fact scare me? Absolutely. But what frightens me more is not being able to protect my children. The fact that the DCI reached out to Thomas means that he knows everything even though we had Hobbes delete what we thought were all traces of their abilities."

"Something else I don't recall doing," Hobbes said offhandedly.

"So let me get this straight," said Julie. "You're actually contemplating the DCI's offer to what, start up a secret branch of the CIA or something?"

"That decision hasn't been made because Emily and Gavin are just finding out about this now. I thought they were too young to make such monumental decisions about their lives, but if recent events are any indication of good decision making skills, I don't know why I was worried."

Laura and Thomas looked at their kids.

"What do you think Em? Gav?"

"I…I don't know," Emily replied.

"Me either," said Gav. "What does it mean? What would we do?"

"We'd use our powers to help fight against the bad people of the world," answered Thomas. "To make a difference. And we'd be kept safe."

"Would we have to move?" Em asked hesitantly.

"Move?" Amanda stated before anyone could reply. "We just put this family back together and now you're talking about moving? I don't like this at all. Why would you think it's a good idea to split our family apart?" She began to pout.

"I don't want you to leave," Sarah whined.

"Me either."

"Don't leave."

Laura put her hand up. "Maybe we should talk about this another time. It's late and it's been a very long d…"

Laura was cut off by the unmistakable sounds of muffled automatic weapons that emanated from outside.

\* \* \*

The eight FBI agents had finished their dinner together in the conference room and had spent the last ten minutes chatting with each other while they waited for their replacements to arrive. Lights danced across the room from vehicles that had just pulled up to the front entrance.

"Time for someone else to take over babysitting," one of them said as they all stood up and began to head out to the lobby together.

"Better them than us. I hate the night shift."

"Yeah, me too."

\* \* \*

Robert Aleman, and five of his men, had been parked on the side of the road, a mile away from SANDBOX, for the last two hours. It had been twenty minutes since the catering truck had driven by, dropped dinner off and then drove back past their location.

"Moving out," the former General said into his radio.

Both Range Rovers pulled back onto the road and began to make the short trek to SANDBOX. Each of his men wore full tactical gear, Kevlar vests and carried CAR-15 short barreled assault rifles with thirty round magazines. In the rear of both vehicles were additional black duffel bags, all filled to the brim.

The two Range Rovers quickly drove up in front of the office and all six men exited. Inside they counted eight FBI agents joking around as they casually walked into the lobby. Three of the General's men raised their assault rifles and began to open fire. The exterior floor to ceiling glass lobby walls shattered. Five agents dropped before the other three could dive behind the reception desk. Bullets peppered the exterior of the desk as the three remaining agents hastily pulled their side arms from their holsters.

"We're fucking sitting ducks if we stay here," one of them told the others as he sized up the situation.

The General's men, who had instigated contact, ejected their spent magazines and inserted new ones as they kept their assault rifles trained on the desk. Five FBI agents lay bleeding and rippled with wounds from the initial barrage. The General spoke up loudly from outside.

"There is no escape. Toss your weapons and come out with your hands up. You have ten seconds."

"Nine."

"I can't go out like this," one of the agents whimpered.

"Eight."

"Seven."

"Fuck this shit," another one said. "We're dead either way so we might as well take some of them with us."

"Six."

"Five seconds."

"Are you with me?" The third agent nodded and then tightened his grip on his weapon.

"Four."

"Go."

Two agents popped up from behind the desk, weapons at the ready, and began to shoot. They each fired three rounds in quick succession before the immense volley from the assault rifles drove them back down. Of the six rounds they collectively fired three missed their mark completely. Two of the other three rounds impacted the attacker's Kevlar vests. The final round entered one of the attacker's eyes and he dropped to the floor, dead.

"Goddammit," Robert Aleman said. "Stop dicking around and frag the fuckers."

One of the two remaining began to slowly fire at the desk, forcing the FBI men to keep their heads down. The other removed a fragmentation grenade from a side pouch, pulled the pin and let the spoon fly. He counted off a few seconds, lobbed the device behind the desk and ducked down. The explosion shredded the three agents and ended the engagement. The stench of blood mixed with the cloud of expended gunpowder; it was the smell of death and it was abundant.

"Clear the area and then begin the operation. And kill their communications ASAP."

"Yes sir," the remaining four men said as they began to sweep the lobby and immediate areas for any additional opposition.

\* \* \*

278

Sam and Bill instinctively reached to their waist for their weapons and came up empty, but that didn't stop them from springing into action. Worried faces appeared on everybody's faces.

"All of you get into the main bedroom, right now," Sam ordered. "It's the furthest away from the elevator and stairwell."

As the families moved with a purpose Sam and Bill then went to the kitchen and armed themselves with large kitchen knives.

"We're going to be sitting ducks up here," Bill said.

"Maybe not," Thomas told him. "We're a wild card. For once we might have surprise on our side."

More weapons fire was suddenly followed by a *thump*.

"That was a grenade," Bill said automatically.

"Yeah, it was," Sam replied. "Try the phone."

Bill headed to one of the phones, picked it up and was rewarded with a dial tone. He gave the others thumbs up as he dialed 911. It rang a few times before it was picked up.

"Nine-one-one operator. Please state the nature of your emerg…"

Bill's face fell as the phone call was cut short. He repeatedly pressed the cradle buttons and then hung in disgust.

"It's dead. They cut me off just as I connected to nine-one-one."

"So there's a chance," Sam replied. "That's better than nothing. In the meantime we need to barricade the stairwell so we only have to defend the elevator."

"Then let's get it done," Bill urged as the three men ran over to the door.

"Bookcase," Thomas suggested.

"And then a couch or two behind it," Bill added.

Three minutes later the men had built a sizeable barrier that would prevent anyone, for a substantial amount of time, from entering the suite through the stairwell.

"Now what?" Thomas asked.

"Now it's a waiting game."

* * *

"Communications are down. I don't think they had time to get a call out."

"No matter," the General replied. "This will all be over soon enough. What's the ETA on setting everything up?"

"Twenty minutes, sir. The elevator has also been temporarily disabled."

"Good. I want a claymore placed on the back stairwell immediately."

"Right away, sir."

* * *

"What the hell are they waiting for?" Bill asked somewhat nervously knowing full well his family's safety was at risk.

"I have no idea," Sam replied. "And that makes me worried. We also haven't heard any sirens, so it looks like help isn't on its way."

The internal intercom system came to life and an ominous voice filled the entire suite.

"Sam Paige and Bill Nicholson, you know who this is. To those family members who are not familiar with my voice, this is General Robert Aleman. Your fathers and I are old acquaintances, long before you were lovingly brought into this world. To the wives; your men were excellent soldiers but don't have the clarity

280

to see the world as I do. However, they took that world away from me and now I am here to repay that kindness.

"I am in full control of your building and the FBI agents that are here are no longer a threat to me or my men. To be honest I thought about not telling you what I've done, but the more I thought about it I realized not knowing about your impending deaths would just be an injustice. To that end you should know that the building has been wired with plastic explosive."

"He's bluffing," Bill said.

"In my hand I hold the detonator. As soon as I press this button a countdown will commence. Ten minutes later the explosives will detonate, sending the building down around you. Oh, and as you can imagine, everyone inside will die horribly."

Over the intercom the audible sound of a button being depressed was heard.

"It's begun. Ten minutes and counting. I'll do you a favor and turn the elevator back on. If you try and use the stairwell you'll run right into a claymore mine, so best be careful trying to go that way. Come on down, disarmed, and we'll go from there. If not, well, BOOM! Toodles."

The intercom went dead and before Sam, Bill or Thomas could say anything their families came out of the bedroom and swarmed the family room. Panic, tears and emotions ran high and the noise level was too high.

"Quiet down everyone!" Sam ordered.

Loud whimpers from scared children turned into quiet ones as they leaned against their mother's legs to be comforted.

"What are we going to do?" Julie asked.

\* \* \*

"Five minutes," Robert Aleman said over the intercom.

The elevator doors closed in the lobby and began their way up to the top floor.

"Get ready," the General ordered. "No mistakes." His men positioned themselves.

After pausing on the top floor the elevator descended back to the lobby. As the doors opened the General's four men, from various angles, easily covered the people inside it.

"Step out with your hands up."

The large group of family members squeezed out of the elevator together. The bodies in the lobby had been removed, but their blood and blood trails remained from where they had been dragged away to. Bundles of explosives had been placed on strategic support columns. Wires ran from each of them and had been hastily taped to the wall so they wouldn't be tripped over.

"Check them," Aleman ordered. "And then I want Sam and Bill on their knees in front of me."

As his men began searching the family members for weapons Robert Aleman looked back at the device in his hand.

"Four minutes."

"Shut it down Aleman," Sam ordered. "Shut it down and let our families go. You have us. You have what you want."

Sam and Bill were forced to their knees in front of Robert Aleman and their wrists tied behind their backs. Tears ran down Kim and Julie's faces as they held their children tight against their bodies. Two guards kept their weapons trained on the them while the other two watched the family.

"Don't presume to tell me what I can do Sam. You brought this on yourself."

"Bullshit Aleman," Sam replied. "There was no need for you to do any of this. Coming after me and my family was a waste of time. You could have taken your money and just disappeared."

"You're right Sam. I could have done just that. But after twelve LONG years you became my only obsession. You took everything away from me and my father betrayed me. There's nothing more I want in life than to see you suffer. It's only fair."

"You decided that's what you were going to do with your life, to be a bad guy. And then when it all goes to hell you blame anyone else but yourself."

"Entrepreneur actually, and now there are three minutes left."

"You're delusional."

"Maybe, but I'm in control." He waved his side arm towards his family. "And I have the power to end one of their lives right now, don't I."

"Don't you fucker dare."

"Touching."

Sam struggled against his bonds. "The person you hate is right here Aleman. Leave them out of this."

Robert smiled at Sam's obvious anxiety. "Perhaps I'll start with your daughter." He turned towards the families and they shied away as he pointed his gun at them. "Which reminds me, how in the hell did you little brats escape from that locked room?"

"Don't call them brats," Thomas said as he stepped up to Aleman. The two guards focused their weapons on Thomas.

"I see. And you must be Thomas Clark, longtime friend of Sam and Bill. It's too bad you're involved in all this; but alas such is life, unfair and poetic."

"Not as bad as you're going to be when this is all over."

Aleman smiled. "I can see why they keep you around. You must be the comedian of the group."

"Something like that."

Thomas twitched his finger, down by his waist, and one by one Sam and Bill's restraints silently popped loose.

"Well, apparently the joke's on you." Aleman looked down at the detonator again. "Two minutes."

"Is it?" Thomas asked. "Penny for your thoughts."

The General looked back at Thomas, met his eyes and instantly distinguished that he wasn't full of fear any longer.

"What d..."

As Thomas voiced the key phrase, they'd all been waiting for, the entire family unit dropped to the floor together, as they had planned together in the suite.

With one hand Thomas pushed Aleman away with such force that he went sailing across the room, while with his other he ripped the assault rifle out of the closest guard's hands.

Sam and Bill, in the split second after Aleman went flying, each sprung at the two men guarding them and they hit the floor hard.

As Aleman was sailing through the air a dark shape formed next to Gavin. It promptly pounced at the last guard with such speed and ferocity that as Aleman hit the floor the man's head had detached from its body.

Thomas pulled his newly acquired weapon to his shoulder and fired a quick burst at the surprised guard's unarmed face. As that man went down Thomas shifted and brought his weapon to bear on the two Sam and Bill had just engaged.

Aleman hit the floor hard and his side arm was knocked out of his hand and it skittered away. The detonator in his other hand, however, had a lanyard secured to his wrist. Pieces of the detonator broke off on impact but the device continued to count down.

Sam, from his crouching position, had launched himself with a tremendous amount of force and raw anger at this target. As his body connected he brought his right knee up into his opponent's groin.

Bill bear hugged his man, wrapping his legs and arms around the torso so he couldn't bring his weapon to bear on anyone.

Sam tumbled to the ground in a heap and began to punch the man in the face repeatedly.

Thomas turned and saw Sam on the ground pummeling his man so he continued to swivel. He and Bill locked eyes and in a matter of moments Bill released his grip and fell to the floor which left his attacker on his feet. Thomas squeezed the trigger and sent another quick burst of bullets in to that man's head, who then pitched over onto the floor next to Bill and didn't move.

After a chain of quick punches, Sam pulled a tactical knife from his opponent's tactical vest and then rammed it under his chin, up and into his brain. The man instantly went limp.

"Clear!" Thomas yelled.

"Clear!" Bill said as he removed the CAR-15 from his enemy.

"Clear!" Sam said as he collected himself, exchanging the knife for his adversary's weapon on the way to his feet.

"Not clear!" Aleman yelled.

Thomas, Sam and Bill instantly trained their weapons on their nemesis and saw that he now held a grenade in his hand that once held his side arm.

"Drop it!" Sam ordered.

Aleman took a few steps towards everyone. "Are you sure Sam? It's a live grenade. Maybe you're right. I'll drop it."

"STOP WHERE YOU ARE!" Sam yelled.

"Why Sam? Why stop?" He took a few more steps until he was two feet away from Sam. Aleman looked down at the crushed and broken detonator. "Oh no. It looks like my toy has been broken, but it's still counting down. They don't make 'em like they used to. Well, just over a minute to go now. Time's a'tick'n."

"You're insane," Bill said.

"Thomas," Sam said without taking his eyes off Aleman, "get everyone outside right now."

"NO!" Aleman screamed. "You move and I will drop this grenade. Your family will die right in front of your eyes."

"Thomas, can you work your magic on this situation?"

"Your magic Thomas? Interesting. How did you throw me across the room?"

"Wouldn't you like to know."

"Well, I'm a quick learner so I guess you'll be occupied after I do this…"

Aleman tossed the grenade into the air and the spoon popped off. It would blow up in seconds.

Sam and Bill followed the arc of the grenade with terror in their eyes.

Thomas dropped his weapon and used both hands to propel the live grenade towards the front doors and away from everyone. He ran after the grenade as fast as he could.

Aleman reached behind his back, produced a second handgun and took advantage of Sam's distraction to close the distance and jam the weapon into his ear.

"DROP IT SAM!" Aleman shrieked.

"GET DOWN!" Thomas screamed as the grenade exploded outside. Something grazed Thomas' head and he fell to the floor, dazed.

"THOMAS!" Laura yelled, clearly concerned.

Bill turned back towards Sam and saw that Sam was now at the mercy of Aleman.

"Drop it. Both of you."

Sam's weapon slipped from his hands and clattered to the ground.

"Now you Bill or I'll drill your boy here right now."

Bill let his drop.

Aleman turned to the family members. "Roberta. Roberta, come to my side."

Roberta, wide eyed and fearful, got up from the floor and walked over to him.

"Roberta, tell me that at least you haven't forsaken me."

Roberta's mouth moved up and down but no words came out.

"I understand," Aleman told her. "There are only forty seconds left before it's all over. I want you to pick up that rifle and fulfill your destiny. Pick it up and kill Sam. Kill the man who took your son away from you. Take his life like he took your son's."

Roberta bent down and picked up the CAR-15. She pointed it at Sam. Aleman stepped away.

"Now shoot him," he commanded.

Roberta twisted the weapon towards Aleman but he anticipated her treachery. He shot her in the stomach and she fell to the ground.

"You sonofabitch!" Sam bellowed.

"There's no time like the present Sam," Aleman said. "Now it's your turn."

General Robert Aleman pointed his handgun at Sam's head, but the shot that rang out had come from Roberta's weapon. The bullet caught Aleman in the upper arm and his gun was knocked away. Sam instantly punched Aleman in the face and he dropped to the floor as Bill immediately went to Roberta's side.

Sam looked at the detonator that was still counting down.

"GET THE FUCK OUT!" Sam yelled. "EVERYONE GET OUT OF THE BUILDING! WE ONLY HAVE EIGHTEEN SECONDS!"

The family scrambled to their feet and began to run towards the front doors. Hobbes, Julie and Kim went to Thomas and half lifted, half dragged him out the front door as fast as they could manage.

Bill, in the meantime, tried to help Roberta up but she weakly turned the assault rifle on him.

Sam turned away from Aleman and towards Roberta just as she pointed the weapon at Bill.

"What the hell…" Bill began to say before she cut him off.

"I deserve this," she said as her other hand gripped her stomach. "Get out."

"But…"

Roberta coughed up blood. "There's no time to argue. Go."

Sam pulled Bill by his shirt as the two of them sprinted to the exit, took a left and ran into the parking lot in front of their building. All of their family was still running away, past the range and towards the motor pool. Thomas had partially come to and was now on his own two feet.

Time stood still for a brief moment as if the world stopped and took one final breath.

BOOOOOOOOM!!!!!

The plastic explosive detonated as the timer reached zero.

In the span of milliseconds the internal support beams were pulverized and the exponential energy from the explosive rippled throughout the building.

Sam and Bill were tossed forward by the shockwave and tumbled helplessly around in the air. They landed on the asphalt and rolled over and over again until they came to a stop, scraped up, bloody, stunned but alive.

As the family rushed to Sam and Bill's side they watched in horror as an ominous screeching sound filled the air. The building, or what remained of it, began to collapse in on itself. They couldn't turn their eyes away as SANDBOX went from everything they had worked for to a pile of useless rubble. Tears streamed down dusty and dirty faces as each of them bore witness to its destruction.

* * *

Thirty minutes later the entire scene was a madhouse of medical personnel and first responders. Firefighters worked to put out the blaze as police cordoned off the area. Multiple FBI agents were also on scene and had just learned that another eight of their own were dead and inside the destroyed building.

The family members had taken refuge inside the motor pool. They sat in a couple of Suburban's, turned on their motors and kept themselves warm. The children, even though they had just been through a terrifying experience, had fallen asleep against their parent's sides. There would be significant fallout to deal with in the upcoming weeks for all of them.

Special Agent Packard found Sam and Bill and pulled them aside.

"What the fuck happened here?"

"A goddamn nightmare," Sam replied, very dejected. "A travesty."

"What a fucking waste," Bill muttered.

"You told the other agents that Robert Aleman attacked you and your family, is that accurate?"

"He was out for blood," Sam answered. "And he almost got what he came for."

"Our building is gone," Bill mumbled. "It's just fucking gone."

Agent Packard backed off. Anyone could tell that Sam and Bill were still in shock; processing what had just happened.

"I'll coordinate some hotel rooms for everyone. We can go through all this tomorrow."

"No, we're going home," he told Agent Hartin who reluctantly decided not to argue.

"What do we do now brother?" Bill asked after Agent Packard had departed. "I mean, shit, what the hell do we do now?"

"I don't know," Sam said. "It goes without saying that our reputation will be ruined; tainted forever regardless if and when the truth comes out. This isn't over. The indictment is still very much alive."

Bill shuffled his feet. "I'm not ready to give up on our dream; our reality. I know we just lost everything, but it's all I know."

Sam put an arm around his best friend. "For me as well but we need to let it go for now. The only thing that we can ultimately take away from all this is that our family is safe and back together."

Bill looked Sam in the eyes. "I'm sad. I'm really, really sad." He hugged Sam.

"You and me both brother; you and me both."

## 41
## Saturday September 22, 2001

In the wee hours of Saturday morning three very tired and emotionally wrung out families were escorted back home. After they arrived it was quickly decided that, at least until morning, everyone should stay together. Thomas and Laura volunteered their house and sleepily prepared places for everyone to fall asleep. Gavin and Emily were thrilled to be back in their own beds and in no time Stickers curled up beside him.

While Sam and Bill's children had cried themselves to sleep, exhausted and fearful, Emily and Gavin had treated the situation through veteran eyes. Whether Thomas and Laura wanted to admit it or not, this wasn't the first time Gavin had utilized Stir to kill someone. And Emily was no stranger to the horror and stench of death either. However, regardless of what those two had just gone through, they both seemed strangely relaxed as they drifted off to sleep.

Out in the family room an entirely different scenario was being played out. Julie was snuggled close in to Sam and Kim was doing the same with Bill. Laura handed out beers to everyone, as the traumatic events repeated over and over in all of their minds, and then sat down next to Thomas and leaned her head on his shoulder. Even Hobbes didn't have anything to say so he just sat there with a faraway stare and drank his beer.

"What….what does it mean?" Kim hesitantly asked.

"What part honey?" Bill replied. "Our indictment, that Aleman is no longer a threat or that our building is now just a pile of rubble?"

"All of it."

"It means we find ourselves in an impossible situation," Sam stated. "We're under the microscope whether we want to be or not. What started as a drug trafficking conspiracy, at least to us, has now escalated into a massive neighborhood firefight; six dead personnel, whose loyalty was to an entirely different organization; the death of Rebecca Cross and nine Federal agents; the loss of Roberta, even though she was deceived; the death of former General Robert Aleman; as well as the destruction of our company headquarters. And on top of that they're not going to forget that our children were kidnapped and miraculously escaped somehow."

"That's a shitload of attention that's not going to go away anytime soon," Bill said as he took a long swig from his bottle.

"So what are we going to do?" Julie asked. "What's the plan?"

Sam finished his beer and then stood up. "The plan is to get some sleep and then take it one day at a time until all this is behind us."

## 42
## Sunday September 30, 2001

The family unequivocally decided to remain together, in somewhat close quarters, to provide comfort and safety for one another. It's what they all needed even though they said they were doing it for the children.

Throughout the weekend and into the beginning of the next week crews worked to remove the building's rubble. Truck after truck hauled away the building that used to be known as SANDBOX. Tuesday afternoon the first of many bodies began to be removed from the demolished structure. News crews had been following this story very closely and captured each body bag as it was carried from the wreckage to awaiting Coroner vehicles.

Information about the drug smuggling and money laundering indictment had been leaked, and combined with the deaths of so many Federal agents the public opinion and outcry against SANDBOX was overwhelmingly negative. People kept questioning how such atrocities like supplying drugs to school children could happen right under their nose in Marin County. In no time at all Sam and Bill's family name had been dragged through the community mud and everyone cried out for blood.

\* \* \*

Wednesday morning there was breaking news as financial details, from the indictment, were also leaked to the press. Contained within was the fact that SANDBOX had received a substantial amount of money four years prior, in the tune of half a billion dollars, from an anonymous source. That sent the news stations on a whole new tangent. Opinions and allegations that it was drug money ran rampant all over the newscasts.

On the Federal side of things, and due to the tremendous story coverage, lawsuits began to trickle in from the families of the deceased agents. Without having the chance to defend their name about what actually transpired, across the United States and the world, Sam and Bill had already been pronounced guilty. To make matters worse Marin County pulled SANDBOX's permits and immediately condemned their property. It was just another blow in what seemed like an endless downhill spiral. Even though their parents tried to hide what was being said about them on the news, the children saw it anyway. It was disheartening.

"Why do they hate us so much?'

"We're not drug dealers."

"They think we're bad people."

"My friends don't want to be my friend anymore."

* * *

On Sunday, September 30, the family's gathered to say goodbye to both Rebecca and Roberta. They were the only ones in attendance due to the fact that the funerals had been kept quiet to avoid the onslaught of media. Rebecca and Roberta's service was closed casket, due to the violent nature of their deaths and the condition of their bodies.

Sam spoke first.

"Rebecca was, and has always been, a prime example of humanity. She was a medic in the service and came to us wanting to give more. And she did just that, time and time again as she selfishly protected us all. It goes without saying that she touched each of us deep in our hearts. She was family and she will be missed.

"Roberta's deception surprised me, but at the end she realized what she had known all those years with us, that she had become family and we weren't the bad guys we were made out to be. She worked long hours and always went above and beyond what her role required to make sure we were taken care of. I'm saddened by her loss and I'll always remember how she touched and enlightened our lives. Rest in peace."

Sam stepped down from the podium. The rest of the family stood and individually walked by both caskets to say their final goodbyes.

Laura put her hand on Rebecca's casket. "Thank you," she whispered. "You have no idea what you meant to us or how much you'll be missed. We love you."

At Roberta's Laura said, "I hope you finally found the peace you were looking for."

Emily stopped next to Rebecca. "I love you Becca. You were the big sister I never had and will always miss."

When it was Gavin's turn he put his head down on Rebecca's coffin. "You were the best Becca. You looked out for Em and me. I know I'll see you again, and maybe then it can be my turn to look after you. I love you."

Rebecca tried to console Gavin by kneeling down. She tried to place a hand on his shoulder but it passed right through his body. He didn't move a muscle as she stood back up.

*I love you too Gav.*

## 43
## Monday October 1, 2001

Everyone was unprepared when someone knocked on the
Clark's back door. Gavin ran halfway to it before he remembered
it couldn't have been Rebecca coming across the lawn from the
guest house. Thomas, knowing it had to be a trespassing reporter,
opened the backdoor with gusto.

"How dare you…"

He stopped in mid-sentence when he recognized the man who
stood in front of him was none other than Robert Duncan, the
Director of Central Intelligence. *What the hell is he doing here?*

"Hello Thomas. May I come in?"

"I…I guess…sure."

Thomas stepped sideways, the DCI walked in and Thomas
closed the door behind him.

"I hate to be so bold but I don't have a lot of time. I'd like to
address everyone at once, if that's alright with you?"

"What's this about?" Thomas asked.

"Your future."

"Is that right? Interesting." Thomas pointed to a chair at the
head of family room. "Please take a seat."

"Thank you."

Sam, Bill, Julie, Kim, Laura, Hobbes and the children slowly
gathered from various parts of the house as curiosity spread about
who had knocked on the door. All eyes were locked on the
mysterious stranger. Thomas spoke up before anyone asked who
he was.

"This is Robert Duncan. He's the head of the CIA."

"This is highly unusual, sir," Sam said as he sat down on one
of the couches.

"What brings you to our neck of the woods Director?" Bill asked with a slight edge to his voice. "We're drowning in a ton of litigation already so I hope you haven't come to add to the pile."

The DCI smiled and took no offense at Bill's attitude. "Please, everyone take a seat. I need to make this quick before I catch my plane back to Virginia."

"What's this all about?" Laura asked as she and Thomas sat down. Emily and Gavin came over and they put them on their laps.

Bill and Kim also found seats next to each other while their children sat on the floor. Hobbes and Julie were the last ones to settle down before their kids also found a spot.

Robert Duncan spoke up. "The media is having a heyday with your reputations."

"Tell me you didn't come all this way just to tell us the obvious," Bill spat out.

"No, Mr. Nicholson, I did not come to San Francisco on a whim just to rub your face in what is obviously a very painful and unnerving time in your lives." Bill settled down. "However, I did make the trip to hopefully talk you all in to a future together."

Laura cut him off. "We haven't had time to discuss it as a family yet."

"Fair enough, but since I'm here I'd like to make an argument for it, if I may."

Laura looked around the room and then finally at Thomas. Surprisingly she wasn't met with any resistance.

"Please continue Mr. Duncan."

"Thank you. Now Laura, before I begin, I need to ask you and Thomas one question."

"Which is?"

"To be vague, is anyone in this room, the children included, not in the know?"

"Proceed Mr. Duncan," Thomas replied as a confirmation.

"Very good. Thank you." The DCI looked around the room at everyone before he continued. "I'll be blunt. You are the future and I want you to work for me."

Sam addressed the DCI. "Are you referring to all of us or just the Clarks?"

"A valid point, Mr. Paige."

"Sam. Call me Sam."

"Very well, Sam. My offer goes out to all of you."

"But before," Thomas said, "when we met you only wanted my family and I."

The DCI nodded. "That's true. But as you're well aware, things have drastically changed in that regard. May I be brutally honest Sam?"

"It's the best policy."

"SANDBOX is all but a distant memory. Rumor has it that when you are summoned to D.C. next week to face your indictment, you'll ultimately lose your business, your reputation and your money."

"We'll fight it and we'll win," Bill declared adamantly.

"No, Bill, you will lose and lose badly. The American public wants blood and the U.S. government has already decided to make you an example in an effort to elicit confidence in the governing body."

"That's bullshit. We didn't do anything wrong."

"You were complicit, regardless that any wrongdoing was happening under your noses. But let's say, for arguments sake, that you could win. Your reputation has and will forever be stained with that complicity, not to mention any incompetence they wouldn't hesitate to place on your shoulders."

"What's your point then sir?" Sam pressed. "Did you come here today to offer us all a job or something?"

"Indeed. Exactly that; jobs."

"Doing what?"

"I want to create a separate compartmentalized division of the CIA; one that only reports to me. My vision is to reinvent how the CIA conducts its business, from interrogations to information gathering. I call it PsyOps, or Psychological Operations. This family cohesively works very well together and I want that trend to continue."

"I'll ask the same question," Sam said. "Doing what?"

"Laura Bond, now Laura Clark. For years you worked as a psychiatrist running your own business. That changed drastically when you met Thomas and when you discovered your children had special abilities. Based on the quick conversation we had over the phone I'm going to deduce that perhaps you can tell when someone is lying or not."

Laura didn't reply and maintained her blank poker face.

"And since that's not a no you would be perfect as the PsyOps shrink. My apologies if that's too derogatory a term.

"Thomas, with his telekinetic power which have unlimited applications, will be utilized as the situation fits. The same thing can be said of Emily and Gavin. Their unique abilities drastically change the playing field that we're all used to."

Laura countered. "You want my children, who are only eight and ten, to put themselves through even more heartache and nightmares?"

"They would only be allowed to engage in what you both deem as acceptable levels of participation."

"Sounds fishy," Bill said.

Laura leaned back. "No. He's not lying."

"No, I'm not," the DCI replied.

"Please continue."

"Thank you." He turned to Sam. "You and your partner would be brought on as PsyOps security."

"And what would that entail?"

"Basically anything and everything security related, from keeping everyone safe to going on missions."

"Missions?" Julie snarled. "Our men have an agreement with us to do no such thing."

"To continue my bluntness and to apologize in advance Mrs. Paige, how's that worked out for them?"

Julie stiffened but remained quiet.

"Hobbes will be in charge of the technical side of the operation, assuming of course that he wants it."

Hobbes smiled.

"Here's the bottom line," the DCI said. "I can protect everyone and in turn you can protect each other. In all fairness, it's going to take a lot of effort to get Project Zelda, aka PsyOps, up and running. But the benefits from the idea of its success alone are breathtaking."

"And what about the significant problems we're currently facing?" Bill asked. "How do you propose we shed that weight and start all over working for you?"

"One step at a time, but I have some thoughts on that issue. In the meantime, none of this is a done deal unless the four core members," he said gesturing to the Clark family, "are in."

"And if we are," Thomas asked, "then what happens next?"

"You'll move to Virginia and remain together as a family unit in the coming weeks. SANDBOX is finished but I guarantee that each of your employees will be well compensated in their exit packets. Financially you're facing substantial fines which will basically drain your entire business and life savings, which are still frozen."

"And our wives and children?" Sam asked.

301

"Schooling and whatever they want to do. The sky's the limit. The important thing is that you'll all be together. Anyway," the DCI said as he stood up, "that's my pitch. The details will work themselves out on their own if you decide to move forward."

The DCI made his way towards the backdoor as a multitude of eyes followed his progress. He turned with his hand on the doorknob.

"I'm excited that this might be coming together and I think you are too. I await your decision."

"One more thing Mr. Duncan," Laura said.

He paused and turned around. "Yes?"

"What's stopping us from just wiping your mind now or just making you disappear?"

"Absolutely nothing," he replied without missing a beat. "And yet I decided to come here anyway."

And with that he opened and then closed the door behind him. Everyone turned back around and looked over at Thomas and Laura.

"Soooo," Laura said, "who wants a beer?"

## 44
## Friday October 5, 2001

A man, his right arm significantly scared from fire, picked up the ringing phone.

"Yes?"

"The DCI has convinced them."

The man smiled. "Excellent. When will they arrive?"

"They're scheduled to leave on Monday as a family. The indictment hearing is on Tuesday, the following day."

"Good. Keep the updates coming while I continue to work on my own lab results."

"Of course," the female voice replied. "That's what you're paying me for."

Dr. Yamato Takuma Matsushita slowly placed the phone back on its cradle. "Welcome back Thomas, I missed you."

\*   \*   \*

## Monday October 8, 2001

SANDBOX's Cessna Citation was forced to take a more southern flight path to avoid a large mid-western storm front. Currently it was cruising over the Gulf of Mexico with all family members safely on board, although very anxious about what they had agreed to. On top of that the indictment hearing was scheduled for the next day and Sam and Bill thoroughly dreaded it.

"They're going to bury us brother," Bill said.

"Probably."

"I don't like it. This is all wrong."

303

"Tell me something I don't know. But unfortunately this is the hand that we've been dealt. We can either run from it or face the music."

Bill half smiled. "Running doesn't sound like that bad of an option right now."

"I'll see what I can do," Sam joked.

Sam got up from his seat and began to walk down the aisle to check on everybody.

"Daddy?" Amanda asked as he approached.

"What is it sweetie?"

"Are we there yet?"

"Don't make me turn this plane around young lady," he replied as they teased each other.

She laughed and then said, "Are you sure we're going to be okay?"

*From the mouths of babes.* "We're going to be just fine. It's going to take some time to adjust of course, but in time you'll make new friends. We have each other and that's what's important."

She nodded and he kept moving down the aisle. He stopped at Thomas' seat. Laura was across the aisle.

"You good?" Sam asked.

"I think we made the right decision, but only time will tell."

"I hear you."

"You must be nervous about the hearing Sam?"

"More than you know. It's going to be fun to get crucified on national television."

"Ugh. That sounds horrible."

"Yeah, I'm sure it will be. Anyway, can I get either of you anything?"

Thomas shook his head. "I'm good, thanks."

"Nothing for me Sam," Laura added.

"No problem."

Sam stopped at Hobbes' seat. He had the armrest in a death grip.

"Nervous?"

Hobbes nodded. "I don't like flying."

"You'll be fine, trust me. Just think about the new opportunity. You're going to be great at it."

"Thanks."

As Sam left Hobbes behind the plane jolted violently to the left and then dropped a good hundred feet. Sam was thrown off balance and barely managed to avoid injury.

"WHAT THE HELL IS GOING ON!" Bill yelled to the pilots.

The children began to scream as the jet continued to bounce around haphazardly.

Sam clawed his way back to his seat and strapped himself in.

"WE'VE GOT MULTIPLE WARNING LIGHTS ALL OVER THE BOARD!" they yelled back.

The jet suddenly veered right and tipped over into a dive. Magazines and refreshments went careening off the inside of the plane as the strong inertia yanked at each person's body, trying to pull them from their seats.

"MAYDAY! MAYDAY! THIS IS SB845 DECLARING AN EMERGENCY! I REPEAT, THIS IS SB845 DECLARING AN EMERGENCY! OVER!"

"SB845, this is Houston. We have you on our radar and see that you're rapidly losing altitude."

"NO SHIT HOUSTON! WE'VE LOST HYDRAULICS AND RUDDER CONTROL IS NOT RESPONDING!"

"25,000!"

"SHIT! WE'RE LOSING IT!"

"22,000!"

"19,000!"

"COME ON, WORK GODDAMMIT!"

"15,000!"

"SB845, you need to pull up! Pull up SB845!"

"WE'RE IN A STEEP DIVE THAT WE CAN'T PULL OUT OF!"

"10,000!"

"6,000!"

"MAYDAY! MAYDAY! THIS IS SB845! WE'RE GOING IN HARD! BRACE YOURSELVES BACK THERE!

"Roger that SB845. We're right here with you. God bless."

\* \* \*

Search and Rescue were dispatched immediately to their last known coordinates in the Gulf of Mexico. Five hours later pieces of the destroyed Cessna were discovered floating in a large slick of fuel and oil. There was zero chance that anyone onboard survived.

Visit my website at

http://www.dwneuman.com

If you enjoyed this novel please consider
taking a moment and writing a quick review
about it (on Amazon).  It helps me out more
than you know and fuels my motivation!
Of course, word of mouth
works wonders too! ;)

Thank you!

And you can look forward to book seven,
**Shadows of the Future**,
sometime in 2015.